"You two planted the seed back then,"

Gram said. "It's just taking awhile to grow and flower."

Jenna looked at her grandmother's confident smile and almost burst into tears. If Gram only knew what kind of seed had been planted back then, it would break her heart.

"Gram," Jenna said, wearily, "Rob's only here temporarily."

"No one knows how things will work out for him."

"Rob Fagan is a roamer. He'll be chasing rainbows until the day he dies. Just like his father."

"He's more like his mother, dear. Solid and dependable. Salt of the earth. His father gave him his charm and quick wit, but his mother gave him two feet, planted solidly on the ground."

Jenna saw her grandmother grow misty before her. Poor Gram. She wanted something that could never happen, something Jenna had stopped dreaming of long ago.

Dear Reader,

Welcome to Silhouette **Special Edition**... welcome to romance. Each month, Silhouette **Special Edition** publishes six novels with you in mind—stories of love and life, tales that you can identify with—romance with that little "something special" added in.

November brings plenty to be joyful and thankful for—at least for Andy and Meg in *Baby, It's You* by Celeste Hamilton. For with the birth of their child, they discover the rebirth of their love... for all time. Don't miss this compelling tale!

Rounding out November are more dynamite stories by some of your favorite authors: Bevlyn Marshall (fun follows when an abominable snowman is on the loose!), Andrea Edwards, Kayla Daniels, Marie Ferrarella and Lorraine Carroll (with her second book!). A good time will be had by all this holiday month!

In each Silhouette **Special Edition** novel, we're dedicated to bringing you the romances that you dream about—the type of stories that delight as well as bring a tear to the eye. And that's what Silhouette **Special Edition** is all about—special books by special authors for special readers!

I hope you enjoy this book and all of the stories to come.

Sincerely,

Tara Gavin
Senior Editor

ANDREA EDWARDS

Home Court Advantage

Published by Silhouette Books New York

America's Publisher of Contemporary Romance

SILHOUETTE BOOKS
300 East 42nd St., New York, N.Y. 10017

HOME COURT ADVANTAGE

ISBN: 0-373-09706-9

First Silhouette Books printing November 1991

Printed in the U.S.A.

Books by Andrea Edwards

Silhouette Special Edition

Rose in Bloom #363
Say It with Flowers #428
Ghost of a Chance #490
Violets Are Blue #550
Places in the Heart #591
Make Room for Daddy #618
Home Court Advantage #706

Silhouette Intimate Moments

Above Suspicion #291

Silhouette Desire

Starting Over #645

ANDREA EDWARDS

is the pseudonym of Anne and Ed Kolaczyk, a husband-and-wife writing team that concentrates on women's fiction. "Andrea" is a former elementary schoolteacher, while "Edwards" is a refugee from corporate America, having spent almost twenty-five years selling computers before becoming a full-time writer. They have four children, two dogs and four cats, and live in Indiana.

WARSAW STAR RETURNS TO COACH BOYS BASKETBALL

WARSAW, Ind.—Rob Fagan, the star of the 1978 Warsaw High School championship basketball team, has returned to town to take over the boys' high school basketball team for ailing Don Parsons. Fagan starred at UCLA for four years, then went on to play in Europe for seven years. He is best remembered for shooting the winning basket in a tight championship game against arch-rival Northwood High. Jenna Lauren, coach of the girls' varsity basketball team and former high school classmate of Fagan's, admitted her surprise at his return, but would only comment, "I'm just glad the boys finally have a coach. Now we can all concentrate on the upcoming season."

Chapter One

"Good Lord! It's the middle of October and those kids are walking around barefoot."

"They're country girls."

Jenna Lauren smiled but said nothing to her two assistant coaches as they all stared out into the dim morning light. Teenage girls, wearing gym shorts, sweatshirts and disheveled mops of hair, tumbled out of cars. Most were shoeless and carried their basketball high-tops in one hand, duffle bags of clothes and schoolbooks in the other. A mist from the low area to the west of the high school hovered about them, matching Jenna's moodiness.

"Uh, when do they start wearing shoes on a regular basis?" Rita Benjamin asked.

"A few will start in another couple of weeks and by the first snow you'll see all of them wearing something on their feet," Peggy Schmitt informed.

Peggy, like Jenna, had lived in Warsaw, Indiana, all her life and could trace her family tree back to the first German farmers who'd settled the area. Rita had just moved to town this past summer when her husband took a job with one of the biomedical companies there.

"She's pulling my chain, right?" Rita asked.

Jenna turned around in time to see total innocence flashing from Peggy's soft blue eyes and rosy cheeks, and threw her hands up in mock surrender. "I don't want to get involved."

"You're the head coach," Rita argued. "You're supposed to get involved."

"But, as has been rudely pointed out to me any number of times, I'm also the shortest," Jenna said. "So you two can fight your own battles. I'm not letting you giants beat up on me."

At five feet six inches, Jenna was taller than average, but she'd played basketball since grade school and had been shorter than most teammates and opponents. She still felt as though she were the runt of the litter.

The girls came in, murmuring their sleepy good mornings, and stumbled on toward the gym. A few filed off toward the locker rooms.

"Girls," Jenna shouted after them. "In the gym, please. We start at six sharp."

"We'll round them up," Rita said. "Let them get in front of a mirror and they'll start on their hair. Practice will be half over before we get them out on the floor."

Jenna sighed as the two women hurried after the girls, leaving her alone in the lobby. She was tired. It was a good thing the season was starting; she needed distractions in her life.

Actually, Jenna couldn't ever remember a time when she hadn't been glad basketball season was starting. She'd begun playing in the fourth grade, then played through junior high, high school and on into college, but high school ball would forever remain her favorite.

Of course, all of high school had been special, a time that her memories treasured. From that first homecoming dance she shared with Rob when both were freshmen, to cheering him on in the state basketball finals in their senior year. Their friendship had been like gold dust, making everything it touched magical.

Everything? Clouds started to shadow her memories, and she closed the door on her thoughts. Those days of endless happiness were followed by ones of empty misery, but all that was gone. She was better off without either the highs or the lows; her life was fine now.

A car door slammed, adding emphasis to Jenna's mental assertion. As Jenna watched, a barefoot, red-haired girl ran from a pickup truck, bags bouncing on her ribs. Jenna opened the door for her.

"You're late, Sara."

"My mother didn't get me up in time," the young girl explained breathlessly.

"The captain of the varsity team shouldn't need her mother to get her up for practice."

The girl's smile was a mixture of the charm and cockiness that epitomized seventeen. "Why do we have to practice this early anyway? The boys should have this slot. They don't need as much time to get ready for school."

"The boys don't even have a real coach yet," Jenna said. "Get your shoes on and get into the gym."

Sara padded off to join the team, leaving Jenna staring off into the shadows of the past. Things hadn't changed much in the last twelve years. She and Rob had bickered over whose team got more gym time and who should have the 6 a.m. practices, but when the games started, they cheered each other on.

Jenna could feel a warmth stealing over her heart. The mist outside seemed to swallow up time, tugging her back into the past. She could feel that cold blacktop under her own bare feet as she had run from the car into the gym for her early morning practices. She could feel the racing of her heart as each new day had begun, a day holding so many chances for happiness that she felt she would burst with excitement. She could feel that delicious tingling as she hurried from the locker room after practice to the cafeteria where the early arrivals gathered.

What she and Rob had talked about all those mornings, she couldn't remember, but she could remember how he'd been the center of her life, the sun around which everything revolved. It had been that way right up to the time he left for college without knowing she was pregnant.

A car pulled into the parking lot, its headlights splitting the halfhearted darkness and brought Jenna back to reality. She should be getting her team into shape for the season, not getting nostalgic just because it was the start of a new season. She turned and hurried into the gym.

"Let's go, ladies," she shouted. "We have a lot of work ahead of us and time's a'wasting. Give me five laps around the gym."

Rita took off running with the girls while Peggy stayed behind with Jenna. "You act as though you have your marine drill instructor hat on," she said to Jenna.

"We have a young team," Jenna replied. "We're going to have to work hard just to be respectable. Besides, it'll give them something else to grumble about. I'm getting tired of the 'Why do we have to get up this early?' song."

"They'll be singing it until Arthur gets a coach for the boys' team," Peggy said. "After school is the only time the volunteer fathers can practice."

Jenna nodded. Don Parsons, who had coached the boys' team here, even back in Rob's day, had had a heart attack the week before and would be out for at least half the season. Maybe longer, for the latest word was that his heart attack was more severe than they had first thought.

"It's gonna be tough to find somebody now," Jenna said. "The season's about to start. They may have to settle for—"

"Goodness, Arthur's here," Peggy said. "I didn't know he got up this early. And who's that with him?"

Jenna turned to look toward the door, mild curiosity taking her attention from the stragglers trailing in after Rita. The stragglers, the team, and everyone else was soon forgotten though, as her eyes took in the tall, dark-haired man standing next to the principal. Rob? No, it couldn't be.

But her sudden lack of breath indicated that her heart knew better than her eyes. She'd never in a million years expected to see him again, certainly not here in the gym where they'd first kissed. Her heart raced, making her feel like a silly high-schooler again, while her cheeks flushed with remembered heat.

The giddiness passed faster than she could blink her eyes, and a cool wariness took its place. She wasn't a teenager anymore, believing in fairy tales. She was an adult who knew better; she was in control. She stood still, waiting for Arthur and Rob to join her and Peggy.

"Morning, Jenna. Morning, Peggy," Arthur said, carrying a grin as big as an Indiana cornfield. "Hi, Rita."

Jenna glanced over her shoulder to see that her young assistant coach had stopped running and was coming toward them, along with the entire basketball team. Varsity, junior varsity, and freshman. Great, almost forty girls to witness her little reunion.

"I just thought you should be one of the first to know," Arthur said, his arm around Rob's shoulders. "We got ourselves a new boys' head basketball coach and athletic director for Warsaw Senior High School."

Double great. It wasn't a one-shot visit, in and out like a trip to the dentist; he was here for a longer spell.

"Hello, Rob," Jenna said with a short nod. Her voice was quiet, but in control. I'm a new person, Rob, not that silly little girl who thought you were everything.

"Hello, Jenna. It's good to see you again."

His voice had grown deeper, aging like fine brandy. His hair had remained as black as coal and his blue eyes were still as blue as the Indiana sky on a bright summer's day. She had to fight not to let memories awaken.

"Hey, that's right. You guys would know each other. You went to school here at the same time." Arthur sounded as if he'd stumbled over a gold mine. "This is great."

Peggy coughed suddenly, or was she smothering a laugh? Peggy's eldest daughter and Jenna had been good friends in high school, and Jenna didn't dare look her way.

"Rob's gonna help us out while old Don's laid up in the hospital," Arthur went on, resting his eyes neatly on Jenna and no one else. "And seeing as how he's stepping right into the middle of things, I thought you wouldn't mind giving him a hand for a while, kinda show him the ropes."

Triple great. Not only was Rob Fagan back in town, but she was expected to be his tour guide.

"Sure," Jenna said. "I'll help him reschedule the practices so he and the boys will have the joy of getting up for a 6 a.m. session."

Arthur laughed and shook his head. "Some things don't change," he said. "Jenna, she's as tough as she's always been."

Jenna finally dared to meet Rob's gaze and his blue eyes washed over her, a cool lake lapping at her hot feet on a dog day in August. But unlike the lake, those eyes increased the warmth around her.

"The boys and I will be happy to do our fair share and more," Rob replied. There was murmur among the girls.

"It is nice to see that some other things haven't changed either," Peggy said lightly. "Rob's still as charming as ever."

Rob, Arthur, and Peggy chuckled while a few of the older girls tittered. The seniors on the team had a lot more savvy than Jenna had at their age. Had they somehow gleaned something from the somewhat strained exchange between the two coaches? Could they somehow know that she and Rob had been an item all those years ago? Well, they weren't an item now. That was in the distant past, when they'd been kids without any sense. She was an adult now, a teacher, a coach. And she had a practice to run. Best to remind everybody of both those points.

Jenna looked toward the girls. "What are we standing around for?" she said. "Are we here to play basketball or air our mouths out?"

Rita and the girls stared at her, but Jenna didn't care. She could feel Rob's eyes on her; she needed to escape from their spell a while so that she could think.

"See you all around later," she said to Rob and Arthur, then turned back to her girls. "Ten times around the gym. Double time." To show how fair she was, Jenna took off to lead.

Rita moved easily to her side. "I've got a feeling that Rob fella is going to be a big help," she said.

Jenna glared at her.

"I mean with him around, it looks like our girls will be the best conditioned team in the conference."

"Hi." Rita sat down at the table across from Jenna and put down her lunch tray.

"Hi." Jenna mumbled, barely looking up.

She'd given her first-hour algebra class a pop quiz and had spent any spare moments that morning going over the papers with a fine tooth comb. Her grumpy mood was due solely to the fact that she apparently had not taught her students a thing in the first six weeks of the quarter.

"Do you want me to go sit on the other side of the room?" Rita asked after a moment.

"No, stay here," Jenna growled. "That way I won't have far to reach and smack you when you start slurping your milkshake."

"Certainly can't turn down such a charming invitation." Rita pulled an egg salad sandwich out of her brown bag.

"How can you stomach egg salad every working day of your life?" Jenna asked.

"I like egg salad."

Damn. Jenna circled a simple, straightforward question that someone had solved backwards. She didn't care what Rita or anyone else had for lunch. No more than she cared what Rob Fagan did with his life. So she had been thrown for a minute when he'd come into the gym. That was because she just hadn't expected it. Nothing else.

"Heard you and the new temporary athletic director used to be an item," Rita said, trying for a look of innocence but failing.

"About thirteen years ago."

"You're kidding."

"Nope. That was back when we were seniors in this very same high school."

Rita appeared slightly confused. "I thought the way people were talking that it was just a couple of years ago."

"That's one of the advantages of a small town," Jenna said. "We hold dear our gossip, nurture it, if you will. Thirty years or thirty days, doesn't make any difference to us. We give it all the same care and concern."

Jenna found another student unable to add and wondered if she and her students had been in the same classroom the last six weeks.

"Hello, Jenna."

Jenna looked up to see her grandmother walking into the teachers' lounge and felt some of her orneriness melt away. "Hi, Gram. What a nice surprise. How was your morning?"

"Just dandy. Had one fine walk." The elderly woman was clad in her usual fall outfit of boots, jeans, and heavy mackinaw shirt with her short gray hair stuffed into a stocking cap. Eighty-one years old and she still walked four or five miles daily, no matter what the weather.

"I don't think you've met Rita yet, have you?" Jenna said. "She's a new history teacher here and one of my assistant coaches."

Gram nodded. "You and your husband bought the Millers' old house."

Rita shook her head. "Millers? We bought the house from the Lenskis."

"They only lived there a short while," Gram said.

"They said eight years," Rita said.

"Like I said, dear. Just a short while." Then her grandmother turned her crooked smile back on Jenna. "I imagine you've heard by now, Jenna. Rob Fagan's back in town."

The cloud of grumpiness returned to settle over Jenna's head again. "I know," she mumbled. She should have known Gram was here for a reason. And she should have known what that reason would be.

"Poor boy," Gram said. "Bouncing all over the world like that. Never knowing from one day to the next where he'd be laying his head."

"He played pro basketball in Europe for a few years," Jenna explained to Rita.

"Oh."

"Poor, poor man," Gram said. "He's so lonely."

"I can't see Rob Fagan ever being lonely," Jenna pointed out, pulling her papers back in front of her.

"Ain't no other reason for a man to come home," Gram said, her voice schoolmarm-firm. "He wants to settle down and raise a family."

Rita's eyes flipped from one to the other as she slowly ate her sandwich. Amusement danced in them, making Jenna wish she'd eaten her lunch in the grungy athletic equipment room by herself.

"Rob's lived all over," Jenna said. "I don't see why he'd call Warsaw, Indiana home."

"Where else would home be?" Gram asked.

Jenna gave a short sigh of exasperation. "Maybe any of the hundred other towns he's hung his hat in."

Gram rolled her eyes to the ceiling. "Jennifer, Jennifer." She turned to Rita. "This is the man who shot the winning basket with two seconds left on the clock. The basket that beat Northwood High in 1978 and brought the state championship to Warsaw. Now tell me. Does a body do that for any town, or their hometown?"

Rita stopped chewing her sandwich, her eyes shifted from one to the other, laughter flooding her features. "Hometown?"

"Absolutely," Gram replied.

Jenna glared at her young assistant but the woman continued to munch innocently on her sandwich. Society frowned on manhandling a sweet old grandmother, but Jenna was sure that no jury in the world would convict her for punching out a smart-aleck assistant's lights.

"Jenna, could we—"

Great, just the person she was hoping would join this party. She steeled herself to look up and face Rob, but discovered he wasn't looking at her.

"Gram?" Rob stepped toward Jenna's grandmother. "Grandma Lauren?"

"Yes, it's me," Gram snapped. "What the matter? Surprised I'm not dead and buried yet?"

"Of course not." His smile was broad, and his voice deep. Gathering the old woman in a warm embrace he said, "I'm just happy to see you."

Gram's face shone with pure joy for just a moment as he hugged her, then she pushed herself back and pinched Rob on the shoulders. "Gosh almighty, young man," she scolded. "You're nothing but skin and bone. Ain't you been eating proper?"

Rob shook his head. "Traveled the world, Gram, but I couldn't find anyone who cooks like you. Do you still make chicken and dumplings on Sunday?"

"I certainly do," she replied. "That's the way the Lord wants it. And you're welcome to eat with us this Sunday, isn't he, Jenna?"

Jenna could only stare at her grandmother. She didn't want Rob coming to their house to eat. She didn't want him hanging around, taking up their relationship where they'd left off. But it was Rob himself who rescued her.

"I can't do it this Sunday," he said. "I'm only going to be here for a couple more hours, then I've got to get back to St. Louis and finish moving."

"Any Sunday then," Gram said, as she turned to leave. She stopped at the door and looked back. "Course you ain't restricted to Sundays. You can come out and eat any day of the week. Ain't that right, Jenna?"

Jenna's vocal cords were paralyzed and the silence in the room grew as everyone stared at her. Well, they could stare until it snowed in July. There was no way in the world she was going to start anything up with Rob. Like her Daddy always said: first time is a mistake, second time is stupid.

Rob stepped in smoothly to rescue her as he always had, his Irish charm ever ready. Jenna refused to let the memories in. "We need to get together and settle the practice times," Rob told her. "How about sometime Monday?"

"I'll be here," Jenna said.

He nodded, smiled at Rita, then joined Gram over at the door and went out with her. Gram was laughing and chattering like a schoolgirl.

"You know," Rita said, breaking the heavy silence that hung over the room. "I bet he is lonely."

Jenna stared hard at her assistant.

"He has these little stretch marks at the corners of his mouth," Rita said, pointing to her own lips. "My grandmother told me those were sad muscles straining against a man's smile. It means he's carrying a burden he doesn't want the world to see."

Sighing, Jenna looked down at her watch. "I've got a class in five minutes." Time enough to plan a pop quiz.

Rob leaned against the door frame and stared into the office. A battered old wooden desk, a vinyl-clad swivel chair with one tattered arm torn and trophies lining the shelves on the back wall. Off to one side was a barrister's bookcase that was filled with every high school text known to man.

The scene before him grew blurred as he remembered the endless hours he'd spent in this very office, a windowless cubbyhole guarding the sports equipment storage room. He had squirmed in one of the scratched wooden chairs positioned in front of the desk belonging to Coach Parsons, who had sat opposite him. Rob had been anxious to discuss his jump shot and old Parsons wanted to talk algebra.

Even back then, Parsons had been athletic director and basketball coach for what seemed to be forever. Of course, anything over five years was near to forever for a high school kid.

The coach had been a short man, on the heavy side, with chubby cheeks that made him appear soft. His looks were both true and misleading at the same time. The coach had a soft heart, too, but he was known as a stern disciplinarian. You listened when he talked X's and O's and you listened when he talked algebra, English, or world history. You also listened when he talked morals and values.

That was one of the reasons Rob had come back here. He owed this place, and Don Parsons, a great deal. They'd given him a chance that his big mouth never would have gotten him. Agreeing to a stopover here was no big deal. Pay a few debts, see a few friends, then be on his way. That was the blueprint of his life anyway.

He walked into the office, sat in the comfortable old chair and put his feet up on the desk. From this position of power Rob could see the brown tiled hallway and the scarred set of doors leading to the boys' locker room. Hell of a view.

Closing his eyes, Rob leaned back and tried to remember what color the walls were when he'd walked these same halls. They must have been painted once or twice in the past thirteen years but for the life of him, he couldn't remember them ever being different. It was as if nothing had changed.

In a lot of ways nothing had. The basic layout of the school was the same and so were many of the teachers. The feel of the place hadn't changed and probably never would. The classrooms pulsated with the same rhythmic ebb and flow of noise and silence.

Jenna's hair was shorter now though, a lot shorter. Easier to take care of. That would be why she cut it. The lady had always been a practical sort. Nothing happened to Jenna that she hadn't planned on.

Serious and steady. Two words that described Jenna to a T. The type that did her homework and drilled hard each and every practice. She even took her fun seriously. Planning out beforehand what she would do at the parties, dances and picnics they went to.

Not that he'd ever blamed her. Things had always been on the heavy side around her house. Her father worked hard and was away a lot as a traveling salesman. Her mother had that damn kidney disease, moving in and out of hospitals a good part of her life, then was on dialysis for years before passing away. Grandma Lauren had been the only one in that family who seemed to remember Jenna needed to smile.

Rob smiled to himself. Not that he hadn't tried. He remembered teasing her constantly. Clowning around in class and on the school bus. Doing almost anything to drive the seriousness out of her eyes and make her laugh.

Jenna had always been a beauty with her bouncy step and that sleek mop of blond hair, but it had always been her eyes that had drawn him. They ranged from stormy gray to the peaceful deep blue of a backwoods lake, and when she laughed, it was as if the angels had smiled on him.

In many ways he wished he hadn't been good enough to get that scholarship to UCLA. If the opportunity hadn't presented itself, he would have gone with Jenna to some small school here in Indiana. She had been smart and tough, but a step slower than the big time programs wanted. They could have stayed together and come back to Warsaw together. Things would have been very different for him. No bouncing all over hell.

Then sighing, he rubbed his face wearily. But would they have? Rob doubted it. He was just blowing smoke like he always did when he got down and moody. Wandering was in his genes, he'd come to accept that.

His dad had been a wanderer. He had been a good mechanic who could get a job anywhere, so the family wandered from town to town. His mother always stood up for the old man, no matter how many dumps he'd led them into. No matter how many times he blew his money on dice and booze. She'd smile and say the old man was just chasing his rainbows. Then she'd wear her knuckles raw cleaning other people's clothes and houses.

Then one day the old man went off chasing a rainbow on his own. Walked out one night without leaving a forwarding address. They never heard from him again. There wasn't any money for them to move on, so they stayed. Rob and his two younger brothers helped out with odd jobs, and protected their self-respect with Irish charm and big-knuckled fists . . . legacies from a man he'd grown to hate.

"Hey, Coach."

Rob looked up, eager for a diversion to escape the demons that mocked him in his private moments. He found himself looking up at a tall, thin boy. The kid had a military cut—they called it a buzz now—and a solid bone structure. Looked like he needed some weight training to beef him up.

"Mike Sherwin. I'm your first string forward and team captain." The kid wore a mocking little grin that seemed to laugh at himself as much as at the world at large.

"Oh, yeah?" Rob replied. "Have a seat."

"Just dropped by to meet with you," Mike said.

"And check me out."

The kid's smile grew broader.

"How do the guys look this year?" Rob asked.

"Great. Just great. We're gonna go downstate. You can take that to the bank."

"Have we got some players?"

"A whole team full."

"Are they good students?" Rob asked.

Mike blinked and hesitated a moment. "Yeah. Pretty good."

"I don't want to lose anybody because of academic ineligibility," Rob said.

"We'll be okay."

The bell rang but Mike didn't move, so Rob did. He stood up. "As students, we're going to be more than okay," Rob said. "You can take that to the bank. Now get to class, I don't want to start by getting in trouble with one of your teachers."

The kid blinked at him.

"Now," Rob said quietly.

"Right." Mike stood up and started walking out. He stopped at the door and turned, obviously forcing the uncertainty from his eyes. "Later," he said, pointing at Rob.

Rob nodded and waited until Mike left to pull out some posters he saw peeking from behind a file cabinet. They were large pictorials of teams from years back, ones that used to line the hallway and entrance to the gym before they were replaced with smaller versions. He flipped through and stopped at the shot of his senior year basketball team. They all wore the same cocky smiles that Mike had worn.

He flipped through a few more and stopped at the picture of Jenna's team. Her blue eyes were calm, serene, open to the world. They were more shadowed now, as if the waters had been churned up and unhappiness lay beneath the surface. Times had changed. Best if he kept reminding himself of that fact.

Chapter Two

"Swell," Jenna muttered as she surveyed the empty office. Rob'd said they had to talk and that she should drop in any time Monday. Here it was almost four o'clock, as well as her fourth time down, and he still wasn't here. She was determined not to be preoccupied with his return, but he was making it hard to think about much else.

She was about ready to stomp out of the office when she noticed the door to the equipment room was open, light spilling out onto the floor. She walked through the office and into the large, musty-smelling room.

"Damn," Rob muttered, throwing a shirt on the floor.

For a moment, she watched him with an unguarded heart. As a boy, Rob had been good-looking, but as a man he was devastating. He was broader in the shoulder now and there was a stronger look about him, but it wasn't just from muscular bulk. He had a steadiness about him, a solid sense that seemed to promise dependability. But then, if she remembered correctly, he resembled his father who'd been built in much the same way.

Shielded by that thought, she took a step in closer. "Having fun?"

Rob started slightly, but he was smiling by the time he'd turned around. "Hi, Jenna."

"I've been trying to see you all day," she said.

"Sorry." He shook his head. "I had a breakfast meeting with the boosters club, lunch with my assistants, as well as the first time through my health and gym classes. Then Arthur tells me they need an inventory of the fall sports uniforms by this evening for the school board meeting. And I still haven't laid out a plan for tonight's practice."

His voice did strange things to her equilibrium, as if she were trying to balance on the top of a tall tree in the midst of a tornado. She planted her feet firmly on the ground and let that same firmness take hold of her voice.

"Looks like you better quit grumping and get to work."

"Thanks," he replied, grinning as he always had from her scolding.

He turned back to his box of uniforms, allowing her to take a few steps closer. "What are we going to do about a practice schedule?"

"Oh." Rob ran his hand through his tousled locks. Another flashback. "Turns out, we really don't have much to decide there. Our wrestling coach has a part-time job teaching a remedial math class at the Biomet plant. If we don't give him the early bird shift, he won't be able to coach."

"That leaves afternoon and evening for us."

"We could alternate," Rob suggested. "Gives the kids that need it the opportunity to work part-time."

"Fine," Jenna said. "I'll take the afternoon shift tomorrow and then evening on Wednesday."

"Sounds good," Rob said with a nod.

Jenna returned the nod and turned to go.

"Uh, Jenna."

She turned. Rob was standing there, hair hanging in his eyes, a crooked smile on his lips. Just the way he looked when he was about to ask her to help him with his math homework. Jenna felt an unholy mixture of irritation and tenderness that united to bring a pain to her heart. Why wasn't she immune to him?

"I don't know which of these uniforms are current and which are leftovers," he said, spreading his arms to indicate the piles of game jerseys, in various styles and shades of blue and white.

Jenna looked at him, seeing both the man he was and the youth he had been. Her willpower seemed to turn to mush around him, but that didn't mean he had to know it. If she stood still, he'd never know that his gaze could turn her knees to water. She wasn't a naive high school girl anymore, a soft touch, ready to dance for any handsome blue-eyed stud that walked down the pike.

Still smiling his crooked smile, Rob shook his head as he stared at the shirts. "I don't even know where to start."

Oh, hell. She could hardly stand still and leave at the same time. Better get it over with and leave when he was busy doing something else.

"Those shirts with the white blaze across the front are the home court uniforms for the girls' basketball team," Jenna said. "The white with the blue blaze are the away uniforms. That pile is the boys' shirt, same colors for home and away as the girls. Those other ones are the old volleyball and softball uniforms."

Rob just stood still and smiled at her. "Thanks."

"Neither of us have all night," Jenna pointed out before his eyes turned other things besides her knees to jelly. "Get your clipboard and let's start counting."

Jenna began separating the shirts and with the two of them working, they were able to inventory the uniforms quickly. Then they assessed the condition of the jerseys and developed a list of replacements needed.

"We have a lot of old uniforms here," Rob said.

"We should offer them for sale at one of the athletic booster club's spaghetti dinners," Jenna said. "Lots of people would like to buy back their old jersey."

"Good idea."

They boxed up the uniforms and walked out together, carrying the silence between them, as if in completing the job, they'd used up their store of conversation. Or maybe just safe conversation.

"I was surprised to see you're still here," Rob said, as he locked the equipment room door. "I thought you had other ambitions besides teaching in your old high school."

Jenna shrugged and looked away into the distance, seeking someplace that was safe to rest her eyes. "You knew that my dad was in an automobile accident," she said. "A few weeks after you left for California."

"Yeah." Rob nodded. "Mom wrote me about it but it was already more than a month after the accident. By the time I called, you were away at school, so I just sent that card. Mom said you were in the car with him, but weren't injured."

His silence had hurt at the time, but she'd never considered the idea that he hadn't known. They'd been so close, it seemed that he should have known whenever she'd been hurting.

Jenna took a moment to put a lid on her painful memory. "A drunk driver ran a red light. Hit our car on the passenger side. I was driving." She paused a moment to swallow the lump in her throat. "Dad was killed instantly. I was hurt some, but not too badly."

"You had a basketball scholarship to Manchester College, didn't you?"

"Yeah." She checked the scarred tile in the hallway outside Rob's office. "I passed on that. Mom was getting sicker with her kidney thing and I didn't want to be too far away from her and Gram. So, I went to St. Joseph's College in Rensselaer. They needed a point guard and were willing to take a chance that I'd heal in time for the season."

"And you did?"

"I had fun." She paused a moment, wondering how so much pain could be condensed into so few words. And how it was that the things she'd left out weren't obvious. But he said nothing and she went on. "I knew Mom would need me, so I planned on coming back. Sort of drifted into teaching."

"From what I hear you're good at it," Rob said.

Jenna smiled. "I enjoy it."

They stood in the silence for a long moment, long enough for the echoes of their youth to start reaching her consciousness. It was time to move on, in a lot of ways.

"Well," Jenna said brusquely. "I'd better get going. I have some tests to correct."

"Yeah," Rob agreed. "And I have a practice to run. Then I have some studying of my own. Can't let the little kiddies know how much smarter they are than me."

"Doesn't matter what you do. They'll figure they are anyway."

He nodded again. "Ah, yes. The infinite wisdom of teenagers."

Jenna just nodded. After that bit of clever repartee, they stood and shared a long moment of silence, as if neither could break the spell of the past and leave.

"Say," Rob said, as if struck with a bolt of inspiration. "Why don't I run this data down to Arthur and then we grab a bite to eat?"

Her first thoughts issued warnings, but for some reason they sounded faint, almost too faint to hear and certainly too faint to take seriously.

"Sure, I was going to stop someplace for a meal anyway," Jenna said with a shrug. "Tonight's Gram's pinochle night."

He glanced at his watch. "I've got less than an hour before my practice. Where can we pick up a fast snack?"

"How about Pattie's Grill?"

"My God," he exclaimed. "Is Charley still around?"

"Yup," Jenna replied. "And he still makes those grossburgers, smothered in onions."

"And how about the cherry pies?"

"The same," she replied. "Crisscrossed on top with strips of dough and baked so that the sugar and sauce turns into black tar."

"Sounds great. Real down home. Meet you there in ten minutes?"

He hurried off to give the inventory results to the principal as Jenna walked slowly out to the parking lot. She absolutely refused to think about anything. She just took time to help out a fellow teacher and now they were just going to grab a bite to eat. There was nothing to it, nothing at all.

Jenna's feet took her to the booth in the far back of the little snack shop just down the street from the high school. A little bird lodged in her memory whispered that it had been her and Rob's table back in the days when they were an "item" but she quickly squashed that thought. That had nothing to do with why she chose it. It was just quieter back here, away from the noisy bunch of football players up front.

She sat down facing the door, then glanced at the clock on the wall. Rob was late, but then Rob had always been late.

Jenna had always arrived first, then Rob would follow later. It took him ages to move from A to B; there was always someone to stop him, to exchange a few words. Sometimes it took him five minutes to get from the door of the snack shop back to their booth. When he'd finally arrive, he'd be wearing that crooked little grin on his lips, have sparkle in his eyes, and charm oozing out of every pore. She forgave him every time for making her wait.

The chimes hanging on the door rang as Rob stepped in. He had on his crooked little grin and even from where she sat she could see that his eyes sparkled. For a moment, she felt that sudden surge of delight like the sun breaking through the clouds after a storm, then reined herself back in sharply. He might be the same old Rob, but she was not the same old Jenna. Not by a long shot.

"Hi. Sorry I'm late," he murmured, as he slid into the booth opposite her.

Jenna found herself speechless, surprise wiping out the irritation she'd been trying to arm herself with. Rob never apologized for being late.

"I gave Arthur the inventory list. Then he had just a few other questions." Rob shook his head and laughed. "He was almost hanging onto my leg to keep me in there until I answered them."

Jenna felt uncertainly surround her. "Arthur is like that," she said slowly. "He has so many things going on that once he gets hold of you, he has trouble letting go."

"Yeah, he has a tough job."

His voice was matter-of-fact, but his eyes had taken on a softer glow as they roamed gently over her face. It was almost as if he was touching her, caressing her skin until the heat in her heart was strong enough to flush her cheeks. The years and all the tears started slipping into oblivion.

"Hey, Rob. Rob Fagan. How the hell are you, sport?"

His gaze was jerked away, leaving Jenna feeling topsy-turvy for a split second. Just as well, she told herself, taking a deep steadying breath as Rob rose and walked over behind the counter. This was not going as well as she had hoped.

"Charley, great to see you," Rob was saying as he shook hands with Charley Willis, owner, cook and jack-of-all-trades for Pattie's Grill. "And you don't look a day older."

The old man laughed. "Good old Rob," Charley said. "Same old bull flipper he's always been. Right, Jenna?"

Jenna smiled, a bright noncommittal smile that said everything and nothing.

"What'll you guys have?" Charley asked.

"I hear you still make grossburgers," Rob said.

"Sure do," Charley replied. "Go out early in the morning, scrape up the road kill, mix it with whatever's too slow to run away and I got me a new batch of grossburger. The kids love 'em."

"Give me one with everything," Rob said. "And a large cola."

"Swiss cheese on rye and lemonade," Jenna said.

"I'll bring them out," Charley said.

Even Rob remembered things well enough to be amazed. Charley never served anyone. If one of his daughters wasn't there to wait tables, you came to the grill and picked up your own order. Rob sat back down, shaking his head.

"How does it feel to return home a conquering hero?" Jenna asked him.

Rob just shrugged. "Lotta nice folks here. They remember me to have been better than I was."

A modest Rob Fagan. This was getting scary. She could fight the old Rob, full of bravado and cockiness, but this one was different. This Rob could catch her unawares, finding cracks in her walls she hadn't thought to shore up and attack her heart in ways she'd never expected.

"Well, you are a world traveler," Jenna said.

He shrugged.

"Hey, you've been to California, Europe."

He frowned slightly. "To tell you the truth, Europe hadn't been anywhere in my plans. I had a good career at UCLA. Starter for three years." He looked around the half-empty snack shop for a moment. "I was sure that I'd be drafted by some NBA team. Maybe not in the first round but I was absolutely positive that there was a team out there who needed a good point guard." A grin flickered on his lips. "Like myself, of course."

The smile was a flash of his old self. The one she could handle. "Of course."

"I wasn't drafted at all." He shook his head and smiled ruefully. "Boy, that was humiliation city."

"Didn't you get any invitations to try out?" she asked.

"Oh, sure. A lot of them. No guarantees. No money up front." He made a face. "At first I was shocked. Then I got mad. Decided the hell with them, I'd show them. I'd play in Europe. Make a name for myself and they'd be begging me to come back. Got in touch with an agent and he had me signed with a team in Belgium within a couple of weeks."

"That sounds like it could have been fun," Jenna said.

"It was," he said and paused for moment. "New places, new food, new and interesting people."

Charley brought their order out to them and both murmured thank-yous before turning back to each other.

"You played in other countries, right?"

He nodded. "Yep. From Belgium I went to Italy. Then I got traded to a team in Spain. The money was good and I was able to save most of it. And it was a good education to live in different parts of the world, in other cultures. But I was glad to get back to the USA."

They let silence wash over them while they ate. She wasn't sure where Rob let his eyes wander; she wasn't brave enough to look up and see. She kept her eyes down, though her gaze meandered across the table and rested on Rob's hands as he ate. He still ate his sandwiches the same way—a bite of sandwich, then two french fries and a sip of cola. It began to feel as if she had slipped back through some time warp. A feeling she had to fight.

"How long did you play in Europe?" she asked, as she finished off her sandwich.

"Almost seven years," he replied.

"Didn't any NBA teams call?"

"Yeah, but not loud enough to make it interesting." He stared up toward the front of the snack shop, but not as if he really saw anything there. "Then I ripped up my ankle. Not super bad, but the injury slowed my game, making it impossible for me to continue to play competitive basketball."

"So you came back."

"I went back to UCLA," Rob said. "I needed a few more courses to get my bachelor's degree. As I'm sure you remember, I wasn't exactly a rocket scientist. But I got turned around and stuck it out until I got a masters in education."

"You went into teaching then?"

He shook his head. "No, I went into sales for a sporting goods company. Don't ask me why."

"Sounds like more travel."

"It was. More living in cheap motel rooms and more eating at greasy spoons." Rob grinned. "I guess they're in my blood."

"Would a transfusion have helped?"

"Only temporarily."

His joking nature hadn't changed, that was for sure. Jenna remembered the boy who teased meals out of her grandmother and charmed extra time for completing assignments from his teachers. Assignments that she then helped him with.

What had changed was his attitude toward life. She remembered him being angry so much of the time, mostly at his father for the wanderings he'd led them all on. Now Rob seemed as much of a wanderer as his father, and content with it.

"So what have you been doing with yourself?" he asked, breaking into her thoughts.

"Teaching," she replied. "Coaching. Doing some traveling of my own."

"Didn't that itch to move on ever return?" he asked.

"You mean chase some rainbows?"

His mouth grew tight and his eyes remote, and Jenna didn't know what to think. She'd touched some raw spot obviously, though she didn't know where. Before she could regroup her thoughts, Rob's smooth smile was back on his lips.

"I meant like having a life of your own," he said, with sparkle in his eyes. "Like how is your love life?"

Something snapped inside Jenna. She'd felt as if she were a yo-yo since Rob had come back, a yo-yo that was on display with everyone watching and analyzing her every reaction. It was bad enough that half the town expected she would fall back into his arms, while the other half probably figured her "week at Diamond Lake" each summer had really been spent with Rob, wherever he'd been at the moment. It was intolerable that Rob should be thinking along the same lines. There was no vacancy waiting to be filled in her life, at least not one that could be filled by him.

"Quite fine," she snapped. "Though I don't see where my personal life is anymore your business than yours is mine."

His eyes reflected his surprise, and she felt a funny feeling in the pit of her stomach. She'd overreacted, primed to slay fire-eating dragons where there was only smoke. He'd only asked a simple question of an old friend.

"You're right," he said softly, looking at her with eyes considerably dimmed. "I was totally out of line."

"Let's forget about it." It was probably better that way. Let him think some knight in shining armor was waiting just up the road in Fort Wayne, not that her empty arms still ached for their child she'd been unable to carry to term.

They finished their meal in silence, sipping at their drinks as if they were each searching for a way to slip away.

"There you go, folks." Charley dropped a dish of pie before each of them. "Cherry pie with a double scoop of ice cream for the fella and banana cream for the lady." He stood back and smiled. "Just like the old days, huh?"

Jenna and Rob could only stare at Charley in surprise, though a cold flash of fear rippled through Jenna. *Just like the old days.* Things couldn't be just like the old days, never again, and she didn't want them to be. She never wanted to feel so sick and all alone, or in need of someone as much as she needed Rob once he'd gone. Thank goodness, Rob's stay was going to be temporary.

"Dessert's on the house," Charley was saying.

"That sure isn't like the old days." Rob laughed as he picked up his fork and began eating. "It does bring the memories back though, doesn't it?"

"Sort of," Jenna agreed, taking a bite of her own pie.

"Wonder where a lot of the old gang are."

"Most everyone came back to our ten-year reunion," she said and concentrated on her confection.

"I think I was working in Texas at the time."

"A lot of them are still in town," Jenna said. "Those who moved are mostly in Fort Wayne or South Bend."

"Their roots run deep."

"Yep."

They ran out of dessert and conversation at about the same time. Rob stared into his glass of ice cubes and Jenna watched him with sadness tinging her shadows. In some strange way she wished she could tell him about the baby, about how she had vowed to herself that she'd never tie him down to Warsaw when she found out that she was pregnant, and how she'd longed for him to come home and be with her after the accident. Every secret part of her life had been torn apart, but it was too long ago to discuss any of those things and open old wounds that had healed. The subject was best left alone.

"You guys want anything else?" Charley asked.

"No," they answered in unison.

"Good," Charley said. "Then get out of here so I can clean up and go home."

Rob stood up and walked up to the register. "You're still the same old charmer, Charley."

"Yeah, I gotta watch that." Charley took the ten Rob offered and automatically assumed he was paying for both. "Let it go too far and before I know it the women are all over me. Like fleas on a dog."

Rob laughed as he took his change, while Jenna just muttered, "Cute, Charley."

They walked out into the fall evening, the chill of winter mixing with the smell of burning leaves and pumpkins. Jenna silently offered Rob money for her dinner, but he just shook his head.

"Thanks then," she murmured.

He took her arm and walked her to her car. "Hey, you know me," Rob said. "Big spender."

Jenna laughed, all at once convinced that it was safe to be here with Rob. She leaned into him slightly, liking the feel of him. She could risk it just for the few moments it took to reach her car.

They stopped next to it, and he waited while she pulled her keys from her pocket.

"Thanks for keeping me company," he said.

"Ditto."

She wanted to move to her car door and unlock it, but she couldn't seem to move from Rob's side. There was a stillness in the air, a sense of wonder that Christmas was here unexpectedly.

Rob leaned over to lightly kiss her lips. It was the softest touch that she should barely have been able to feel, yet it rocked her to the core. The joy of Christmas was there, but also the promise of spring, the sense that old fires could glow brightly again, that old loves could grow strong once more. He pulled away from her.

"See you later," he said.

"Right."

Then he turned and Jenna watched him hurry down the block toward the school. With fear tightening her heart, she climbed into her car. It wasn't being here alone in the dark that frightened her though. It was the man who had just left and the power he still held over her heart.

Jenna hung her coat on the wooden peg in the vestibule, then bent down to pat her dog. "Hi, Susie. How are ya, girl?"

Susie rolled out her tongue and wagged her tail. The gray-muzzled old golden retriever couldn't jump around much anymore, but she could still wag a mean tail. And she still was about the best thing around to hug when Jenna felt down.

Why should she feel down? Jenna scolded herself. She had a great job that she loved, family and friends who cared about her, and her health. Just because an old love came wandering through town and awoke some vivid memories with a kiss, didn't mean she should get all mopey and sad. Or that she should become as indecisive as a willow branch, blowing whichever way the wind wanted.

One moment, she's promising herself she won't fall for Rob's line and the next, she's falling into his arms. She tells herself the past is past, but then she wants to tell Rob about the baby. What good would it do to be hurt all over again by him? Was she trying to make this into some sort of ritual? Once every thirteen years she would let him into her life and then be torn apart when he left.

Susie's love was the safest, a sure thing. Jenna heard a noise in the kitchen and stopped petting the dog, suddenly conscious of the warm, delicious aromas in the house.

"Gram?" She stepped into the kitchen in time to see her grandmother pulling two apple pies from the oven. "I thought you had pinochle tonight."

"Della's cat caught a mouse and she's all worried that her house is full of them. Doesn't want any company until she calls an exterminator." Gram closed the oven door with a solid thud. "Land sakes, as if everybody doesn't have mice coming into the house this time of year. What does she think she has a cat for?"

Jenna smiled at her grandmother's impatience as she sat down on the stool in the corner. "City slickers."

"She's lived here for going on ten years. Think she'd learn. Want some stew or do you want to clean up first?"

"I already ate," Jenna said. "I didn't think you'd be cooking."

"What'd you have? Some of that drive-through, pretend food?"

Jenna sighed. Gram hated fast food places, didn't believe real food could be fast. "Rob and I went to Pattie's Grill. I had a sandwich and a piece of pie."

Her grandmother's sudden smile lit up the room and Jenna's stomach sank down into her shoes. Damn, why had she told Gram whom she'd been with? The old woman's one-track mind didn't need any encouragement.

But Gram just turned a bland eye on the big pot of beef stew. "I'll just freeze this then."

"You should start making less."

"If you'd brought that man home like you should have, there wouldn't be anything left over."

"There wasn't time. Rob had to go back to school for the boys' basketball practice."

"Poor man's near starved to death. Got to put some meat on them bones before he just ups and keels over."

"He didn't have time."

"I can feed him just as quick as that reprobate at Pattie's. And better. Healthier and tastier."

"He has a two-hour practice, Gram. He'd get sick if he ate all you'd have pushed at him."

"He could have come back after practice for seconds. Stew ain't like some of them hoity-toity French dishes. Fact is, it tastes even better after sitting on the back burner for a spell."

Jenna got up from the stool. You'd think she would have learned by now there was no winning an argument with her grandmother. "Just leave the pot there," she said. "I'll put it away in a little bit."

"Don't worry about it, child. I'll take care of things after you eat."

"I already ate, Gram."

"One little bitty sandwich ain't enough to keep body and soul together." Gram's eyes glittered and snapped, warning signs that another storm was about to descend on the household. "Least-wise, not so you're strong enough to attract a man."

"If I ate all you wanted me to, I'd be a blimp."

"Men don't like skinny women. They don't find sharp edges all that comfortable."

Jenna said nothing, but vowed silently that Rob wasn't getting close enough to feel any of her edges, sharp or otherwise. She learned from her mistakes. Maybe not fast, but she did learn.

"Ain't that wonderful, Rob Fagan coming back to town?" Gram suddenly took off on another track. "Your Mommy and Daddy always liked him. I liked him, too."

A sudden pain shot through Jenna's breath. Would they have if they'd had to deal with the truth? "I have a lot of papers to correct," she said. "I gave quizzes in algebra and geometry today."

"He's such a funny boy. Carries the sunshine with him everywhere he goes."

"I'll be in the den," Jenna said.

"Your special guardian angel's been watching over you."

This was getting to be too much. She couldn't let her grandmother hope and dream. "Gram, Rob and I were just high school sweethearts. That's all over now. We just work at the high school. We're not students there anymore."

"You two planted the seed back then," Gram said. "It's just taking a while to grow and flower."

Jenna looked at her grandmother's confident smile and almost burst into tears. If her grandmother only knew what kind of seed had been planted back then, it would break her heart.

"Gram," Jenna said, weariness dragging down every word. "Rob's only here temporarily. He'll be gone as soon as Don Parsons recuperates."

"Don's up in years. No one knows how things will work out for him."

"It doesn't make any difference. If Don doesn't come back, someone else'll take his place permanently. Rob Fagan is a roamer. He'll be chasing rainbows until the day he dies. Just like his father."

"He's more like his mother, dear. Solid and dependable. Salt of the earth. His father gave him his charm and quick wit, but his mother gave him two feet planted solidly on the ground."

Jenna saw the kitchen scene and her grandmother grew misty before her. Poor Gram. She wanted something that could never be, something Jenna had stopped dreaming of long ago.

Chapter Three

"Hi."

Jenna paused, leaf rake in hand, and took a deep breath. Rob's voice still had the power to tingle the hair on the back of her neck. It didn't mean anything and certainly wasn't a sign that she was weakening in any way, but she took a moment to cool her cheeks. There was no need to give him the wrong idea.

"Hi, stranger." Jenna kept a tight grip on her rake as she turned around. "Looks like things are keeping you hopping. I hardly saw you at all this past week."

"Hardly saw myself."

"Something wrong with your car?" Jenna asked, looking up and down the empty street.

"It's parked over back of the hardware store. It's such a beautiful day that I decided to walk over."

Decided to walk over? Why would Rob need to come over at all? She hoped he wasn't taking all of her grandmother's invitations seriously; seeing him at school was hard enough on Jenna. She leaned on her rake and looked at him.

His jeans and blue-checked flannel shirt did nothing to hide his trim athletic physique. Though the dazzling warmth of his smile sure could distract a person from it, if a person let it. Which she didn't, of course.

"There were some changes in the girls' varsity and JV schedule," Rob said. "I marked the new dates."

She took the new schedule from him and quickly glanced at it. "The changes are all for the latter half of the season. You could have given this to me Monday."

Rob ran his fingers through the hair on his forehead. "I know, but things have been hectic and I was afraid I might forget."

Unexpected urges swept over Jenna and her grip on her rake tightened for a moment to keep her fingers from wandering into places they didn't belong. There were certain things, such as brushing back errant locks, a woman had to let a man do for himself. That is, if she wanted to stay out of trouble. Once she felt she could trust her fingers again, she let them fold the schedule and stick it in the back pocket of her jeans.

"Thanks," she said, suggesting the gesture of resuming raking, but Rob continued to stand there. "If you need any help with anything, just let me know."

He nodded. "Don had been feeling poorly for months, so some equipment and schedules weren't up to snuff." Then he smiled broadly, catching her heart by surprise and almost causing it to break into song. "But I've almost got things under control now."

She went back to raking, only glancing up at him for split seconds. Tiny doses of his smile, minute exposures to his charm, that was the ticket to keeping her heart healthy.

"Don should have eased up a while ago," she said. "Might have kept himself out of the hospital."

Rob shrugged. "Yeah, maybe. But the school and its sports programs have been everything to him for a long time. Letting go would have been like letting go of life itself."

"I hear he's coming home next week."

"Yeah, but he's got a long recuperation ahead of him."

So how was that going to effect Rob? But she wouldn't ask, wouldn't let herself wonder if he might stay. Instead, she joined Rob in staring at the large lot, the old Victorian house, and huge oak trees surrounding it.

"You've got tons of leaves here," Rob said. "Makes for a lot of work in the fall."

"They give us great shade in the summer. Raking leaves in the fall is a small price to pay."

Rob just grunted.

"Daddy always said, nothing's free in this world."

"Isn't that the truth?" Rob replied and looked up to the bare tops of the towering trees. "These things were big when we were in high school. How old are they?"

Since high school was a couple thousand years ago, the trees had to be at least that. "About a hundred-twenty, hundred-thirty years old," Jenna replied.

"How can you be so precise?" he asked.

"My great-grandfather planted them when he came here soon after the Civil War. He wanted these branches to shade his children, his children's children, and on until the final judgement."

In the light of such longevity, her problems in remaining objective about Rob seemed minor. She relaxed slightly.

"Is that one of your family fables?"

"Nope." She shook her head. "My great-grandfather kept a diary. Gram has it."

"Did your great-grandfather build this house?"

"No. My grandfather did. My great-grandfather's house was a little thing that got burned down."

Jenna watched him stare at the yard, an unreadable expression on his face as his eyes swept the landscape before them. Finally, he spoke. "How could he be so sure that his descendants would occupy this property?"

"I don't think he could imagine anyone ever wanting to leave," Jenna replied. "In his mind, he had everything anybody could want right here. Good soil for farming, fair and loyal neighbors, and the chance to raise his family in peace."

"The land could just as well have been turned into a shopping center." A dark cloud seemed to be drifting into Rob's eyes. "Then these trees would have been all hacked down and the land buried in concrete and asphalt."

"I guess we were lucky."

"Yeah, I guess you were." Suddenly his face brightened and the sparkle came back into his eyes. "Want any help with the leaves?"

"That's okay."

"Come on, Jenna. I used to help you, remember?"

Jenna snorted. "I remember you jumping into the piles."

"I was just having a little fun."

"And you'd dump leaves on my head."

"Just trying to bring a little cheer into your day," he said. "You always had trouble lightening up."

"Then you used to wrestle me down into the neatly gathered piles."

"Gee whiz, Jenna. If I'd known you were going to be a grump about things, I never would have put myself out that way."

She stared at him a long moment, at his black hair hanging in his eyes, infringing on but not hiding those sparkling blue eyes. For just the teeny, tiniest moment, Jenna ached for those wild carefree moments of their youth, when Rob made her heart come alive and she could find a world of joy in his eyes.

But sanity came rushing back and she quickly pushed the memories away. She not only pushed them, she stomped them into the black Indiana dirt. Stomped them until there wasn't a shred of life left in those foolish little girl thoughts.

"Thank you for bringing the schedule changes." Jenna started raking vigorously. "But I'd better get back to my chores."

Jenna pursued her task, eyes safely on the ground, brow furrowed in concentration as if it could shield her from the charm of his smile. She studiously waded through the silence, the absence of the sound of shoes on the sidewalk telling her that Rob hadn't walked away yet. Finally, she could stand it no longer.

"Are you afraid to cross the street by yourself?" she teased. "Want me to ask Gram if she'd be willing to walk you down to your car?"

He looked at her yard and sighed, putting only a glint of a smile into his eyes. "I can't remember the last time I had a chance to rake and bag leaves," he said.

"Sad. Almost enough to make me cry."

"They don't have autumn in Los Angeles," Rob said. "And in Europe I lived in apartments." He shook his head sadly. "I think the last time was on this very yard, back when we were in high school." He shook his head again. "That was over thirteen years ago, Jenna."

"You just said there were a million things to do," she reminded him. "Aren't there more uniforms in the storeroom that need counting?"

"Why can't I help you, just for a little while?"

Jenna frowned at him for asking a question she couldn't answer, at least not to him.

"I'll just rake and bag," he said. "No fooling around. I promise."

Her gaze turned skeptical.

"Scout's honor," he said. "Cross my heart and hope to die, poke a stick in my eye if I lie."

Jenna sighed and went back to her chore. "Even though I don't remember you ever being a Boy Scout, there's another rake in the garage."

She didn't know what to expect but once Rob returned with the rake he worked diligently and industriously. They chatted a little about things in general: new stores on main street, how the biomedical companies were making strides in prosthetics, and how the shopping malls were expanding on the edge of town. But most of the time they were quiet, just working and enjoying the fall day. The leaves disappeared and the number of full bags grew.

With every minute that passed, it seemed that another knot was untied somewhere around Jenna's heart. It wasn't that she felt ready to take up with Rob again; she just didn't see so strong a challenge in his smile. They were old friends and that friendship had been strong enough to last over the years. They'd been lovers, too, but only for a short time, a small percentage of the time they'd known each other. And it probably had been more of a sexual attraction than love. The friendship, though, had been deep and strong and true. It was right that she should discover it again.

Suddenly Jenna noticed they were down to one huge pile. As she took a moment to catch her breath, Rob jumped into the mound, leaves flying out in a spray of gold and red. He sat up, grinning.

"You promised," Jenna said, but her voice wasn't nearly as stern as she'd meant it to be.

Rob said nothing, but got up slowly, a bunch of leaves clutched in each hand. His eyes gleamed with mischief.

"Hey, now wait a minute," she cried, but laughingly darted away from him.

She felt wild and alive, a child again and free of all the shadows that had haunted her over the past years. The wind ruffled her hair as if it too were laughing.

She raced around a tree and back over to the heap of leaves, ready to capture her own ammunition, but Rob was there waiting for her. He tried to grab her arm to make her drop the leaves she'd gotten, but instead they both lost their balance. They tumbled into the drift of leaves, Jenna on the bottom and Rob landing on top of her.

The laughter died from both their eyes, fading away slowly like the dew under the heat of the sun. Rob looked at her, his eyes caressing her cheeks and her lips before coming back to stare deep into her soul.

She stared back up at him, seeing his face framed in sunlight, yet finding the heat of his gaze more blinding. She couldn't look away though, mesmerized by the longings that were waking in her soul. Some were distant memories from yesteryear that woke slowly, stretching as if rising from a sound sleep. Others were new hungers, deeper needs that had nothing to do with the past, only now. Only with the man pressed against her body, not with the boy he used to be.

"Ah, Jenna," he sighed, his breath mingling with hers and he moved in to take her lips.

They kissed, their mouths and hearts mingling. She felt a completeness in his arms, a sense of having found something that was lost. A fire began to smoulder, sparks lapping out to warm every part of her. This was being alive; this was what she had been waiting for.

Rob moved slightly, his hands sliding beneath her to pull her closer to him. She'd needed the feel of his hands on her and when his touch came, it seared her soul into happiness.

Suddenly, amid a flurry of barks, they had a guest. Susie arrived, greeting Jenna and Rob with a few friendly nuzzles. Both of them looked up, moving with the stunned sluggishness of having just woken up.

"Calm down, Suze," Jenna finally said, sitting up.

Rob had moved to sit next to her. "Susie? This is that little squirt of a puppy you had senior year?" He didn't wait for an answer, but scratched the dog behind her ears as he spoke to her. "Hey, girl, remember me?"

Susie looked as excited and eager as Jenna had felt a few moments earlier, Jenna thought while taking a deep breath to shake all the cobwebs from her mind. What had she been thinking of? Or had she been thinking at all? Maybe that was the real trouble.

She waited a moment for Susie to calm down, then she turned to face Rob, scooting back away from him slightly as she did. "We need to talk."

He looked at her, his eyes free of mischief, but still holding traces of desire. "Okay."

She picked up a leaf and curled it into a tight ball, its edges dried and flaking. It would never be green and giving shade again. Some things were meant to last for only a season, not a lifetime.

"We had a close relationship back when we were in high school," she said. "Everyone in town certainly remembers it and seems to expect us to take up where we left off, but a lot of things have changed."

He watched her, his eyes searching hers, but she just looked away, refusing to let him read answers in her gaze. "Maybe what's changed the most is me," she continued. "I have a life of my own, a profession, and . . . and my cup is full."

Rob nodded as he looked off down the street.

"So." She let the leaf fall to the ground. "I really don't thing we should make that much of the little kiss we exchanged after our snack at Pattie's Grill or this one. It's not the start of anything. It's not the return to our past. I mean, old habits might rear up, but that wouldn't do anything except make things awkward."

Jenna watched him sit silently, crumbling dry leaves in his hand as he stared off down the street. She was quiet herself as she got to her feet and went to pick up her rake.

When she looked back, he was standing also, and though she couldn't see his face, there was something still and hurting about him. Her resolve quivered. Had he hoped they would get back together? Could he have come back, wanting to find her still single?

But when he turned around, he was smiling and she could see no shadows hovering about him. "Guess we'd better quit gabbing and finish bagging this pile before Susie scatters them over the yard."

Jenna nodded and picked up the bag while he raked the errant leaves back into the fold. "We've both changed, Rob," she added, feeling that there was more to be said.

He smiled. "Sure. I know I have."

They finished bagging the remainder of the leaves, then exchanged goodbyes, after which Rob walked off toward the hardware store to get his car. Jenna picked up both tools and walked slowly back to the garage. Clouds danced on the far western horizon and Jenna felt tired.

"I should be home around ten, Gram."

"I still think you should have called Rob," her grandmother said. "He'd probably enjoy going to the football game. After all, it isn't every year that Warsaw High makes the sectional playoffs."

After Jenna's speech of this afternoon, calling Rob up for a sort-of-date was the last thing she wanted to do. "He's a basketball coach, not a football coach."

"He's also athletic director," Gram pointed out. "That means he's interested in all the school's sports activities."

"Good night, Gram."

"Be more fun to have a date," Gram grumbled.

"I'll see you around ten," Jenna said.

By the time Jenna'd backed her car out of the garage and was on her way to the stadium, she was humming. Poor Gram. It wasn't her fault she wanted to see Jenna married. Gram had just grown up in a different time, a time when most women needed a man to survive. Things were different now. There weren't bears lurking in the woods. And most jobs these days required a nimble mind rather than a strong back. There were jobs that a woman could do as well as any man.

Jenna wasn't getting rich on her teacher's salary, but she was certainly comfortable. Her car was paid for and so was the house. She didn't need anything else. A little voice tried to mock her, reminding her of the melting surge of heat that had washed over her in Rob's arms. A momentary weakness, that was all that had been.

Jenna parked her car and joined the crowd inching its way toward the gates.

"Hey, Jenna," someone called out. "How are the girls going to be this year?"

"Competitive."

"Hey, Jen," someone else said. "Can you help chaperon the Halloween Dance? I really need a couple more people."

"Sure. I'll be glad to."

The crush of people and greetings banished the moodiness that had tried so hard to capture her thoughts. There was no way she could ever be lonely around here. She showed her teacher's activity pass at the gate and climbed the steps to the banks of seats.

"Jenna. Hey, Jenna."

She turned, arm automatically half-raised for another greeting, but it froze in place. "Hi, Rob."

"Come on up," Rob said. "I saved a spot just for you."

Jenna hesitated, staring at him. This wasn't what she wanted, wasn't what she ought to be considering. She'd spent all afternoon congratulating herself on the way she handled that awkwardness with Rob, but she knew she wasn't ready to spend an evening at his side. Being tough when she had five minutes left with him was a good beginning, but the next round should be ten or fifteen minutes, not a couple of hours.

"For heaven's sake, Jenna. Go sit by the man so the rest of us can get through and find some seats."

Jenna turned to find Rita and a whole gaggle of people, grinning wickedly at her.

"Thanks, Rita," she hissed.

"Don't mention it." Her assistant coach smiled sweetly at her. "Give the hunk a squeeze for me."

Jenna tried to fix her with a glare, but the crowd was getting restless. Jenna stepped aside and walked up the stands to the seat beside Rob. This was no big deal, she told herself.

"I didn't know you were interested in football," Jenna said as she sat down.

"I'm the athletic director," Rob answered. "I'm interested in all the school's athletic activities."

"That's what Gram said."

"That grandmother of yours is a wise woman, a very wise woman."

"Wise as in wiseacre," Jenna growled.

They sat in silence, Jenna absently waving to friends in the crowd as she tried to think of something safe to talk about. Rob moved, his thigh resting against hers. They were barely touching, but awareness of it consumed her. Warmth spread, melting her resolve. She wanted to press closer and knew she should jump away.

"Did she tell you I was interested in intramurals?" Rob asked.

She started, at least mentally. "What?"

"Your grandmother," Rob said sharply. "Did she tell you I was interested in intramurals, too."

"That's nice."

"Yep," he said. "As athletic director I want to see that every child has the opportunity to develop his total person. Intellectual, physical, as well as moral."

His silkiness took some of the tension from the moment. "That's not only nice, that's noble."

"Did your grandmother tell you I was noble?"

"No," Jenna said. "She probably figures there's no need to emphasize the obvious."

"Your grandmother certainly is a very wise woman."

Jenna grinned, relaxing completely. "Oh, stop it," she said, swatting Rob on his arm. "The game is about to start."

They both stopped to watch the kickoff. Warsaw was receiving and their man on punt returns made a good run to their own forty-yard line. The Warsaw fans all stood and cheered, then settled back down as the offense came on the field. She was sometimes her own worst enemy, Jenna told herself. Seeing problems where none existed. It was as if she were still afraid of the dark.

"I always liked to make you laugh," Rob said.

"How decent of you," Jenna said. "You were noble even back then."

"And would you believe that I didn't even realize it?"

His smile seemed to pull strings in her heart and she turned to concentrate on the game. The Warsaw quarterback threw a pass that just sailed over the fingertips of his teammate streaking for the end zone. A collective groan erupted from the stands, but she was more aware of the man sitting next to her than a missed play.

Rob squeezed closer to her, even though there was room enough in the stands, and took her hand. "Who makes you laugh now, Jenna?"

She turned to face him. His gaze seemed to hold her eyes prisoner, locking the two of them together in a world that no one else could enter. But it was also a world that didn't exist any longer. She looked away.

"I read the funnies," she said.

"The funnies?"

"Every day," she said nodding.

"Are they as good as I was?"

No, never, her heart cried out, but she was too smart to listen to it. "They don't start any arguments," she said.

"That's one point for me." His teasing broke the spell. "Every stew needs a little spice. Anything else?"

Jenna laughed again and punched him on the shoulder. "You're just as full of yourself as you've always been."

"You've got to put your best points forward," Rob said. "Never get to first base if you don't."

And so it went. Jenna tried to concentrate on the game, but Rob was always there, pushing himself into her consciousness. She had never watched a game harder, though she couldn't recall from the first to the fourth quarter what had occurred. Warsaw's boys did the town proud; they played well and won. But Jenna couldn't have intelligently discussed the game to save her life.

"The crowd still go to Ricco's?" Rob asked, as they crept along toward the exit, the crowd undulating like one giant worm.

"Yep." She sensed his next question and rushed in to forestall it. "You coming too? Want me to save you a spot?"

"Yeah. Great."

With a smile and a nod, she took off for her own car. Maybe saving him a spot wasn't the smartest thing to do, but it was far better than riding with him within the close confines of his car. Alone in a car with Rob would awaken old memories, old longings. She'd play the good friend and maybe that's what they could be.

But Rob pulled into Ricco's parking lot right behind Jenna, so they went in together. It made them feel like a couple, a feeling that Jenna liked down deep inside her. Don't get to feeling comfortable, she scolded herself. There were too many secrets that lay between her and Rob for any real relationship to develop. She was kidding herself if she thought otherwise.

The restaurant was full and they had to search for a spot to sit down. Jenna was glad for the crowd, lots of noise and distractions.

"Hi, Miss Lauren," a group of sophomore girls chorused as she and Rob passed their table. Whispers and giggles came a moment later.

"I have a feeling we're going to be the subject of gossip among the sophomore class," Rob said in her ear.

Jenna just laughed. "They'll just be more obvious about it. Everyone else in town will play it cool, but the results will be the same."

"The joys of small town Americana."

"Hello, Miss Lauren."

"Hi, Sara," Jenna said as she and Rob passed the small table in the back where Sara and Mike were sitting.

Jenna and Rob sat down across the aisle from them. "That's Sara Jacobs," Jenna said. "She's my team captain, plus a good, hard worker. I think I should be able to get her a scholarship at some smaller school."

"Are she and Mike Sherwin going together?" Rob asked.

Jenna looked around, to see Sara smiling up at the tall boy sitting next to her. "Yes, they are." She turned back to Rob. "He's your star player."

"I know. He's told me that, several times."

Jenna smiled. "He puts on a bold front."

"Yeah?"

"Yep. His parents are divorced. The father moved away ages ago. There's a little sister at home, grade school age, and the mother works in packing and shipping at one of the biomed plants. Mike has to help out with the finances."

Rob stared a moment at Mike Sherwin, the boy talking and waving his hands, holding the attention of his group. "Sounds like somebody I used to know."

Jenna looked at Sara, cheeks flushed, a glowing smile on her face. The boy talented enough to play at a major college, while her hardworking captain would probably play at a small place close to home. Sara was a nice kid. Mike was...Mike was an opportunist. Uneasy butterflies danced in Jenna's stomach. It sounded too much like a replay.

"I know where my car is," Jenna protested.

Rob pulled Jenna closer as they walked across Ricco's parking lot. Mostly everyone else was still inside, and they were alone in the darkness. No witnesses to make Jenna self-conscious.

"Hey, let me play the gentleman once in a while. Okay?"

"This isn't a big city." She continued protesting, although she made no effort to pull away. "A woman doesn't need an armed escort to get to her car."

They came to Jenna's car and Rob leaned back against her door, looking up at the sky. She couldn't very well knock him to the ground to get in, so it was a way of holding on to her a bit longer.

"Indiana stars sure are brighter than any others I've seen recently."

"You see the same stars no matter where you are," Jenna said. "We just have dim streetlights."

He looked at her in the half-light. She was still as pretty as she'd always been, with her high cheekbones and full mouth, but she was different, too. Her edges seemed to have sharpened. The years changed everyone.

"You always were such a wide-eyed, romantic soul," Rob said with a sardonic laugh that also held a touch of sadness.

She shrugged and Rob thought there was an additional tightness around her eyes. Had his big mouth gotten her mad at him again?

"I'm just a country girl. We calls them the way we sees them."

The way he saw her was beautiful, though he thought it best not to tell her that. He was still getting used to her short hair. She'd had such beautiful long hair yet she complained about it all the time, about how much trouble it was to take care of. Whenever Jenna talked about getting it cut, he'd pleaded with her to keep it long. But once he was out of sight, the long hair went. Jenna had always been a practical sort.

"Ever find your father?"

The question came out of the blue and stung. "Never looked for him," he said.

Never had to. He saw pieces of his old man every time he looked in the mirror and felt the hatred awaken all over again. He'd inherited his father's charm, smile and wandering feet. Rob couldn't do anything about that, but he could choose what he did with them.

He avoided relationships that would lead to commitment the way a recovering alcoholic avoided bars, for he was addicted to the traveling life. Knowing that, he was careful not to let anyone lean on him so he'd never let anyone down.

He glanced up to see Jenna watching him. "Joe told me he died about ten years ago in LA," he said quickly.

"Sorry. About your mother, too," she said. "She was fairly young when she died."

"Life had been hard for her," he replied.

That was an understatement. Working to support and make a home for three boys. In some ways, the kind of man his father was just made things easier. When he'd finally disappeared over the horizon, no one noticed he was gone. The family had continued to scrimp and scratch as they had before to get by.

"Some folks were upset about the funeral arrangements—the town's people wanted to properly pay their respects.

"She wanted to be buried with family," Rob explained.

"I know, but a little service would have been nice. You know, just for friends."

"We hadn't been here that long."

"She still had a lot of friends. Folks respected her. We all considered her one of us."

"That wasn't my perception."

Jenna looked hard at him, concern was obvious in her eyes. "Why was that? Did anybody say anything?"

"No." He shook his head, not wanting to have placed a burden on her. "It was all inside my own head. You know how I felt about my father. I hated his cavalier ways and felt that everybody was pointing a finger at us. I even was angry at my mother for always standing up for him, thinking that we'd be able to live like everybody else here if she'd just made him toe the line."

He was young then and still thought he could fight his destiny. He hadn't yet experienced the imprisoning sensation of friends and habits, making his feet restless and the horizon look so tantalizing.

"No matter what he did," he went on. "She had an excuse."

"Sounds like she loved him."

Rob's throat was tight. He had never known what that was. Love, a sense of duty, or just plain stubbornness. Whatever, it wasn't something he could easily talk about.

"Hear from your brothers?" she asked quietly.

"We keep in touch," he replied.

Jenna looked up at the stars and he looked at her. Her body had remained tight and lean and muscular. It looked like she took after her grandmother. The old woman still stood tall and trim, and Rob could see Jenna doing the same when she reached her eighties. When he'd kissed Jenna earlier, her lips had fit his just as snugly as her body had fit his body. She'd always been perfect for him, igniting the same fire, too. Time to think of something else.

"I'm really surprised to see that so many people still remember me," he said.

"You're a legend," Jenna said. "After all, you shot the winning basket that beat Northwood High in 1978."

"Here I thought it was my world travels," he said with a laugh. "You always did like to prick my balloon."

"Only when you needed it."

Her smile was as soft as the moonbeams dancing in her golden hair. His lips turned dry and his loins turned tight.

"You know what the main thing was that I learned from all my traveling?" Rob asked.

Jenna shook her head.

"What a real treasure friends are."

She continued looking at him.

He took a step in closer to Jenna, her soft perfume casting its spell, and bound her to him. "You've always been one of my best friends."

She stood there, soft and cool like a spring breeze. He remembered how hard and aggressive she was on the basketball court, but off the court— "I know I was your standard issue teenage stud." He paused and swallowed hard. "But I've thought about us a lot and I know that we really were devoted—close. I hope we'll always be."

"I don't see any problems with that," she said slowly.

"It was always so good to talk to you." He went on, getting strength from the quiet peace in her voice. "I'd probably be in jail or dead by now, if you hadn't let me talk." Toward the end, she'd let him do more, but that had been his fault. A young stud with raging hormones, pushing at somebody who cared for him and taking advantage of it.

Rob reached out and took Jenna's hand. "Friends?" he asked.

"Sure."

"Forever?"

"That's a long time," she said, laughing.

He kissed her gently on the lips and it was like sipping sweet nectar.

"That's being friends?" she asked.

"It is in Europe."

"You've gotten to be quite continental."

"I've been told that." He wanted to take her into his arms, to hold her so close that the night couldn't come between them.

"I have to go," Jenna said. "It's getting late."

Rob leaned forward slightly, but then pulled back. He and Jenna were just friends, and friends didn't take advantage of people they care about. Certainly not once they'd grown up.

Rob put Jenna in her car and stood there watching her red lights disappear down the street. The stars appeared to dim once she had left, as if she had taken all the radiance with her.

Chapter Four

Jenna'd had it. She blew her whistle, ending practice, and sent the girls off to the locker room. Sometimes she wished she coached the freshman team; those girls were serious, were constantly worried about playing well and winning games. She gathered up a few stray balls and put them on the cart.

"Did you know it takes more muscles to frown than to smile?" Rob asked.

Jenna jumped, not having heard him enter. She felt as flighty as her girls. This was silly; she wasn't going to let him think he had any effect on her at all. "As a matter of fact," she said slowly. "I remember a smart-aleck teenage boy telling me that, and also telling me that he frowned because he needed the exercise."

"Boy, those smart alecks must be hard to take."

Jenna frowned toward the varsity boys' team straggling into the gym. "You should know by now. You've got fifteen of them to deal with."

"Did they screw up your practice?" he asked.

"One hundred percent." Jenna sighed and sank onto the bottom row of the bleachers. "Actually your guys were pretty quiet going into their locker room, but once they were in the building, my scrimmage went to hell in a handbasket."

"Teenagers have very sensitive antennae," Rob said, sitting down next to her. "I've heard that they know when a member of the opposite sex is within fifty miles."

Jenna just laughed. "I'm not sure that any of these young lads and lasses are ever farther than fifty feet from each other," she said.

"Old Mother Nature certainly didn't program them for separation."

Maybe that was who she could blame for her awkward, stumbling feelings around Rob. And for the fact that her feet kept taking routes through school that passed the athletic director's office or by the classes he was teaching. She tried telling herself that she was just putting a little variety into her life, but maybe it was all Mother Nature's fault. And she would deal with the old mistress's effect on herself just the same way she'd deal with the lady's effect on her girls.

"I'm going to reorganize my practices a bit," she said. "Instead of ending with a scrimmage, I'm going to end with wind sprints."

"Do you think that will help?"

"I hope so. The wind sprints will be easier to control. They won't have to think." And if she joined in, she wouldn't have to either. "Besides, it's good to close practice on a stern note. Give the girls an evening to mull over how rotten I can be if they don't buckle down and work hard."

Rob chuckled, a soft, comfortable sound that felt like a fuzzy robe on a cold winter's night. "You're going to run them until their tongues hang out."

"You've got it."

They stood and Jenna began to push the cart of girls' basketballs toward the equipment room. Rob walked along with her, his eyes on one of the boys' assistants trying to help a kid with his jump shot. The man's efforts weren't successful and the kid continued having trouble.

"My assistants are rather short on experience," Rob said.

Jenna stopped to watch also. "They were good ball players."

"Playing and coaching are two different things. In some ways, it would be better if they had been just average athletes who had a love for the game."

Jenna nodded. "You mean somebody who had to study the game and use his head to make the team."

"Exactly," Rob said. "I remember someone fitting that description, who has turned into a terrific coach."

He looked at her with a light in his eyes that she couldn't quite fathom, or maybe she was afraid to. Was she the moth and he the flame? Careful, careful, she cautioned herself.

"You got the max out of your natural talents," Rob said. "There aren't too many people in this world who can boast that."

Jenna felt her cheeks warming under his gaze and his praise. She looked away, watching the team shooting baskets. He'd always been generous with his praise and support back when they were in school, but now it seemed even more special. He hadn't said it because they were going together; he must have believed it to be true. The warmth spread through her heart giving her a glow deep inside.

"I enjoyed myself," she said.

"Can't ask for more out of life," Rob said.

The young assistant was still working with the boy who trudged over toward them to get the ball after a shot. It was obvious patience was wearing thin on both sides.

"Some of these kids have potential," Rob said. "But they need work on the basics."

"True," Jenna agreed.

Rob was silent for a moment, but she could feel a question hanging in the air. She pushed the ball cart into Rob's office. He followed her.

"I know you have your own responsibilities," he said, his voice hesitant. "But if you could spare some time—"

Jenna felt that glow burst into a deep satisfying pleasure. She put the cart into the equipment room before she turned to face Rob. "Wouldn't that create problems with your present assistants?"

"I doubt it," he said. "We have three teams and there are three of us. We'll take all the help we can get."

Jenna wasn't sure what to say. The very fact that Rob asked her to help must have meant that he respected her professional ability, her incentive to turn cartwheels on the front lawn. But spending more time with him could be risky. Was professional pride reason enough to take the chance?

"I don't want to shortchange the girls," he said. "I could lend a hand with them when you need it."

More time with him. She'd better answer quick or he'd be offering to move in with her so he could make her bed and wash her back while she bathed. The ideas were enticing and she looked away for fear that he'd be able to read her errant thoughts.

Professional help, that's all he wanted and that's what she could give. It was an honor to be asked, a responsibility to accept. The kids needed her and she couldn't put her own immature worries ahead of that.

"I could probably spare a couple of hours a week," she said. "And we could always use help with strategy."

"Good." His smile broadened and he stuck out his hand. "Deal."

"Deal." She shook his hand, wanting to linger in his strong grip, but pulling away quickly as if to prove to herself that she knew what she was doing.

"This should work out great," he said, then with a nod went back out into the gym.

Right, she thought and let out her breath slowly. Sanity returned like a wave washing up on the shore. This would work out really great. She'd just be running wind sprints from now until kingdom come.

The first thing that hit Jenna as she entered the gym Saturday evening was the smell of burning leaves. Someone had brought in a grill earlier and let a small mound of damp leaves smoulder for a while. The scent still lingered faintly in the air. Jenna paused at the gym door and smiled, letting waves of nostalgia wash over her.

Halloween descended from the ancient Celtic New Year, which marked the division between the warmth of summer and the cold death of winter, but in Jenna's little part of the world, Halloween was the transfer from football to basketball. The time to move from open stadiums, crisp air and golden leaves to indoor gymnasiums, packed cheek to jowl with fans and cheers rattling the rafters that held up the roof.

"Hi, Miss Lauren." Sara bounced to a stop in front of her. "Ain't it neat?"

Jenna gazed with her at the pumpkin lanterns hung from the ceiling, and the scarecrows draped across the fan barriers in front of the stands. There were several rows of corn shucks mixed in with wrapped bundles of cornstalks, which were scattered about the floor.

"You guys did a nice job," Jenna said, then frowned at the corn shucks. "There are an awful lot of shucks out there."

Sara just giggled. "We have them all over the hallways, too."

"You've got make-out dens all over this school?" Jenna shook her head. "Did Mr. Fidler approve these decorations?"

"He said we were old enough to make those kinds of decisions, so we didn't need to check with him."

Jenna just gave the girl a look.

"Besides, we have a whole bunch of chaperons." Then the girl startled giggling. "But who's going to watch the chaperons?"

"I don't think we need anybody to do that," Jenna assured her.

"Right," Sara said. "You wouldn't want to grab Mr. Fagan behind one of those shucks and give him a squeeze?" The girl's giggles were replaced with a mocking snicker. "Sure."

Jenna bit back a sigh. She was trying so hard to treat Rob like she would any friend, regardless of the occasional lapses of control, yet no one seemed to notice. "Mr. Fagan and I are just friends."

"That's not what my cousin says," Sara said. "She graduated in 1978 so she knew you guys real well."

"She knew us back then," Jenna pointed out. "This is now. Thirteen years later."

But Sara didn't seem to see there was any difference. "So you aren't kids anymore, but you sure ain't dead." She stopped talking to jump up and down, and wave frantically. "Hey, guys. Over here."

Before Jenna could protest, flee or even frown, Rob and Mike Sherwin were coming over. Sara grabbed Mike's hand.

"One for me and one for you," she said, grinning broadly at Jenna. "Now, have fun and watch out for those chaperons." With a wicked grin, Sara pulled Mike across the gym.

Jenna watched them disappear into the crowd before she turned to face Rob. The dim lighting and the crowd moving around them should have made her relax. They weren't exactly alone. But the look in Rob's eyes, that all too familiar gleam, shook her. In the middle of a crowd or alone together on a deserted island, she didn't think there was much difference.

Rob had played a special part in her growing up, and the years couldn't change that. That time ended in pain, but that couldn't completely alienate the feelings that had bonded them close. She just had to keep a rein on them, and make sure they stayed feelings from the past, not part of today.

"What was that all about?" Rob asked.

Jenna just shrugged. "A young lady with some definite ideas about relationships."

Rob laughed. "That's an attribute of the teenage female."

"The teens aren't the only ones," Jenna grumbled. "Everyone seems anxious to tie us together. Maybe we ought to separate. No use giving them fuel for thought."

"Yeah, we could do that." Rob pulled down at the corners of his mouth with his thumb and forefinger. "But wouldn't that be giving others control over our lives?"

Right now, others might do better than she was, but she knew what he meant. "I guess it might start even more rumors. If we make a big deal about staying apart, everyone will think we're hiding something."

"We're damned if we do and damned if we don't."

So what did she do? Did she follow her head or her heart? The trouble was, she wasn't sure which was giving which message.

"Want some cider?" Rob asked.

"Sure." She'd decipher the messages later, when she had time enough to think.

They strolled over to the snack bar, where Rob got in line for their glasses of cider. As she waited, Jenna glanced around the gym.

"Things seem locked up fairly tightly." Rob had returned with the glasses. "With the instructional wings locked off, we won't have to check the classrooms for passionate couples."

"But we have the men's and women's locker rooms, the balconies, the stage, and the cafeteria downstairs."

He grimaced. "I don't remember using all those places."

She ignored the cry of her memory, wanting to replay pieces of the past to remind her of just what places they did seek out. And just what feelings were awakened there. "And you see all those corn shucks," Jenna said, pushing on. "There's a zillion of those darn things. And they make great hiding places."

"Now, those I do remember."

The look he gave her took her back to the past, to the days when she lived to be in his arms and found heaven there. Her heart raced and her cheeks flushed, and she swore that she could almost taste his lips on hers. There was nothing the future could hold but wonder and joy, no shadow so dark that Rob couldn't brighten it. The innocence of youth.

"Let's start patrolling downstairs," Jenna said, and dumped her empty cup into the trash, carefully avoiding Rob's eyes. "That's where most of the kids sneak off to."

They went down the back stairs and checked out both locker rooms, sending two couples back up to the dance.

Neither she nor Rob said much. The only sound was the soft plodding noises of their shoes on the tiled floor.

As they walked side by side down the deserted hallways, Jenna felt the urge to take his hand like she would have in the old days. But it wasn't the old days, so she kept her hands to herself.

The cafeteria was safer to patrol with its wide aisles and sense of openness. She didn't feel the walls closing in around her, pushing her and Rob closer together. They went to the far end, next to a row of soda machines where they found Mike and Sara.

"Oh hi, Miss Lauren." Sara pulled out of Mike's arms, her face flushed and her T-shirt disheveled. "Hi, Mr. Fagan."

Mike just grunted.

"People are looking for you upstairs," Jenna told them.

"Who?" Mike asked.

"The world, man," Rob replied. "Like everybody."

Mike blinked.

"Scoot," Jenna ordered.

Jenna waited until the two kids had trudged through the cafeteria and up the stairs before she took her eyes off them. This was the same corner she and Rob used to hide in. Was it just the best necking corner, or were Sara and Mike following in her and Rob's footsteps?

"Cozy," Rob said and Jenna turned to look at the corner where Sara and Mike had pushed some chairs. "Care to sit down?"

Back in the cozy corner with Rob? The idea was appealing, too appealing, and Jenna looked frantically around for a reason to say no.

"Afraid of being caught by the chaperons? I think we're the only ones who have been checking down here," Rob said.

Not only were they the only ones checking down here, they were the only ones down here period. At least for the moment they were out of the public's matchmaking eye. That in itself was an enticement.

"For a minute," Jenna said, sitting slowly down and kicking off her shoes. "My feet are killing me. I hardly ever wear heels."

Rob reached down and pulled her feet up on his lap, just as if he thought it was still his job to help her relax. Jenna was about to jerk her feet away, but he began massaging them. It felt so good, she had no choice but to leave them to his touch.

"Why do women wear heels anyway?" he asked.

"I don't know. I think when early man and woman divided things up, we got heels and you guys got ties."

Rob didn't reply, he just kept massaging. Jenna felt her toes relax and her whole body wanted to follow suit. She wanted to curl up in his lap like they did so long ago. To be held in the safe harbor of his arms and have his smile drive the cold blues away.

She had been so in love with him back then. It had seemed so natural and right when they finally made love. That summer had been magical, she'd felt as if they really could make time stand still.

Then reality intruded; she was pregnant. The more devastating circumstance was that she felt alone. Her mother was getting sicker, requiring more and more time in that Fort Wayne hospital, her father had no time or thought for anything but his wife's illness, and Rob was getting ready to leave to start his big-time college basketball career, and escape from Warsaw and its memories.

Her parents had borne enough troubles. To tell them how she'd jeopardized all their hopes for her would have been brutal. And Rob, well, she couldn't take his dream away from him.

Frozen in indecision, Jenna finally concluded that she would return the basketball scholarship she'd received, but knew she'd have to give her father a reason. Then one day, when they were driving into Fort Wayne to see her mother, she told him.

He hadn't been angry as she'd feared, but sad. Just terribly, terribly sad. He didn't suggest dragging Rob back to marry her, or hiding her away with some distant relative until she had the baby. He just said they'd manage. She'd never loved him more.

But only a few blocks later, a drunk driver ran a red light, hitting their car square on the passenger side and her father was killed instantly. Jenna was taken to the hospital where she miscarried.

She didn't know how the social worker who talked to her did it, but no one else in the family ever found out about her pregnancy. She shared a room with her mother for the next few days, where they both grieved together, then one of Jenna's cousins drove her home in time for her father's funeral.

That night she went home to the big old empty house and sobbed her little heart out, guilt and pain all warring together. Had she been distracted by their talk about her pregnancy and missed warnings of the drunk driver? Had she not only failed her father by getting pregnant, but caused his death as well?

Gram moved into action the next day, hassling Jenna and the high school counselor into action. Jenna was offered a last-minute scholarship to a small school in Renssalaer, not too far from home. The day before she left, her mother was released from the hospital into Gram's care.

It wasn't right, Jenna thought, that all this misery, should fall on others because of her carelessness. From then on, the only way to avoid all the pain was hard work both in the classroom and on the court. Whatever free time she had, she would run home to help her mother and grandmother.

She had friends at school, but let none of them get close and all her dates had been casual. She'd learned that love carried a high price and she would never pay it again. Jenna pulled her feet from Rob's lap.

"We better get back upstairs," Jenna said, even though her mind wanted to argue.

Rob's nearness, the soft scent of his aftershave, the melting touch of his hands . . . all warred with her common sense. Who would know if they lingered down here? Even if they were concealed from the world, she wasn't ready to replay the past. That was something she couldn't do.

"Hi, Gram," Jenna said. "You're up pretty late."

"Gol dang it." Her grandmother spat out the words. "Slam him on his big fat butt."

Jenna stared for a moment at two large, overweight men pushing and pummeling each other around a ring.

"Whatever did you do with all those aggressive emotions before cable came to town?" Jenna asked.

"Choke. You big dummy, he's got him in a choke hold." The curly-haired wrestler broke away from the mean masked villain, but got knocked to the floor again. "Dumb ref. He's as blind as a bat."

Suddenly, the curly-haired hero erupted from the floor, and in a series of dazzling moves proceeded to put the villain down. The referee counted to three and her grandmother threw both hands up into the air.

"Hot dog," Gram said as she stood up and turned the TV off. "I knew that Curly would do it. How was the dance, dear?"

"It was okay," Jenna replied.

"Just okay? Why? Wasn't Rob there?"

"Yes, Rob was there, but that doesn't mean chaperoning wasn't a lot of work. We have around four hundred little teeny-boppers that we need to encourage to have fun, but not too much."

"Doesn't mean you can't have a little fun yourself."

Jenna didn't say anything. She didn't need that kind of fun anymore. The price was too high.

"Did you drive home by yourself?" Gram asked.

"I drove down there alone. Why shouldn't I drive home by myself?"

Gram snorted. "In my day, a gentleman wouldn't let a lady go home all by her lonesome."

"In your day, neither of you had a choice. Most women didn't drive."

"I'm not talking about choice. I'm talking about what's right and proper."

"Well, we're not shackled by conventions anymore," Jenna said. "These days women have their freedom."

"With all that freedom comes a whole lot of loneliness."

Jenna sighed inwardly and went to sit in her chair. Nothing was free. And loneliness was like a touch of the flu. It left you a little worn at times, but it sure wasn't a deep down excruciating pain. She had experienced the worn-feeling and the pain, but she would take loneliness any day of the week. Jenna picked up a book of basketball drills.

"Hope you're not expecting to find any answers in that thing," Gram said.

"As a matter of fact, I am. My team is having trouble with the fast break and I'm looking for some drills to help them."

"I'm talking about answers to your life's questions."

"Gram, basketball is my life. I'm a coach. That's my profession. It's not just something I enjoy, it's also my job."

Her grandmother didn't say anything, but Jenna could feel her agitation.

"I have a young team this year," Jenna went on. "But they're truly talented athletes. We have a real chance of making the Final Four."

"You're running away from life," her grandmother said quietly.

"We live in Indiana, Gram. Basketball is our life."

"I know it's your job. But a job isn't the sum and total of a person's life." Gram paused a moment. "At least it shouldn't be."

Jenna opened her book. "Good night, Gram."

"Good night, dear."

She'd heard her grandmother sigh, but kept staring at the figures and words before her. Gram was wrong. It wasn't life she was running away from. It was pain. A pain that she could neither cope with, nor do anything about.

That's why she was making a drive for the Final Four. There would be disappointment if they didn't make it, but she could cope with that. There would be a spring and summer to relax and then another fall to try again. Love didn't work that way.

Chapter Five

Rob shifted the phone to his other ear while he looked through Mike Sherwin's folder. "He's still six feet four inches," Rob said. "But he's put on twenty pounds of solid muscle."

"That's good," the college recruiter said. "He was a bit of a beanpole. Definitely needs that extra weight for college."

"His shooting and rebounding are improving," Rob said. "Still has to work on his free throws."

"As I remember from last year, his academics could stand a lot of improvement."

Rob scanned Mike's academic record. A lot of C's and D's from his freshman and sophomore years had been replaced by B's in his junior year, but his GPA—grade point average—wasn't great. Not where his test scores indicated it should be.

"I'll keep on him," Rob promised.

"Good," the recruiter said. "Tell the kid those grades will determine whether he plays in a quality program or not."

"Will do," Rob assured him. "Thanks for your interest."

They exchanged goodbyes and Rob hung up. He could barely restrain himself from jumping up and hollering for joy. The kid's good fortune felt almost like his own. The DePaul University athletic program was first class. He hoped that Mike was mature enough to recognize the opportunity and work on his grades as hard as he did on his basketball skills.

No better time than the present to find out. Rob called the office to get Mike out of class.

The kid was down in a matter of minutes. "Hey, Coach. What's happening?"

Rob indicated one of the chairs with a nod of his head. "You got here fast."

"I was in chemistry."

"I take it you don't plan on being a chemist," Rob said.

"No way, José."

"But you're going to get a good grade in it."

Mike stared at him.

"In fact, you're going to get good grades in all your subjects. You're going to work up to your full potential. Got it?"

The boy nodded uncertainly.

Rob leaned forward and let the grin he was holding in slowly surface. "I just had a conversation with the recruiter from DePaul University." Mike's eyes opened wider. "You're near the top of their short list."

Mike was speechless. He could only shake his head and grin like a little boy at Christmas, getting the train set his father had told him they couldn't afford.

"I don't have to tell you it's a big-time, quality program," Rob said. "Located in Chicago, national TV exposure."

"It's my ticket out of here," Mike said, finally able to speak. "Out of this one-horse town and into the pros."

Ticket out. One-horse town. Gateway to the pros. Young and cocky, with a disdain for his present circumstances. Rob felt a tightness in his stomach, as if he were staring in a mirror and seeing an image from thirteen years back.

"Want to listen to a little advice?" Rob asked quietly, then didn't wait for answer. "I've already been down the road you're headed for. On the one hand, you have recruiters buttering you up, and on the other hand, you have a home situation that isn't the greatest."

The shadows across Mike's face darkened but he stayed still and attentive.

"There are a lot of pitfalls between here and playing in the NBA."

"You played pro, didn't you?"

"Just in Europe. Only about two percent of the top college players in the country make it to the NBA." Rob leaned forward and put his elbows on his desk. "All I want to tell you is don't concentrate on a single goal so hard that you don't enjoy the trip. That means take advantage of everything that comes your way, especially school."

"Yeah," Mike said nodding.

"I mean it," Rob said. "That's the only thing the recruiter is concerned about. If you don't bring up those grades you'll be scrambling. Right now, you're borderline for the junior college route."

He thought he saw the kid gulp a bit, but Rob couldn't be sure.

"I'm really working on it this year, Mr. Fagan. Sara's helping me. She's a real good student."

"Good." Rob stood up and stuck out his hand. "I want you to have only two things in your life the rest of the year. School and basketball."

Mike took Rob's hand, grinning. "Yes, sir."

He watched as the tall boy disappeared down the hall. That misty mirror full of old images floated up before his eyes. The kid's girlfriend was helping him with his studies. Jenna had helped him. That was the good news and the bad news.

But the image of Jenna today, soft and womanly behind that tough facade, was what stayed with him. Jenna would be as excited about this news as he was.

He hurried down to the teacher's lounge. Jenna and her assistant, Rita, were the only staff there.

"Jenna," he said. "I've got great news." He dropped down in the chair next to her.

"Good." She paused in her eating. "What is it? A new gym so we won't have to play all these scheduling games?"

"Hardly." He leaned forward. "DePaul has their eye on Mike Sherwin."

"Wow," Rita exclaimed.

Jenna just took a drink of her diet soda. "That's wonderful," she said after a moment. "Really wonderful."

She wasn't jumping up and down, even mentally, but then maybe she was used to this type of victory.

"I think I'm more excited than Mike is," Rob said. "I guess this is what coaching and teaching is all about."

"Yep. Seeing the kids grow and mature."

No one said anything more as the two women cleaned up the remains of their lunch. Rita took Jenna's garbage with her own and left the two of them alone.

Rob didn't know what else to say. This wasn't going the way he had expected. His first instinct had been to share the news, somehow picturing he and Jenna exchanging high-fives or hugging each other with excitement. The old Jenna would have reacted that way, but he was starting to see that the old Jenna was gone.

"Mike's going to have to concentrate on his academics," Rob said slowly.

Jenna nodded. "Sara's helping him."

"Yeah, that's what he said."

"They're going steady."

"Like we were."

Jenna gathered up her papers into a neat pile, then picked them all up. "The University of Dayton is very interested in Sara," she said.

"Oh, yeah? That's great."

Jenna stood up. "Yep. It sure is."

For some reason, that seemed to end the conversation.

The girls on the bench groaned and Jenna sprang to her feet. That was the third turnover Sara had caused.

"Sara," Jenna hollered at the girl. "Concentrate."

Rob leaned over from his seat at the scorer's table. "She played superbly in the first half. What's with her now?"

Jenna just shrugged, though she had an idea. Not because she could read minds, but because she had a good memory.

Their center grabbed a rebound and threw a rapid outlet pass to Sara. The ball went right through the girl's fingers and out-of-bounds.

"Cindy," Jenna called down the bench. "Go in for Sara."

The freshman guard ran over to the scorer's table where Rob checked her in, then went into the game. Sara came out.

"Sit down and get yourself together," Jenna told her.

The girl took a towel and went to the end of the bench to sit down as Jenna turned her attention back to the game. Cindy was doing well, but was tentative as any freshman would be. Jenna couldn't really leave her in too long, and turned toward Sara. Maybe a quick talking to and she'd be ready to concentrate.

Except that Sara wasn't event watching the game. She was turned toward the stands. "Sara," Jenna snapped. "Get your mind back on the game."

The girl quickly turned back to the game as Jenna looked up into the stands. The focus of Sara's attention smiled and waved at Jenna. Damn. Mike hadn't been there at the beginning of the game. He must have come in during the second half, just when Sara had crumbled.

Jenna stalked over to Sara. "You and I are going to have a private conversation after you shower," she told the girl.

Jenna sat back down and tried to concentrate on the game, but her hands were clenched, and her jaw was tight with anger. Anger at herself and at Sara. Why had she been so stupid at seventeen as to think Rob was her whole world? And how could she stop Sara from making the same mistake?

No answers came, but mercifully the end of the game did. It was only a practice game, but Rita and Peggy had accumulated a lot of statistics and notes on what they needed to work on. None ranked higher on Jenna's list though than getting her point guard straightened out. She waited around as the girls showered and departed in bunches until just she and Sara were left.

"Let's go, Sara." The girl was still poking around, brushing at her hair. "I'm sure we both have other things we'd prefer to be doing."

Sara made a slight face and quickly slipped into her shoes, giving her long red locks a last finger-combing.

"Sit down," Jenna ordered and took a seat on a bench across from Sara. "You had a rather poor game, young lady."

"It was just a practice game," Sara replied, with a shrug.

Same reasoning Jenna used to use. "It doesn't matter. Once you tell yourself it's all right not do your best, you'll come to rely on it. It'll start with a practice game, but before you know it, you'll do it for all games and then in the important parts of your life. Like school. And later on, your job, taking care of those you love. Forming good habits is important, though we all have to constantly fight to keep from falling into destructive modes."

Sara looked down at the floor away from Jenna's penetrating gaze.

Jenna knew what was happening to the girl, and some of her anger faded. "You had a good first half. It's the second half where you went to pieces."

"I know and I'm sorry."

She looked up and Jenna saw a load of trouble and pain in Sara's eyes. She also saw that Sara knew exactly when and why her play deteriorated. What more was there to say?

"Can I go now?" Sara asked.

"That scholarship to the University of Dayton is a good opportunity," Jenna said. "You don't want to mess it up."

"Miss Lauren, please. I have a lot on my mind right now. Can't we just cut this short? I promise to concentrate in the real games."

Jenna wished she could reach into her soul and pull out magic words to make Sara see the light, but no words were there. No right ones, no wrong ones, either. She nodded and got to her feet, letting the girl go by.

The door slammed shut after Sara's exit, but Jenna just sank back down on the bench, staring at the long rows of lockers. Sara had always been a hard worker, dependable and solid as a rock. She and Mike had gone to school together since first grade, dating casually for a couple of years now. When things had turned a little more serious late in their junior year, Sara had been very happy, but her work ethics hadn't changed. Something had happened.

Perhaps what had happened was a repeat of the past. It did every year like the leaves falling in autumn and the new green life coming in the spring. Graduation was on the horizon for the seniors. Mike would probably get a scholarship to a school in Chicago while Sara's opportunity was in Ohio. They would have to separate.

Jenna got up and turned off the lights, a leaden weight growing in her stomach. Mike was an exceptional player. Sara was good. Mike was dreaming of the NBA however, there weren't many alternatives for women's basketball after college. Sighing, Jenna made her way to the door.

"Hi," Rob said, straightening up from the wall. "I was starting to get worried. You were in there quite a while and I was sure that everyone else had already left."

He wore a tentative smile with more concern in his eyes than sparkle. It hurt to feel his caring, his watching out for her. Jenna's first reaction was to retreat back into the locker room. She wasn't feeling very strong right now.

"I was just checking things out. The girls have a tendency to leave their stuff in the lockers."

"They're old enough to pick up after themselves," he said.

Jenna just shrugged.

"You look tired."

Jenna shrugged again.

"Hey, it was just a practice game," Rob said.

"I hate it when someone doesn't do their best."

"You mean Sara?"

Jenna nodded.

"No big deal," he said. "She had an off day. We all have those from time to time."

"I hope that's all it is."

Rob looked at her with a penetrating frown.

"I'm sure she's not in trouble," Jenna hastened to explain. "Yet."

"Is that supposed to mean something?"

Jenna's fists clenched for a moment and she wished that Rob hadn't waited for her. In her present irritation, she felt reckless and foolhardy. She should be alone, rather than here with him while she was nurturing an anger that had festered over the years.

"What kind of trouble is she going to be in?" Rob persisted.

What kind of trouble? Her boyfriend was headed for some big-time college program where zillions of beautiful coeds would fawn over him. A boyfriend Sara will have given everything to. But come next fall, her world was going to come apart. What would she do to try to hold onto Mike?

"She's losing her concentration and focus," Jenna said. "And this isn't the best time for that."

"True," Rob agreed. "Although the beginning of the season is a better time for that to happen than at the end."

Jenna winced. That made it sound like her concerns were selfish ones. "She's got a good college interested in her," Jenna said. "I'd hate to see her ruin the opportunities she has available to her."

"Hey, ease up. They're kids." He moved to her side, put an arm around Jenna's shoulder and pulled her to him. For a moment, she let herself lean into him. "In a lot of ways, they sound like us and we survived."

Oh, Lord. Her vision blurred momentarily and she pulled away, standing back on her own two feet, where she felt safe.

That was the whole thing in a nutshell. That was what hurt so much. These kids today were just like she and Rob had been yesterday. And it looked like Sara was bound and determined to travel the same road to pain that Jenna had taken.

"I suppose all adolescents are sort of the same."

"We can, and certainly should, advise them," Rob said. "But in the end, they each have to work things out for themselves."

Work things out for themselves. That's exactly how it had been. She'd had to work things out for herself and she had. She had come through fine and was stronger because of it. Going back would just make her weak and vulnerable again. She turned and began walking to check the exterior gym doors.

"My girls are still having trouble with that fast break," she said.

He followed her, checking one door while she checked another. "Maybe your team is a half court type of team."

"I don't think so," she said, shaking her head. "They have so much speed and they love to run. Their timing is just off."

"I've got some drills that might help. I'll diagram some of them for you tomorrow."

"Okay."

After checking the last door, they went to the control box. Jenna turned off the lights, then they went out into the hall.

He took her arm in his, pulling her back into his warmth. "You really do look tired."

"Yeah, I guess I am." Maybe that's why it didn't feel so scary being alone here in the school with him. It felt more comfortable, more right.

"Why don't you let Doctor Fagan work his magic on you?"

"Doctor Fagan?" It was all Jenna could do to keep from laughing.

"Come into my office. You'll see."

She ought to be going. She had piles of papers that needed correcting and a hot bath sure wouldn't hurt. But then, maybe a little bit of Rob's nonsense wouldn't hurt either. She needed a little rest from soul-searching and he was skillful at brightening her mood. They went down the hallway to the worn little office.

"Madam," Rob said with a bow, letting her enter first.

"This is very convenient," Jenna said. "I mean, if you need any equipment for your magic. Like a basketball or a wrestling mat."

As soon as she said it, her cheeks flared with color. She didn't want to give him ideas. Or give him the idea that she had ideas.

But Rob pretended not to misread any of her silly comments and just pulled a chair around, indicating she should be seated.

"I don't need anything but my magic hands."

Even as he spoke, the magic hands started kneading her shoulder muscles and up into her neck. She'd thought she'd play along with his game for a moment, then head for home, but that idea quickly fled. His hands were warm, his movements sure and the tension started draining from her body truly like magic. She felt her muscles grow more and more relaxed. She closed her eyes.

It was like waking up from a sound sleep. The world was peaceful and safe, warmth was all around. The day promised sunshine and laughter. No clouds would dare come by.

But even as her body let the tension of her day wash away, another type of tension flowed in, filling up her psyche with awareness. Her shoulders were relaxed, but oh, so conscious of Rob's hands on her...of his strength and power...of how lonely she'd been, and how afraid she was to let anyone get close.

Rob's hands shifted as he came around her side. She opened her eyes to gaze into his. The teasing laughter was gone and an echo of her own emptiness stared back at her. He stopped his massage, his hands sliding down her arms to take hold and pull her into his embrace.

The world exploded into a million pieces consumed by fire as their lips met. She was burning, her heart ablaze. Rob's touch was everything she needed, everything her life was missing. She wished she could revel forever in his touch.

Their earlier kisses had been gentle, teasing little reminders of times gone by. But this was passion. Not of the past, but of the present.

Rob's hands pulled her ever closer, his arms were like iron that threatened to hold her prisoner forever. The idea delighted her, teased with the wonder and joy of belonging, of having someone to hold you in the sunshine and in the rain. Then suddenly Rob jerked back.

Jenna blinked in bewilderment, then she heard the clunking sound, too. They separated. Rob walked to the door, with Jenna following.

"Hi, folks." It was Wilson Abernathy of the night cleaning crew pushing a large bucket and mop ahead of him.

"Hi, Wilson."

"Working late?"

"Yeah," Rob said with a ragged little laugh. "A coach's work is never done."

"That's what they say about janitors," Wilson said solemnly. "Well, don't stay too late." He pushed his equipment into the boys' rest room.

Jenna stood still for a long moment, staring intently at the far wall. She'd been walking a tightrope since Rob had come back, and she had the feeling she'd just fallen off it. Would she go crashing to the floor or would there be a safety net to catch her?

"You okay?" Rob asked.

"Yeah. Sure." Jenna forced a little perkiness into her voice. "But I'd better head home. Got a load of papers to correct."

"Yeah, me too," Rob agreed. "Let me lock up and I'll walk you to your car."

She wanted to rush out while his back was turned, but besides being immature, it would look like she couldn't handle being with him. That kiss had really rattled her. It had rattled her to the core and beyond but he wasn't going to know that. No reason to compound a mistake by being stupid.

"Let's go, girls," Jenna said impatiently. "I don't want to be here all evening."

The girls straggled into practice about two percent faster after her nagging, but Jenna chose to see that as a moral victory and turned back to her assistants.

"Rob's here," Rita said before Jenna could tell them what she'd planned for practice.

Jenna bit back her sigh and slopped honey all over her voice. "As I understand it, he works here. And since he's the athletic director, he might even be interested in things that are going on in the gym."

"Excuse me," Rita replied with the slightest of knowing smirks. "But he was waving at you. I just thought you might want to know."

Actually Jenna had seen Rob wave out of the corner of her eye, but she had chosen not to wave back. It wasn't that she was feeling unfriendly. It was just that she didn't want to be distracted. If Sara wasn't supposed to be distracted, then it was only fair that Jenna didn't allow herself to be.

"Don't let it bother you," Peggy said to Rita. "They were always like that. A body didn't know from one minute to the next whether they were at peace or at war."

"Oh, yeah? Lovey, dovey one minute and duking it out the next?"

Jenna glared at Rita. "You're really getting into this small town stuff, aren't you?"

"Huh?"

"Getting involved with personal stuff that is absolutely none of your dad-gum business."

Rita grinned a bit broader—or had she smirked a bit broader? "I just want to be accepted by the community."

Her assistant's snide little remark and Peggy's snicker drove out the last lingering feelings of friendliness. "Would it be too much to ask you ladies to get practice started?"

"Come on." Peggy tugged at Rita's arm. "The only thing you can do when she gets the grumpies is leave her alone. Being nice will just aggravate her."

As they turned to walk away the words "the night of the big game with Bremen" drifted back to Jenna and she knew that Peggy was giving Rita a blow-by-blow description of an eventful argument she'd had with Rob. Jenna considered throwing her clipboard at them, but Rob had walked to the front of the gym by then and waved to her again. Since she was facing him straight on, there was little else she could do but force a smile to her face and return his wave.

Darn man, she thought as she tried turning her attention to the notes on her clipboard, he was everywhere. She really didn't mind seeing him in the halls or the gym. After all, she'd confided to Rita once, the man did work here. What she did mind was having the man walk into her thoughts. He was with her even when he wasn't physically around, and that was worse than aggravating.

It wasn't as if she were some weak, little prissy miss who couldn't do anything without a man. She was a capable, strong person with a life of her own. She was a respected professional, a valued member of the community, and was fully able to take care of herself.

"Hi, Miss Lauren. Sorry I'm late."

Sara provided Jenna with a welcome diversion and she pounced on it like a cat on a helpless mouse. "I thought we had discussed a captain's responsibilities before, young lady."

"I'm sorry," Sara said. "I was helping Mike with his algebra."

Oh, Lord. Jenna felt a pinch of pain in her heart. "Maybe you ought to let Mike take care of his responsibilities himself. He's not going to have you around to help him all his life and he's never going to grow up if you keep holding his hand."

Sara didn't say anything, but her expression had taken a definite turn toward sullen.

"Besides," Jenna continued. "You're not doing yourself any favors either. You've got your whole life ahead of you. You should be taking advantage of opportunities right now so that when you're my age, you'll be strong and competent and able to take care of yourself."

"And all alone," Sara snapped, before she hurried off toward the locker room.

Jenna could only stare after the girl. A burning sensation seared in her eyes and she had to fight to keep it from spilling over into tears.

Chapter Six

"Oh, Good Lord."

Jenna couldn't believe what she had done. She was supposed to be correcting a freshman algebra test and she had drawn a heart with initials on one of the papers. This was insane. She hadn't done anything like this since junior high. Plus it was on Larry Warner's paper. His father was the president of the school board and could not only get her fired, but could have her drawn and quartered in the town square for contributing to the moral decay of his one-and-only son.

Luckily she'd been using a lead pencil and hadn't pressed down too hard. She erased it as best she could, then blew off the shavings and examined her work, holding it up to the light to see if there were any indentations or other marks.

Damn that Rob Fagan. Why did he have to come back to town anyway? She'd had her life under control until he showed up with his devilish smile, dangerous blue eyes, and the most cheerful attitude she'd ever seen. Jenna wondered if she could have the man run out of town. Trouble was, part of her liked having him here. Part of her jumped and danced every time she saw him, every time she thought of him.

The phone rang before Jenna could decide whether it would be better to run him out of town or leave herself.

"Hello," Gram said into the receiver. "Rob Fagan. It's so nice to hear from you."

Her grandmother's voice had gone from brisk and no-nonsense, to a sweet, warm-enough-to-melt-butter-in-your-mouth tone in less than the blink of an eye. Jenna forced herself to go on to the next student's test.

"How come you're not coming by to eat?" Gram demanded. "A vigorous young man like yourself needs to eat proper to keep his strength up."

Jenna put her fingers over her ears and stared hard at the page in front of her. She absolutely refused to let her mind entertain such words as vigorous, young, strong or man.

"Of course, I still cook as good as ever." Gram's voice easily slipped past Jenna's censoring fingers. "If you'd come over like you should, you could see for yourself."

Jenna's face scrunched up, anticipating the blow.

"Ain't no reason to wait for an invitation. You know how flighty that child gets. You just come over any old time. Every day if you like. Give an old woman some company before she dies."

Great, she could just imagine what Rob would have to say on Monday. Maybe she could jump off the edge of the earth, just disappear forever. But no, she couldn't. She'd made a commitment to the school and the kids on her team. And she'd never been able to walk away from a promise.

She would just have to deny everything. If Rob asked her about Gram on Monday, she'd pretend that she didn't know what he was talking about. Tell him that he just dialed the wrong number and got some crazy old woman by mistake. Tell him Gram hadn't been home all Friday evening. That would take care of it.

"Nope, she ain't doing anything useful. Just staring out the window at the terrible weather."

Jenna glared down the hallway, her ears vibrating like some rabbit's sensing danger in the woods. What was that woman up to now?

"Sure," Gram said. "I'll send her right over. Send you an armload of vittles, too. At least enough to tide you on through the weekend."

Jenna almost ran to the kitchen but her grandmother had already hung up the phone.

"Gram, what are you—"

"Rob needs some help with things. I said you'd go over now."

"What things?"

"I don't know. I expect he'll tell you when you get there."

"Gram."

"I need to put some things together for you to take over. Man is near starving to death." Her grandmother started to bustle off to the back room where the freezer was, but stopped at the doorway. "Wouldn't hurt for you to dress up a bit. More like a lady."

Jenna glared at the now empty doorway and then at her outfit of lumberjack shirt, jeans and gray wool slacks. Dress up a bit? For Rob? She turned to look out the window at the freezing rain beating down.

Why wouldn't Gram let her lead her own life; choose her own friends and her own occasions for dressing up? She wouldn't lead Rob or herself into believing that spending an afternoon with him was anything special.

When she returned to the kitchen, two large paper sacks sat on the table. Jenna checked the contents while ignoring her grandmother's pointed glare at her clothes.

"Does he have guests staying for the weekend?" Jenna asked.

"I don't know," Gram replied. "All I know is that you're staying for dinner."

"What?"

"I have some lady friends coming over tonight. I can't have you running around underfoot."

"I don't run around underfoot," Jenna said. "I'm not a child any more."

Her grandmother's face grew grim. "That's for sure. And you're not getting any younger."

"What's that supposed to mean?"

"Drive carefully, dear," Gram cautioned her. "It looks slippery out there."

As Jenna drove along the slick, wet streets her mood went from irritated to angry. There was no doubt about it. She was going to have to have a talk with her grandmother. Sure, she was old and concerned, but she was just going to have to butt out of Jenna's life.

By summer at the latest, Rob Fagan would be out of town and out of her life. In the meantime, it was hard enough fighting her own hormones and memories; she sure didn't need Gram shoving her into his arms. Certainly not just because he was some handsome hulk who'd shot the winning basket in the high school championship game.

Jenna pulled into the parking lot at Rob's apartment building, then grabbing up the bags, stomped through the puddles to his door. What in the world would he want help with? If it was cleaning his apartment, she knew exactly what she'd do. She'd kill the man.

The doorbell was high and her arms were filled with the two packages, so she just kicked the door. Within moments, he opened it and his smile grew bright as if he were glad to see her. Probably had some really rotten job.

"Get in here before you catch a death of cold," he said, grabbing the two packages and hurrying her into the apartment. "You want something hot? Tea, coffee, hot chocolate?"

"Hot chocolate would be nice," she said, looking tentatively around as he nodded her into the living room.

It was sparsely furnished and had a temporary feel to it, but it was neat and clean. No obvious grimy chores that she could see. No obvious trophies from his playing days either. That kind of surprised her, made her uneasy, as if the Rob she was sure she knew wasn't really the one here with her.

"I'm making some instant chocolate in the microwave," he said, coming to stand in the kitchen doorway.

"That'll be fine."

Somehow, without even coming into the room, he seemed to fill up the space. Maybe it was that his eyes seemed to capture hers so she couldn't look anywhere else, or maybe it was because her heart was beating so loud that she was sure he must hear it, too.

The microwave buzzed and Rob disappeared into the kitchen, giving her a chance to breathe again. Jenna stood for a moment in the middle of the living room, feeling uncertain and wary. She suddenly felt foolish for acting as though she'd never been in a man's apartment before. Jenna took off her wraps and hung them on the hall tree just as Rob entered balancing the two mugs of hot chocolate.

"You can take off more if you like," he said.

Sure, wouldn't that be a great way to prove she'd learned from the past? "What is it you need help with?"

"I mean anything wet," he said. "Like your shoes." His eyes were innocent, all the more reason to distrust him.

"I have some tests to correct, so I don't have a whole lot of time to waste." She kept her voice polite, but not overly friendly.

"Gram said you weren't doing anything."

"She doesn't always pay attention. Now what is it you want?"

He sat down on the sofa and patted the place next to him, his eyes softly inviting. "I'd like you to be comfortable," he replied. "And I don't want you to get a bad chill from wet feet."

A chill was about the last thing she'd get, being here with him. A warmth had surrounded her whole body and the air felt heavy like a tropical night. She wasn't comfortable, but getting chilled wasn't the problem. Not by a long shot. She took off her boots.

"I bet your socks are wet," Rob said. "Get them off, too." He disappeared into his bedroom, reappearing a moment later with a pair of thick, warm socks.

"Rob, I don't—"

"These are warm and dry."

Sighing, she pulled off her socks, which truth be known, were a bit damp. Not that it gave the man any reason to run roughshod over her, but that had always been his style. He took her boots and socks into his bathroom while she slipped into his socks.

"Now," she demanded when he returned. "What is it you want help with? I can't stay here all evening."

"Gram said you could stay for dinner. She said she had guests coming."

Sure she did. She was probably calling them right now. Jenna just stared at Rob.

"I just have some basketball stuff." He turned, waving toward a pile of brochures on the end table. "We need to pick the holiday tournaments you want your teams to participate in. And then I have some summer camp brochures. Some of them require a letter of recommendation from you."

Jenna felt her heart contract. Was she so worried about falling prey to Rob again that she was ready to cheat her girls out of participating in a series of games?

"I'm sorry," Rob said, misreading her silence. "If you have other things you need to be—"

"Of course not," Jenna said. "The tournaments or camps are the only place most of my girls will get noticed by the colleges. I don't want to deny any of them an opportunity."

He stared at her a moment and she sank onto the sofa, but not too near him.

"I guess I should have answered the phone," Jenna said softly. "I had no idea what you wanted and Gram was acting weird, playing matchmaker."

His eyes caught hers for just a moment. Their look seemed sad, regretful. Or was that just what her overactive imagination wanted to see there?

"Would you rather do this somewhere else?" he asked. "We could go over it at school on Monday."

"When? Between our practices?" She took a sip of her chocolate, then moved over to sit on the floor near him. She was here for a real reason and she would not be affected by his presence. To prove just how businesslike she was, she grabbed up the pile of brochures and began to sort through them.

"Here's a couple for the girls," Rob said, handing her some from another pile.

Their hands brushed slightly, enough to send tremors along her skin, but not enough to break her concentration. She just kept paging through brochures as if her life depended on it, or at least her sanity.

"The Fort Wayne tournament for boys is always a good one," she said. "I was thinking of taking the varsity girls up to South Bend though."

"Maybe that's where the boys should go also," he said.

He leaned over to show her the tentative tournament schedule just as she was turning toward him. They were suddenly close, too close to allow breathing space, and Jenna remembered so many nights in the past when they'd been sitting just this way doing their homework together in her living room. He'd have a question and would lean over, then the question would be forgotten for a few splendid moments as they kissed.

She shook the memories away and shifted slightly, hopefully looking like she wanted to get a better view of the brochure and not like she was a timid mouse.

"Yeah. That one could be pretty good." She went back to paging through the papers. "I sure wish I could find something for the freshman girls' team. They get so few games as it is."

"I thought there was one in here someplace."

It took them a while to find it, and by the time they had, they'd both finished their hot chocolate. When Rob suggested making some spaghetti, it seemed a sensible suggestion. After all, they still had work to do. And the work lasted through the meal and into the start of a pro game on television.

"Well, that's that," Rob said as he gathered up the brochures and entry forms for their choices. "That didn't take very long."

"No."

Jenna leaned back against the sofa, stretching her arms over her head. She accidentally brushed Rob's leg. Hunger raced through her, like a tidal wave engulfing the shore, and she trembled. Would even such an accidental touch always cause her such aching?

Rob hadn't seemed to have noticed, and to keep him—and herself—distracted, she quickly began to gather their notes together. "We went over budget just a bit. I hope that won't be a problem."

"Nah. Some of our old buddies are pretty successful businessmen in town," he said. "I'll get them to spring for an extra tournament for each of the teams."

"Sure you can persuade them?"

"Hey, I'm the guy who shot the winning basket in '78," he reminded her. "They'd do anything for me."

His absolute certainty made her laugh. "Now, this is the Rob I remember," she said. "The one no one could say 'no' to."

He slipped down to the floor next to her. "Are you saying I was a bit pushy?"

His teasing grin took her back to the days when love was joy, not pain. When her heart skipped at just the sight of him and every day held a promise of magic.

Then suddenly, his arms were around her and her heart was captured, locked back in those wonderful days. His touch was special, bringing only laughter and excitement into her life. He could do no wrong and his slightest smile fueled her laughter for hours. His lips were as sweet as sunshine on hers and all the happiest moments came rushing back to drown her.

She held him, feeling the iron muscles of his back move under her hands. She pressed herself against him, her need of him as great as his hungers for her. There had to be ways to hold him closer, to erase the space between them, the time that had passed when they were alone.

But then the more recent past came up to claim her, dragging with it its burden of pain and misery. Rob seemed to sense the cloud and pulled back slightly, enough to let her lean back against the sofa, but not so much as to really be apart. His hand still held hers.

Silence came into the little apartment totally dominating everything. Jenna stared at the basketball game on television, but even the crowd noise and game commentators barely intruded into her world. It was so quiet that she could hear her own heart beat.

Nothing could erase the past, nothing could take away the pain that she'd had to face. All she could do was keep from suffering that pain again.

Rob was looking at her, as if trying to read a message in her eyes.

"The Bulls are doing well this year," she said, though for the life of her she didn't know what the score was of the game they were watching,

"I guess." He waited a moment, trying to read her mood. "Look, Jen, I'm sorry. I hadn't meant for that to happen. I guess I'm just as susceptible to you now as I was in the past."

She just shrugged. For some reason, her throat seemed all choked up. "We aren't in high school anymore," she finally said.

"I'm not sure that isn't an advantage."

She smiled a bit, not too much though because any little crack that would let sunshine into her heart would also melt that wall she'd built around it. "I think I ought to go."

"Can't you stay and watch the rest of the game?"

"I shouldn't." She hadn't intended to sound as if she were running away from him, so she added, "I really have a ton of papers to correct."

He nodded and got her boots and socks from the bathroom. Then, when she was ready to go, he got an umbrella and walked her to her car. They stood for a moment at her car door, listening to the rain beat against the umbrella fabric.

"Well, see you Monday," she said.

"Yep."

He leaned forward for the quickest of kisses, and she wanted to forget the cold and rain. In his arms, she wouldn't be cold or wet or unhappy, a little voice tried to persuade her, but she was too wise to listen. She pulled back slightly and unlocked her door.

"Thanks for the meal."

"Thanks for the help."

She pulled away, conscious that he stood there watching as she drove down the street. We can't go back, she told his silent figure as it was lost in the darkness. We really can't.

Chapter Seven

Rob tried to concentrate on his driving but his mind kept drifting back to yesterday evening and all the ways he'd fouled it up. He'd been pushing with Jenna. That was why she'd backed off. He was sure of that.

But on the other hand, maybe he hadn't been pushy enough. Why had he told her that he'd see her Monday? Surely she knew that they'd both be at the Athletic Booster Club's spaghetti dinner this evening. Why hadn't he asked her to go with him?

Better yet, why hadn't he just told her he'd pick her up? Her girls were serving the dinner and his boys were cleaning up afterwards but they'd both be there the whole time. There wasn't any need for both of them to drive.

He pulled into the parking spot next to Jenna's red sedan and turned off his motor. The drumming on his roof told him the rain had picked up again. Great. He got out of the car and dashed for the closest door, hoping it wasn't locked. Fortunately, it wasn't and even more fortunately, it transported him into the kitchen. The room was filled with adolescent girls, squealing and chattering like magpies, but as the door closed behind him, the place went dead silent.

After a half-eternity of being stared at, someone spoke. "Hi, Mr. Fagan."

A chorus of greetings was released from the rest of them, but all he was aware of was Jenna, standing there in her sweatshirt and jeans looking like a dream come true.

"He's all wet," one of the girls said.

"Somebody get a towel."

"Hurry."

He and Jenna just stared at each other as the words bounced around them, like a multitude of basketballs during dribbling practice. How had he ever had the strength to leave her? She'd been the rock he'd relied on, the anchor that kept him safe. No, she'd been much more than a guardian angel; she'd been the one who gave him strength to hope.

A towel was passed into the kitchen, from one girl's hand to another, until it came to a girl standing in front of Jenna. The girl held the towel out to her.

"I'm not the one who's wet," Jenna pointed out.

"Aw, Miss Lauren," the girls chorused.

Jenna's jaw seemed to tighten a bit, but she came forward and held the towel out to Rob.

"He's soaking wet, Miss Lauren."

"Dry him off, quickly."

"He can get chilled."

"I've heard of people dying from that."

"Take his coat off, it's drowning him."

Giggles surrounded them as strong, but feminine hands snatched the wet coat off his shoulders. He stared deep into

Jenna's eyes. They seemed dark and cloudy, almost smoky. Was there a fire generating that smoke?

She handed him the towel and he dried his face and arms off, much to the sighing disappointment of the girls who seemed to want Jenna to do it. He wouldn't have minded, but he'd thought chances of such assistance were probably slim. He handed the towel back to her with a smile.

"Need any help?" he asked.

"Sure. You can mix salad, boil pasta or stir the sauce. Ricco's donates it. We just have to make sure it doesn't burn."

"I'm not that handy," Rob replied. "I'll mix salad. That way I won't burn anybody if I spill any."

"You always were a cautious sort."

He gazed deeply into her eyes. Was she trying to tell him something? But the smoky pools had turned unfathomable.

"In some things," he said.

Rob walked over to the salad table. It was best he get to work. That way it would be easier to stay out of trouble.

The girls had already cut the ingredients and all he had to do was mix them in big salad bowls. Looked easy enough. A brainless type of task, the only kind he could handle at the moment.

After several minutes, Rob fell into a rhythm of plunging the salad forks in the mixture and tossing from the bottom. His mind began to wander, in exploration of his feelings and emotions.

Did he really want to stay out of trouble? Sort of, but not really. What he really wanted to do was to take Jenna home and love her to pieces. But was that him talking or just his body?

Hell, he didn't know anymore. Maybe he was just trying to recapture the easy, carefree times of his high school days. Although they hadn't been all that easy and carefree. He hated it when his father was around and hated it when he'd left. He hated seeing his mother work so hard. He didn't have much free time himself between school, basketball, and his part-time jobs. The only time he felt relaxed was when he was with Jenna.

"You really mix things up well," Sara said, a big grin pasted on her face. "I mean, you're like, really thorough. You know what I mean?"

"That's because I've always been a mixed-up sort of guy myself."

Sara giggled.

Rob stared a moment into the bowl, whose contents he had been punishing. "I guess I'll beat up on another innocent bowl of salad."

Sara giggled again and took the first bowl away.

Teenagers. They were walking giggle machines. Had Jenna been like that? She'd always been more on the serious side, but he'd usually been able to make her smile. Could he now? He'd sure like to try.

It would make him happy, but what would it do for her? She'd been taking care of herself for a good many years now, and obviously quite well. She didn't need him.

Things just weren't the same. He'd traveled, she'd stayed. Did she resent that? Probably not. She could have moved away after her mother died. Her grandmother didn't really need any help, and if she did, there was a lot of family around.

No. Jenna stayed because Jenna wanted to stay. Her roots ran deep like those damn big oaks on her front lawn. He had no roots, just like a tumbleweed. It was more than time that separated them.

"Hey, looks like you ladies got a new team member," the principal shouted as he moved along the spaghetti line. "Where are you gonna play your new girl, Jenna?"

The whole line roared in laughter, but Rob's grin stayed in place. He'd always been good-natured and wasn't the least bit embarrassed. Of course, a real hunk like Rob never had to worry. There was no doubt he was all man. Jenna certainly had no doubt, her cheeks reddened slightly.

"Center or forward," she said, suddenly aware that Arthur was waiting for an answer. "We can use the height."

"But only as a reserve," her regular center said. "We don't want to give up our speed and quickness."

The crowd hooted.

"Anytime you want a little one-on-one just let me know," Rob said to her center.

Everyone laughed some more, sending a few zingers Rob's way. Jenna looked at him, their smiles mingling. They used to play one-on-one down at the park, pushing and shoving and scrambling for the ball. Until that last summer, when the pushing and shoving and scrambling often turned into another sort of game. A game where they needed to be as one, locked together by their love and their desires. Even their dreams had been part of it, a reaching for the stars that made them feel invincible.

Something appeared to change in Rob's eyes and Jenna quickly looked away. Things had changed. Or at least some things had. She still felt the need to be held at times, to belong to someone special, but knew enough not to be swayed by such weakness.

"For heaven's sake, Rob Fagan. What are you doing back there?"

Jenna sighed. Gram, as usual, was pushing her way into things.

"Jenna said I had to," Rob replied.

"I did not," Jenna protested. "He said he wanted to help so I let him."

Chuckles moved along the line of people, then rippled on out into the hall as people passed back the cause of the merriment. Great. Just what the evening was lacking, a little dinnertime entertainment.

"Well, you shouldn't have accepted," Gram told Rob, then turned back to Jenna. "You know he's got to clean up. The girls serve. The boys clean up. That's the way it's always been."

"I know, Gram." Jenna stacked all the pieces of garlic bread on one platter and slipped the empty one beneath the table. She looked back up to find the whole line of people smiling at her like she was two years old and about to say something terribly clever. Rob just gazed at her innocently.

"You best stay on after and help Rob and the boys clean up," Gram continued.

"I was going to."

"You make sure she does," Gram said. "You hear me, Rob?"

"I surely will, ma'am."

"Why don't you take your plate and sit down?" Jenna said to her grandmother. "You know how you hate it when your food gets cold."

Gram and the line moved along but not before her grandmother called out one last time. "You make sure she really helps," she told Rob.

"Yes, ma'am," he replied.

"Don't let her just sit around and supervise." Her grandmother was down by the coffee table, and shouting.

"Oh, no, ma'am," Rob called back. "I won't let her do that."

Her grandmother was finally gone, sitting at the far end of the hall with her lady friends, and Jenna found that she could breathe again. Except that the people in the line moving along before her—filled with old friends and neighbors that she'd known forever—kept smiling fondly at her. Jenna grabbed up the empty trays and carried them into the peace of the kitchen.

Lordy, but there were times her grandmother was a bit much. Jenna went to stand in the open doorway, letting the cooler outside air bathe the heat from her cheeks. The rain had slowed to a gentle murmur and she felt herself relax.

"Jenna?"

She spun at the sound of Rob's voice. His eyes were so quiet, so concerned. Maybe it would have been safer to stare outside.

"You okay?" he asked.

"Sure. Why wouldn't I be?"

He shrugged and came over to join her in the doorway. "Sometimes Gram comes on a bit strong."

"So what else is new?"

Rob just smiled, but his mind seemed elsewhere. "It's been hard on you since I came back, hasn't it?" he asked. "The way everyone's watching us bothers you."

She wanted to deny it, but that seemed pointless. "At times." She turned back to the night, watching the drops dance into the puddles on the parking lot. "They all seem so certain that we're the same people we were back then, that we'll have the same feelings and react the same."

He brushed some hair back from her face with infinite slowness. "That wouldn't be all that hard," he said.

She just laughed. His touch bothered her, but she sure wasn't about to let on. "I guess what I'm really afraid of is that I'll find out I haven't grown up at all. That I'm still that silly little girl with a mediocre free throw percentage and a fondness for blue-eyed charmers."

"Is that so bad?"

She closed her eyes as if she could close out the world, but she could still feel him beside her. If she reached out her hand, he would take it. Just as in the past, he was there for her. He would have been there for her had she asked him to be. The choices were ones she'd made, not one's he'd forced on her.

"Might be." She opened her eyes and turned back to the kitchen. "I came out here for more garlic bread. If I don't bring some out soon, they'll send the posse after us."

"With Gram in the lead, no doubt, to see who's getting out of work."

She just laughed and let him carry in a tray of bread while she got refills of the salad dressings. The crowd had thinned considerably, with only a few stragglers at the table.

"Most of us have eaten already, Miss Lauren," Sara told her. "So if you guys want to eat now, we can man the serving table." Mike was coming back up for seconds or thirds, and Sara's attention was gone, so Jenna didn't even bother to answer.

"Shall we?" she said to Rob.

They filled their plates and found some empty seats. She was conscious of the eyes turned their way, but it would cause more notice if she went to sit by herself. Besides, she didn't want to.

"Rob, hey man, how's the team going to be this year?" It was Kevin Parsons who'd captained the varsity team the year before Rob.

"Pretty good, long as our grades hold up."

"Some things never change."

Kevin drifted away, but it wasn't long before Dennis Birdsell came over. "So you guys going downstate this year?"

"We're going to try."

Jenna picked at her food. She certainly didn't have to worry about making dinner conversation. Instead, she could eat in peace and wonder if it was worry or age that had put those little gray streaks at Rob's temples.

"Jenna."

She looked up to find her grandmother at her side. "Hi, Gram." But she couldn't keep the suspicion from her voice.

"We're going to the movies tonight." Gram nodded toward her lady friends. "So don't be waiting up for me."

"Okay. Have fun."

But Gram wasn't ready to move. "You ought to be doing something yourself. Susie's been fed and she won't need to go out until I get home. You sit at home way too much."

Thanks, Gram.

"Maybe she and I could do something," Rob volunteered.

Thanks, Rob.

"That would be a good idea," Gram agreed. "You're a decent, kindly man, Rob Fagan."

Rob was trying hard not to laugh, but put on a carefully polite expression. "That is, if Jenna wants to," he added.

"Of course she does," Gram replied. "Ain't got nothing else to do but sit around, watch TV and scratch the dog's ears."

A capsulization of her life. "Thank you, Gram. Now you'd better hurry along or you'll be late for the show."

Jenna went back to her spaghetti, eating with more diligence than appetite until she was sure her grandmother was gone.

"We don't really have to go out," Rob said. "I just thought it would be easier to play along with her."

"Probably."

"We could go to a movie ourselves," he said. "Or we could rent a video and watch it at my place."

At his place? Where they'd be alone with the ghosts of last night's passion lingering in the air?

Jenna played with the few pieces of spaghetti left on her plate. She was tired of this constant running and hiding. In all her determination not to act like a teeny-bopper, that's exactly what she was doing. An adult woman wasn't afraid of desire or of memories. She didn't avoid the bakery just because she'd once eaten too much chocolate.

"Renting a movie would be great," Jenna said. "Then we don't have to worry if cleanup takes a bit longer."

Actually, cleaning up took very little time. Everyone seemed in a hurry to get done, as if they all had more important places to be. After leaving Jenna's car at Rob's apartment, they drove to the video store, but that visit didn't go smoothly. Most of the popular videos had already been rented out, so Jenna and Rob just decided to go back to his apartment and watch television.

"Not very exciting, I'm afraid," Rob said as he unlocked his door.

"Depends on what's on TV," Jenna said.

Actually, it was a toss-up between sitcoms and wrestling on cable, and they decided to try to get a basketball game in on the radio, rather than watch on tape-delay around midnight. Rob fiddled with the dial, trying to find the station when he found, instead, a station playing songs from the late seventies and early eighties.

"Hey, we used to dance to that one," Jenna cried.

Rob left the radio on the music station. "Want to again?"

She wasn't sure she ought to, it was definitely a risky move, but she was tired of being cautious. "Sure."

She moved into his arms like she was coming home. The music, slow and sensuous, relaxed some knot deep in her soul and she laid her head on his shoulder, wrapping her arms around his neck. She was back in the past, lost in a hazy world of laughter and togetherness and joy.

"Doesn't this take you back?" Rob murmured into her hair, his breath tickling her senses, making her feel alive.

"Homecoming, our junior year," she said. "We doubled with Mary Lynn Lewis and Tom Shallcross and they fought the whole time."

"The only place we could escape to was the dance floor."

"Wasn't too bad of a place to be, if I remember correctly," Jenna said.

"It isn't now, that's for sure."

Rob's hands were light on her back, but moved in a slow circle with the beat of the music. Over and over, they barely seemed to be touching her, yet she felt herself moving closer to him all the while. Her heart began to race so that it threatened to drown out the music.

Then the song ended, and they drew apart. Just slightly though, for the mood hadn't been broken.

"Want some wine?" Rob asked.

"Sure."

She followed him into the kitchen, but the bright lights there were jarring. He turned them off as quickly as he turned them on, pouring the wine by the panel light on the stove. He handed her a glass.

"To yesterday," he said.

"To tomorrow."

They each took a sip of wine, and walked hand in hand back into the living room. A new song was on, one from their senior year, and without a word they put their glasses down and came together.

"Homecoming, senior year," Jenna whispered.

She'd made her dress that year, a deep blue, silk-like fabric that Rob said beautifully accentuated her eyes. They hadn't doubled with anyone, but drove to the dance themselves through a blinding rainstorm. As they'd sat in the car, waiting for the rain to let up, this song had come on the radio.

"Mmm," Rob sighed and planted a kiss on her neck. "This song brings back memories."

Too many of them, but she closed her eyes to the sway of the music and the pleasure of Rob's lips on her skin. He kissed her neck, over and over, dancing around the spot at the base of her neck that was so sensitive. It was her turn to sigh, to move closer into his embrace. Her body trembled with passion as Rob was arousing her inner longings and memories she'd long since buried.

She loved the feel of his arms around her. She felt like she'd fallen into a deep sleep when he'd gone and was just awakening. That was it, she was Sleeping Beauty and Rob was her Prince Charming. She smiled at the idea.

"What?" Rob asked.

She opened her eyes to find him smiling down at her. She touched him, lightly running her hand over his cheek. It was so hard to believe that he'd been gone for thirteen years and was back again. But the cheek wasn't the same one she had touched before; this one was rough with stubble. A man's cheek. Just as it was a man that was holding her, not a teenage boy.

"It hardly feels like you've been gone," she said.

"I know what you mean."

His lips took hers and they seemed to soar into the clouds. Her arms tightened, wanting him closer, wanting to be closer herself. They weren't children anymore, experimenting with feelings. They were adults, with adults needs and passions. They could handle the fires now.

Jenna was barely aware that the song had stopped and another had started. It, too, was one from their senior year, one from the time when their passions had been running high. But she didn't need the song to ignite her feelings. Rob's hands had slid underneath her sweatshirt and their cool touch against her skin ignited all sorts of fires.

She kissed him again, opening her lips to the pressure of his tongue. They shared a silent dance of passion and exploring, of seeking to be joined with the other. The movement of his hands quickened, as did her breathing.

"Oh, Jen. You still do things to me," he sighed, resting his head on hers, as they moved in slow rhythm to the music.

They both were silent, but she could feel his heart beating as quickly as hers, feel his breath coming in gasps that matched hers. For all the time they'd been apart, their bodies were getting to know each other awfully fast.

Jenna closed her eyes and let her head rest on Rob's shoulder as they swayed in the dimly lighted living room. Rob just held her for a long time and it was enough. She could still feel the heat of his hands on her from a few minutes back, or was it from the past? She hardly knew anymore. She just hungered for the taste of his lips, ached for the complete feel of him.

Rob's hands began to explore again, as if they could not be still. Or as if her body were calling out its needs. She wanted to feel his touch, wanted him to drive her fires up hotter and hotter until she cried out. She wanted to lay in his arms and belong to him once more.

Rob found the clasp of her bra and undid it, then let one hand slide around to the front to cup and caress her breast. The pressure of his touch weakened her, made her snuggle deeper into his arms.

"Do you really want to keep dancing?" she finally asked him.

His hands stilled. "I can think of better things to do."

Before she could say a word, he swept her up in his arms and carried her into the bedroom. Neither bothered to search for a light, but pushed frantically at the other's clothing.

Rob pulled her sweatshirt up over her head, then tugged at her jeans while she tried to unbutton his shirt. She ached for him so that her hands trembled. He slid out of his jeans and they lay naked next to each other.

"Oh, Rob," she murmured as he covered her with his body. "Take me back home."

Back to the home she had once found in his arms, back to the joy and ecstasy they had shared. His hands were all over her, followed by his lips as he stroked her into a fever. The years melted away. He was her light, her joy, her knight in shining armor and could take her to places no one else would.

Quivering with hunger, she opened her legs to take him into her. They joined like two stars colliding, and clung together through the explosion that seemed to rock the earth. She lay in his arms, peace floating around her like a cloud.

"You're so beautiful, Jen," he whispered as he kissed her cheek.

She just snuggled closer to him and felt the blanket that he pulled up over them. This was where she belonged.

Chapter Eight

The hair on the lean, muscular arm pricked Jenna's cheeks ever so slightly, but it was a good tickling, a comfortable feeling. She sighed and snuggled deeper into the folds of the blanket, letting the darkness and the warmth surround her with peace again. Cold loneliness was gone forever.

Suddenly, Jenna's eyes flew open and her fingers raced madly across the blanket covering her. This wasn't the quilt her grandmother had made, the quilt whose warm softness had covered Jenna for as long as she could remember. This was an ordinary polyester blanket. Rob's ordinary polyester blanket. Her breathing grew more rapid; her throat tightened. She heard a slight sound to her right and sat up. Oh, no!

The bed moved even though she was still, then a light came on. "What's wrong?" Rob asked, pushing himself up into a sitting position against the headboard.

Jenna just stared at him, the last few hours slowly coming back. The memories, the passion, the wonderful ecstasy of his arms and now, reality. She'd set herself up for a repeat of the past. She pulled the sheet up to cover her body as if she could hide from herself.

Rob misread her action, his eyes turning gentle. "You've never had anything to be ashamed of."

Nothing except stupidity. "I have to get home," she mumbled and rubbed her eyes. Maybe this was all a dream and Rob's bedroom would disappear once she woke up.

"Gram won't be worrying about you," Rob said. "I left her a message on your answering machine."

"Oh, great." That was all she needed. She had to get out of here, away from those eyes, those arms. "I just don't feel like sleeping anymore."

Rob slid over, starting to put his arm around her shoulders. "Okay by me. Sleeping is pretty boring stuff."

She pulled away from him before his touch could dull her common sense again. "The only thing I want to do is go home."

"Jenna, it's three o'clock in the morning."

She slid out from under the sheets, grabbed up her clothes, and raced for the bathroom. "Then it's past time for Cinderella to get home."

She reached the bathroom and leaned against the door as if demons were trying to break through. Why in the world had she ever come here?

"Jenna?" Rob knocked lightly on the door. "Are you all right?"

She swallowed hard. "I'm fine."

"Would you like coffee or anything? We can sit and talk."

"I don't want to talk. I just want to go home."

"You act like we've done something wrong."

Not wrong, monumentally stupid. "Just let me get dressed," she pleaded.

The silence stretched out. Rob must have gone, and Jenna found it was possible to breathe again. In and out. In and out. She took slow, steady breaths and finally the tightness eased in her throat.

She should have known that she could fight her feelings for Rob only so long. He'd been everything to her in the past. Why had she thought he'd be nothing to her now? She rinsed her face, splashing cold water onto her eyes until they no longer stung, then slipped into her clothes.

Everyone in town had expected her to fall for Rob again and she'd spent the last few weeks annoyed at their certainty. She was a new person, remade over the last thirteen years with careful precision so that she would never hurt again. Yet all Rob'd had to do was smile and thirteen years of work fell to the wayside. Was she so weak or hadn't she really changed? The thought was scary enough to give her the strength to leave the bathroom.

Rob was waiting for her, leaning against the doorway between the kitchen and the living room. He'd gotten dressed in a pair of jeans and a T-shirt, but what she noticed most were his eyes. They were dark with worry. He was concerned about her, wanting to reach out to her and not knowing how. His changes seemed to have gone a bit deeper than hers.

"Are you okay?"

She brushed the hair from her face. "I'm fine."

"I made some coffee."

"I just want to get home," she said. Home. Solitary and safe. Where she could cry until her heart broke and no one would know.

"Come on, Jenna. Something's wrong and I don't know what. We have to talk."

"There's nothing to talk about," she said. "I got a little carried away last night and it's over."

He frowned and straightened up. He'd always seen through her lies. "I'll make breakfast. Blueberry pancakes made just like you used to love them."

Yesterday's habit for yesterday's Jenna. Doomed to make yesterday's mistakes?

Never. "I don't want any breakfast," she snapped and marched into the living room to look for her purse. "I just want to go home."

Rob went after her, grabbing her arm and turning her to face him. "What the hell is going on?"

"We had sex and now the lady wants to go home. What's so strange about that?"

"I didn't think it was anything like that." His eyes grew hard and his mouth tight. "I thought we made love. Like two people who care about each other."

Jenna looked away. "Two people who used to care about each other. We were reliving the past and got carried away."

"Maybe. But it wasn't an eighteen-year-old Jenna I saw in my dreams."

She felt her control slipping, like she was walking across Donavan's pond in the winter with the ice thin and cracks racing out in all directions. She couldn't stand still and she couldn't move.

"Good night, Rob. Or good morning, whatever the proper greeting is. Take your pick." She tried to step out of his arms and around him, but he wouldn't let her go.

"I want to know what's wrong. What did I do?"

The ice was shifting under her feet. "You didn't do anything. Or rather, nothing that I wasn't agreeable to," she said, her hands gripping her purse. "I'm not angry with you. I'm mad at myself."

"Why? You just said it was what you wanted."

"At the moment." The cracks were growing. She had to get to the door, to the high ground away from him.

"And that's what it was, a moment's pleasure. So why are you torturing yourself?"

"I'm not. You're the one doing the torturing since you won't let me leave."

Rob's face grew dark with impatience. "Come off it, Jenna. Something else is going on here and I demand to know what it is."

"You demand?" Her voice grew louder; the dam had opened into a narrow river of icy water. "What gives you the right to demand anything of me?"

"What we just shared gives me the right."

The ice beneath her feet began to give way. Cold surrounded her. "What we just shared?" She laughed, her heart safely encased in ice. "Since when did you want the rights that come along with sex? This is really a new Rob Fagan."

"What's that supposed to mean?" His grip on her upper arms tightened, his voice edged closer to anger, real raging anger.

"Nothing. Just that it's interesting that you think you can pick and choose what rights and responsibilities you want to claim."

He stared at her a long moment, emotions burning in his eyes but she didn't even try to read them. "What the hell is with you?"

She glanced down at herself. "Nothing, I hope. Or should I say no one? I've already had the pleasure of having a little one with me, thanks to you, and I'm not up to a repeat quite yet."

His eyes grew wide and bored deep into her. Disbelief, confusion, and pain were mirrored in his gaze, but none of it touched her. She was ice; she was the untouchable night.

"You got pregnant when we were kids?" he finally asked.

She nodded.

"What happened?"

"I miscarried."

They stood there, wrapped in silence, for an eternity. She heard a faucet dripping in the bathroom, the buzz of the fluorescent light in the kitchen and a car splashing in the puddles outside, but she felt nothing.

"I would like to go," she said.

Rob's hands dropped from her arms, but he said nothing, not when she got her coat, not when she let herself out the door.

The front doorbell rang and Susie lifted up her head, giving a single, low woof.

"Gram'll get it," Jenna told the dog.

Susie let her head down, but kept her eyes open. Pretty much the same as Jenna did, going back to her papers, but listening to the murmur of voices in the hallway. Gram's footsteps were coming closer and Jenna held her breath.

"Rob's here, dear," Gram said softly.

Jenna let her breath out. Should she tell Gram to tell Rob that she was sick? No, that was ridiculous. She had to work with the man. Sooner or later she had to face him. Might as well be sooner. Or maybe it was already thirteen years too late. Susie pushed her old bones up and followed Jenna out into the hallway.

"Hello, Rob."

He replied with a curt nod. "Jenna."

They traded silent stares for a moment, then Rob dropped to his knees. "Susie, how're you doing, girl?" Susie sniffed his outstretched hand and let him scratch her ears. "You always were the greatest dog."

After several moments, his vigorous scratching slowed down to a gentle, rhythmic petting. "Can we talk?" he asked Jenna without looking up.

"Sure."

He continued petting the dog. "In your den?"

"Your subject has never been discussed in this house," she said and looked outside at the gloomy scene. It seemed damp and miserable outside, but the rain had stopped. "What's it like outside? Can we just walk around the block?"

"It's drizzling. Shouldn't be all that bad."

"I'll get my coat." Jenna walked toward the back door, sticking her head into the kitchen. "We're going for a short walk."

Her grandmother gave them a sharp look but all she said was, "That's fine, dear."

Neither of them said anything as they walked out the back door and down the driveway. There they stopped, exchanging questioning glances. They both seemed to be walking a tightrope, carefully dancing around the other.

"Downtown's quiet on a Sunday," Rob said.

"Okay."

They walked toward the downtown area, hands in their pockets, carrying the silence between them. The rain had tapered down to a mist, and the air even had a hint of warmth to it, but Jenna was chilled through and through.

She had known Rob would come. From the moment she'd blurted out the words of her confession last night, she'd known he'd want more. Why had she told him? The news was thirteen years old; there was no point in telling him except to make him suffer just a piece of what she had suffered. She didn't like to think that was behind her confession.

"I don't know where to start," Rob finally said.

"Neither do I," Jenna murmured.

They stopped in front of the hardware store and its Thanksgiving diorama of turkeys, Pilgrims, and Indians. "In places like LA and Chicago, they're already decorated for Christmas," he said.

"I don't like having the seasons rushed," Jenna said. "Each holiday should be savored as it comes."

He nodded his head and they walked on. What she really wanted to tell Rob was that the past was over and done with. That they both should just leave it in peace. But if she'd truly believed that, she never would have told him about the baby.

"I don't know what to say except that I'm hurt, angry and sad. But mostly I'm sorry." He stopped to shake his head. "I'm a mess."

So was she. "It all happened a long time ago. Everyone lived through it."

He looked at her and twisted his lips halfway between a grimace and a smile. "You're still the tough guy."

"Have to be," Jenna replied as they walked on. The bakery's window was bare, waiting for tomorrow's goodies to make it alive again. As she was, waiting for Rob? No. "Life tramples you down if you aren't tough."

"I'm sorry it all happened."

Jenna shrugged. "Takes two to tango. It wasn't all your fault."

"But why didn't you tell me?" He took her arm and stepped in front of her. "I was part of it. Just as much as you. I should have known. I could have helped."

She looked at him a long moment, trying to drag him back to those times with her. But it wasn't this solemn-faced Rob she saw. It was a laughing, cocky kid who had all the answers. Not someone you could depend on in the long run. Not someone who hurt if you hurt. She began walking again, words bouncing around in her mind. She grabbed at them, trying to put some order to her thoughts.

"Things were happening so fast. I didn't know what to do."

"You should have told me."

She just laughed. "Right."

"Why not? I thought we were close, that we could always talk to each other."

Jenna turned to glance at him. He was so serious now. His eyes narrowed, his lips straight and firm, it all bespoke of maturity. So totally different from the boy who laughed and danced that whole summer. He'd been so full of himself, life, and the bright future that stretched before him. Somehow it hurt more to tell this Rob than it would have the old one.

"You had your scholarship," she said. "You were going to play big-time ball for UCLA."

"Oh, God, Jen."

His voice was so full of agony that Jenna didn't want to look at him. She stopped at the Chamber of Commerce office and stared at the drawing of the new parking garage.

"I could have put that aside," he said.

That lighted a fuse to her anger and she turned to face him. "Put that aside? All you ever talked about was leaving this dumb, one-horse town. Getting out and making something of yourself so that you could live on easy street and take your mother and brothers with you."

The pain stayed on his face. "Things change. If I'd had to, I would have just grown up sooner."

"If you had to?" The cold water of sadness splashed on her soul and washed the anger away. "People may do things because they have to, but they never like it. We would have both wound up hating each other, working in nowhere jobs, dead inside before we were twenty-five."

Rob looked away, but the truth was still there.

"Instead, we both went on to school, got an education, professions we like." She shrugged. "Sure, life isn't perfect but it never is. I know that I got most of what I wanted."

"What about the baby?" he asked, looking across the street at the newspaper office.

Jenna turned and shared his view. "I didn't know what to do. I was all confused, trying to sort things out."

"By yourself."

"Yes, by myself," she snapped. "It wasn't exactly my choice. Mom was sick and Dad was worried about her. Gram stayed with us a lot, but I hadn't found a way to tell her."

"And I was on my way to the promised land."

She hadn't meant to cause the bitterness in his voice and forced a calm she didn't feel. "I did eventually tell Dad. Mom was in the hospital and he was tired. He asked me to drive. I told him on the way down."

Rob turned to look at her and she wished he hadn't. She closed her eyes to hold on tight to herself as she went on. "Not even a mile later, that drunk ran the red light and slammed into the passenger side. They say Dad died instantly. I had the steering wheel as well as a seat belt to hold onto, so I was just shaken up. I miscarried in the hospital."

Rob looked away again. She couldn't breathe.

"A very understanding social worker helped me and agreed to keep the baby a secret. It's in my medical records, of course, but Mom was in no shape to hear about it and Gram had her hands full with the funeral arrangements."

"So the experience just disappeared. Like it never existed."

The pain and anger in his voice tore at her. Tears came, wanting to wash away the hurts, but she just blinked them away. He had to have his turn at anger. She'd had thirteen years to adjust.

"I never forgot about it. Not even for a minute," she said. "But once the pregnancy was over, there didn't seem to be much importance in telling you. You couldn't bring the baby back."

He continued staring down the street. She could feel his torment, shared it.

"It was all taken out of my hands," she said. "Out of our hands."

There seemed to be nothing left to say, only the pain left to endure. An aching misery that the years could only dull, not eliminate. They stood there a long time, locked in their own thoughts, sharing only the cold mist surrounding them.

"Was it a boy or girl?" Rob finally asked.

Jenna shook her head. "They never told me. I didn't even think to ask until later."

Rob nodded, his face tight.

She would have liked to tell him that knowing its sex would only make the healing harder, but couldn't. The only thing they were sharing was space on the sidewalk. Each was suffering in his own little cocoon, for thirteen years and too much pain stood between them. He would have to find his own way through his grief, just as she had. There wasn't a love between them to ease things. There wasn't a well of caring to draw from. When she had needed his strength, he wasn't there. If he needed hers now, there was nothing she could do about it. She'd forgotten how to give.

Jenna looked down the street. "I think it's time to head back."

Rob just nodded and they walked back in silence.

"Oh, shut up," Rob snapped at the electronic beep that screamed for his attention. He threw the Sunday papers down in front of the sofa, before stomping into the kitchen to get his dinner out of the microwave.

It was bad enough to have people constantly telling you what to do. Now modern man, in all his wisdom, had created a whole set of gadgets that could dictate to him. Stoves that beeped their commands. Cars that told you when to put on your seat belts and when you were driving too fast. Another generation and the electronic marvels will take over the world.

Dinner in one hand, he dropped his body back onto the sofa and picked up the TV remote control in the other. After paging through the networks and a zillion cable channels, he settled on a professional football game. A red team versus a blue team.

He turned up the volume, then stared at his meal. Some kind of meat covered with white guck, little green thingies, and mashed potatoes. He stared hard at the plate, but the best he could do was identify one out of the three dinner items.

Closing one eye, he stabbed through the guck and picked out a piece of stuff, presumably meat. Tasted more like "stuff" than meat, though. The TV was loud enough, now he needed a visual distraction. He opened the sports page and scanned it for semi-interesting articles, but found none.

He speared a couple of the green thingies and turned to the middle of the sports section. He found the preseason ratings of the area boys' basketball teams. Warsaw was rated number thirteen in the state. Thirteen. The number of years he'd been gone. Throwing his fork down, he buried his face in his hands.

"Damn, damn, damn."

He looked up with a sigh, gazing at the far wall. He just didn't understand it. She'd been pregnant with his child and unwilling to tell him. Why?

Did she think that he wouldn't care? My God, she couldn't have. They'd been more than boyfriend/girlfriend. They'd been friends. Real friends. There for each other during the hard times.

He dropped his hands and looked down at the floor. At least Jenna had been. Always. She'd helped him with his math and listened to him pour out his rage about his father, at his circumstances, at everything. And when he didn't know what to do with himself, she'd let him vegetate at her house.

Maybe that was it. Jenna had gotten to know him—and his father—much too well. Maybe she saw the signs and knew he'd be his father's son. Just an irresponsible wanderer like his old man had been. She must have figured that if she laid a heavy load on a person like that, he would just squirm around until he could run for the far horizon. She probably thought if she'd told him about the baby, he would have been gone before morning.

He glared at the barely touched remains of his dinner. He wasn't really up to his cardboard rations for tonight. After turning the TV off, he took his plate into the kitchen and dumped it in the garbage.

Closing his eyes, he saw his father before him—a big, strong Irishman with sparkling eyes, a broad smile, and the Blarney Stone never far from his lips. His mother always said that his father had been touched by the little people. Blessed with good looks and charm, but cursed by a restless soul that always needed to wander, to chase the rainbows on the far horizon. As a kid, Rob had always thought the old man was touched more by little bottles than little people, but maybe drinking was the way he coped, the way he kept the demons silent for a time.

Not that long ago, shortly before his mother had died, she'd been talking about his basketball career and how he'd played for five different European teams in four years.

She'd laughed, saying he was truly his father's son, likewise touched by the little people. Handsome, charming, with a glib tongue and a need to chase rainbows.

The anger bubbled even now and Rob threw his dishes into the sink. He'd never asked for that legacy, never wanted anything from the old man. It was just that he couldn't seem to settle in one place. Just when he'd start to make friends, feel at home, something would make him move on. After a bit, the anger cooled, turning into restlessness and Rob decided a walk in the brisk night air was what he needed.

His steps took him down the main street in front of his apartment complex, through a residential area and down past a grade school. His feet slowed as he noticed the lights were on in a church building at the next corner. Did they still have open gym on Sunday nights, like they'd had when he was a kid? He walked back to the long, low building behind the church itself. The door was open.

The unique whappity-whap sound of a basketball bouncing on a concrete floor came from the back, but the gym contained only a single, solitary figure.

"Hi, Mike," Rob said.

The boy set himself up, took a shot, and watched the ball swish through the net. "Hi, Mr. Fagan," he said, as he chased down the ball. He didn't sound as cheerful as he normally did in school.

"Come here often?" Rob asked.

Mike shrugged and he dribbled out to beyond the free throw line. "Beats sitting around the house and arguing with my little sister."

"Got your homework all done?"

"Just about." He took a high arching shot that also went in.

"You got a lot riding on keeping your grades up."

"Hey, no sweat, Mr. Fagan. Ain't no way I'm going to mess up my ticket out into the real world."

Rob could barely contain a bitter smile. The real world. He didn't need too much imagination to see what that meant to this kid. Hell, he'd carried that same picture around in his head for years. Big-time college ball and then the pros. Money, adulation, women, having it all. He wondered whether Mike realized the price of his dream.

"How is Sara taking all this?" Rob asked.

Mike took a shot, watched it miss and then shrugged. "I don't know. She's been sort of grumpy lately." He retrieved the ball. "You know how women get."

Rob sighed. "How about a little one-on-one?"

"Sure."

They played, both working up a good sweat, then called it quits after an hour or so. Rob treated them both to sodas out of the vending machine in the hall. They sat on the gym floor and sipped their cool drinks.

"Not many people here," Rob said.

"Nah," Mike agreed. "The Bears football game is on today."

"How about Detroit or Indianapolis?" Rob asked. "Do they have many fans here?"

"Yeah. Some."

Mike quickly drank his soda. "I better get on home. Got a paper due tomorrow for English."

Rob sat quietly on the floor, not responding immediately. Mike paused a moment, then turned to walk toward the door. Mike and Sara. He and Jenna. Man/woman relationships seemed wedded to a circle.

"Hey, Mike."

The boy stopped at the door and turned. "Yeah?"

"You know a person's life takes a lot of twists and turns."

Mike's brow wrinkled in question. Hell. Now that he started it, Rob wondered what his next words should be.

"Respect everyone you touch along the way," Rob said. "Don't be a user. You might find yourself coming back on one of the roads you went out on and get burned."

Mike blinked in obvious bewilderment. "Yes, sir," he replied.

Hell, Rob thought. He certainly wasn't cut out to be a padre. "See you at practice tomorrow," he said.

The boy's face brightened up when given something he could handle. "Right." He hurried out.

Rob closed his eyes and sighed. How do you tell a kid what's precious? What love really meant? Damn kid wouldn't understand until it was too late.

Chapter Nine

"Hi, Miss Lauren. Are you going inside?"

Sara and three other girls from the varsity team stood near the gym doors. All were in their stocking-feet, arms wrapped around shoes, books, and purses. Jenna nodded, forcing herself to ignore their grinning faces.

"I guess it all depends on who you know," Sara said, her eyes glinting mischievously.

"Or what you know," Jenna said. "One of Mr. Fagan's assistants called in sick, so he asked me to help out to-night."

"Does he need any more help?"

"We'd be great back-up. We're good on defense."

"Yeah," Sara snickered. "We have to defend against their moves every day."

The girls laughed out loud and Jenna just sighed. "Don't you ladies have some homework to do?"

"Yes," they chorused.

"Then maybe you ought to do it," Jenna said.

After taking a moment for a face-making contest, they all turned and walked down the hall toward the open lounge area. Jenna stared after them for a moment, then took a deep breath before going into the gym.

She'd done a good job of avoiding Rob for most of the day, and had been congratulating herself on winning another day to figure out her reaction to him. Then came tenth period and his note, asking her to fill in for Mick Kowalski at practice. No more reprieves. She let the door close behind her.

Rob, in a T-shirt and shorts, was directing the boys in a simple shooting drill at the other end of the gym. Jenna stayed in the doorway, leaning on the frame. He moved with such grace, such strength on the court. She had always enjoyed watching him play in high school, and had to admit the same thrill was there. Was it that some things never changed or was it that some people don't change?

She watched as he demonstrated a shot, his arms raised high, his touch seemingly light and effortless. He'd really been in agony over the baby. She should never have told him.

He saw her in the doorway and waved, a single raise of the hand. She returned it and started to make her way slowly across the gym floor. But he had a right to know; it had been his child, too. Even though she miscarried, maybe she should have told him years ago.

There were no easy, clear-cut answers then and there sure weren't any now. Maybe that was why she didn't know how to act around him anymore. The game of old girlfriend and old boyfriend didn't seem to work. They'd been a lot more than that, yet what were they now? Tiptoeing around each other, that's what.

"Hi, Jen."

She smiled tightly at him, her voice suddenly gone. His eyes seemed so sad, so full of pain that it didn't matter how he pretended to curve his lips into a smile.

"I really appreciate you helping me out."

"No problem." She looked away as if the sight of the boys jogging around the gym was fascinating. "I'm sure I'll need your help down the road."

"Just holler and I'll be there."

She brought her gaze back to him, but he was staring raptly down at his clipboard. Was this a one-time awkwardness or had they completely lost hope of being friends? She prayed not.

"So what do you want me to do?" she asked.

"Work with the guards, if you will," he said. "Three point shots, then run them through some dribbling drills, especially with obstacles."

"Okay," she replied.

"Lou and I will work with the big people," he said, then blew his whistle.

After Rob divided the boys up, Jenna took her group down to the other end of the gym. They worked hard for the next hour, Jenna concluded, but it didn't really help. She kept hearing Rob's voice from the other end of the court. It seemed deeper, darker, drier. The laugh that had always lain just below the surface wasn't there.

She drove the boys harder, wishing that the sound of their dribbling could drown out Rob's questions that had been echoing in her heart all weekend. Why hadn't she told him before? Would she have, had she not miscarried?

A whistle sounded and all of the boys stopped. "Everybody over here," Rob ordered, waving his hand. "Put the balls aside, then get your team assignment from Lou."

Jenna followed the boys over toward Rob. This self-torturing was crazy. There was no point in it. No matter what she decided now, she couldn't undo the decisions of the past. She did what she thought best back then, and that was that.

Rob met Jenna at half-court. "Looks like the guys gave you a workout."

"I enjoyed it," she said. Though it hadn't really helped.

"Well, I appreciate it." Rob seemed to hesitate a moment, then went on. "We're going to scrimmage for the next forty minutes and Lou and I can handle that."

"Well, I'll get on home then."

"See you tomorrow," he said.

"Right."

They stood a moment, as if unsure how to make the final separation.

"The team's all set, Rob," Lou called out.

Jenna dismissed herself from his gaze and his presence, hurrying out of the gym. Things would be less awkward the next time they met. Maybe not back to friendly—they might never reach that point again—but things would be better. Weary beyond all reason, Jenna walked toward her classroom to pick up her books and noticed Sara was alone in the lounge area. Conversation was better than being alone with her thoughts.

"How are things going?" Jenna asked, as she sank onto the carpet-covered bench.

"Pretty good."

"Mike excited about the possibility of playing for De Paul?"

Jenna thought she saw a flicker of a shadow, but Sara kept a smile on her face. "Yeah, pretty much. He's been studying a lot on his own."

"That's the way it should be," Jenna said.

"Yeah, I guess."

Silence intruded for a moment, and Jenna stared at the scratched cover of Sara's math book. "Dayton is still interested in you," she said. "Are you still interested in them?"

Sara hesitated the slightest moment before replying. "Yeah."

Jenna took a deep breath and let it out slowly. "It's not a good idea to push your own dreams aside," she said. "No one cares about your happiness and fulfillment like you do. And nobody will work harder to achieve it than you."

"I guess."

There was some uncertainty in the girl's eyes, but there was also strength. Jenna stood up. She'd done the right thing thirteen years ago, and she did the right thing the other night. There was no reason for Rob to know back then, but he had to know now. If they were to be on better terms, he had to learn who she was and what had formed her that way. But would that knowledge defeat the purpose and keep them from ever being friends again?

"We need to run the girls hard tonight," Jenna said, pulling the clipboard across the luncheon table toward her.

"Yeah, they'll stuff themselves full of turkey tomorrow and then won't be able to move on Friday," Rita said.

"We could take a poll on dinnertimes," Peggy suggested. "And then schedule a practice tomorrow at the most popular time."

"And have all the grandmothers in town after us?" Jenna laughed. "No thanks."

"Yeah, but—" Suddenly Rita began making faint noises like a submarine about to dive. "Squawk, squawk. Hunk alert," she said under her breath. "Hunk alert."

Jenna looked toward the door, her thin layer of good cheer disappearing without a trace. Rob had just walked in.

"Hello, ladies," he said. Without waiting for a response, he went to the bulletin board to check the notices posted there.

"Do we have anything else that needs to be covered?" Jenna asked. She carefully checked off each item she had listed, as if she might find something that had snuck past her. Jenna's eyes wandered over to Rob, noting how tired he looked. She wished she could make him laugh again, a real laugh that came from his heart, not the pretend ones she'd heard lately.

"When I was a girl, we never had anything like a 'hunk alert,'" Peggy said, her voice low. "We used to go 'Dreamboat. Dreamboat coming.'" Then she made a noise like a foghorn.

Rita broke into laughter and Peggy joined in, but Jenna could only manage a smile. Watching Rob in pain was almost like suffering it all over again herself.

"Hey." Rob had turned toward them. "How come my name isn't on this list? It looks like everybody in the school is working on this Thanksgiving dinner, but me."

Peggy turned to face Jenna. "Why haven't you asked him?" Peggy asked.

"Yeah," Rita joined in. "How come?"

Jenna felt as if she were under attack. "Me? I'm in charge of delivery and pickup. I don't have anything to do with personnel."

Peggy just rolled her eyes heavenward. "What difference does that make? The man's waiting to be asked." She turned to Rob. "Rob, would you help us with the Teachers' Association luncheon for the poor and elderly?"

"I'd be glad to," he replied. "Thank you for asking."

"See," Peggy said to Jenna. "It wasn't that hard."

Her two assistants sat there grinning like fools, while Jenna felt like running. She'd been through these little matchmaker scenes before, right after Rob had come, but things were different now. He might not want to be pushed at her.

"What am I going to be doing?" Rob asked.

"There's a whole bunch of ways to help," Peggy said.

"You can take my place on delivery and pickup," Rita said. "I get lost really quickly."

That was Jenna's territory. She wasn't sure she and Rob ought to be on it together. "It's easy to get around Warsaw," she said. "I was going to layout all your routes for you."

"I could be bringing some little old lady over here," Rita said. "And get lost. Then that poor woman'd be missing out on her Thanksgiving meal."

"The old lady would be able to direct you here," Jenna said.

Peggy put down her can of soda pop. "Older people sometimes get confused," she pointed out.

Jenna took a deep breath, feeling the heart strings pulling her tighter. She gathered up the remains of her lunch and stuffed it into the paper bag.

"Jenna," Rita said. "Give the man a chance."

Jenna looked up to find everyone staring at her. "I didn't say he couldn't help."

"You didn't say he could," Peggy pointed out.

Why were they doing this to her? "Fine," she said. "I don't care. He can help any way and anywhere he wants."

Rita wiped at her forehead, as if in relief. "Whew. Now I won't get lost."

"More importantly," Peggy said. "Everyone who's supposed to be here will get here and not lose out on a Thanksgiving dinner."

"Absolutely," Rita agreed.

Peggy and Rita wore self-satisfied smirks while they gathered up their lunch debris. Rob just watched them, looking slightly puzzled.

"Well, I have to get back," Peggy said.

Rita stood up with her. "I have a chapter to review before class."

"I'm glad you're helping us out," Peggy said, taking Rob's hand.

"And now I won't have to worry about getting lost and having some little old lady starve to death. I mean, right in my car." Rita shook her head. "Bummer."

The two women left, leaving Rob and Jenna to themselves. Jenna felt like a kid on her first date, uncertain what she should say, afraid of doing the wrong thing. An absolutely ridiculous reaction, considering all she and Rob had been through together.

"I hope I'm not forcing myself where I'm not needed," Rob said.

His eyes were still and watchful; they made her uneasy because she couldn't read what they wanted. She tossed her lunch remains away.

"I don't know how you were missed. A memo got sent around. I guess you fell through the cracks."

"Happens pretty often to a little guy like me."

They shared a laugh, almost a real one, and Jenna felt something change. Like the sun had come out after a storm.

"Well, thanks for taking me on," Rob said.

"Sure."

Jenna picked up her papers as Rob walked slowly toward the door. She felt a sense of relief. They were dancing toward a kind of friendship again, but not too fast. Her gaze caught him as he reached the door. There was something in the way he held his shoulders, so straight and strong, yet so vulnerable.

"Uh, Rob."

He stopped and turned. "I'm not fired already, am I?"

His eyes tried to laugh, but the shadows ruled. She felt her heart cracking. She wanted to reach out her hand to his and help him bear the pain. She picked up her purse instead.

"Gram was wondering if you'd like to have Thanksgiving dinner with us. It'll be in the evening after we clean up here in the gym."

His smile was polite, but his eyes telegraphed his curiosity. She held her things as a shield over her heart.

"I was wondering also," she said.

"That's very nice of you both," he said. "I'd love to share Thanksgiving dinner with you and Gram."

"Good," Jenna said, and clutched at her papers. "I'll see you tomorrow then."

"Right."

They left the room together, but Jenna turned down the first hall. The matchmakers in town were off the mark. She and Rob weren't a couple anymore, but they might get back to being friends.

"Thank you so much, young man." The elderly woman came over to where Rob was collecting the unused silverware off the long cafeteria tables. "It's so nice to share the holiday with someone."

"It's the same for us," he said. "Do you need a ride home?"

The woman shook her head. "That nice young lady over there said she's got someone to take us."

The "nice young lady" was Jenna, of course, working her way through the few remaining guests at their Thanksgiving dinner. Her manner was gentle, her eyes laughing. These were all her friends, her extended family, even those she barely knew. They were part of a community in a way that he never would be.

Rob put the silverware on a serving cart and moved over to the next table as an older man came by, his tall frame bent over a cane as he walked.

"Say, aren't you Rob Fagan?" the man asked, his hand extended. "Mike Bauer. You made the shot that won that game against Northwood, right? 1978."

Rob shook the man's hand. "That was a long time ago."

"Not as long ago as 1937. That's when I missed the shot that would have won the championship for us." He sighed and the sound seemed to have come from his heart. "A little more spin and I could've had what you had. Everybody fussing over you and colleges all wanting you."

"Wasn't as great as it sounded," Rob said. "I traded a lot of things away for the chance to compete."

"Yeah, but it made you somebody special."

Did it? Rob watched as the man walked away. What made a person special—what he did or who he was? Someone ought to be special because of the legacy he left, not because he could win a game with a lucky shot. Rob's eyes stopped on Jenna who was giving a little girl a paper turkey from the centerpiece of a table.

If their child had lived, it would have been in junior high by now, struggling with independence and responsibility. Would it have been a girl, blond and fiercely loyal, or a boy with a quick mouth and wandering feet? He ached to think that he'd given life to someone he'd never had the chance to know. But even if the child had lived, would Jenna have given him that chance? Or even worse, would he have stayed around to get to be a father to his child? Which legacy was better—the pain Jenna'd suffered or for a child to grow up fatherless? Neither one made him someone special.

He turned back to the tables he'd been clearing, stripping them with fervor to escape his thoughts. He'd made his mistakes. It was too late now to undo them. All he could do was keep from repeating them.

"Hey, I thought you were out there keeping little old ladies from getting lost." Rita came over with a tray to collect sugar bowls. "You get fired?"

"Nah, just ran out of customers. Jenna's got everyone taken care of between herself and Jerry Wray."

"That sounds like her."

Rob looked over at Rita. "Efficient?"

"Doing everything herself." Rita dumped the little packets of sugar into a box, then packets of artificial sweetener into another. "She's a nice lady, but I don't think she's happy. Not deep down inside." She grinned up at Rob suddenly. "I bet you could change that."

Not necessarily, since he was the one who had caused that deep-down hurt. He wasn't even sure they ought to be friends anymore.

"You almost done here?"

He turned to find Jenna by his side. Her pale pink sweater warmed her cheeks, her hair looked like spun gold. He wanted to take her into his arms and hold her until his pain melted away, but what he needed and what she wanted might be two very different things.

"Yeah. Just a few more tables to clear," he said. He looked across the cafeteria where others were stripping the tables and washing them. "You got somebody who needs a ride home?"

"No. I'm taking the last couple now and then I'll go on home if you want to meet me there."

"Sure."

She left with the ghost of her smile lingering in the air. He finished cleaning up with the others and drove over to Jen's house. A light dusting of snow had fallen while he had been in the cafeteria and he offered to sweep the sidewalks while he waited for Jenna.

"Land sakes, Rob Fagan, we didn't invite you here to work," Gram complained. "That little bit'll probably melt by tomorrow anyway."

"Got to earn my meal," he said and started sweeping.

Actually, the cold crisp air felt good. Seemed to clear his head of cobwebs. He worked his way down the driveway and had started on the sidewalk when Jenna pulled in. He felt rather than saw her come over toward him.

"You don't have to do this," she said. "It'll melt by morning."

"You Lauren women are all alike," he said. "Never let a man have his own way."

What a stupid thing to say. He didn't need the sudden flush in Jenna's cheeks to tell him he should think before he spoke.

"Sorry. I wasn't exactly thinking."

"No problem," she said with a careless shrug that would have worked had she been able to look him in the eye.

She started to move away, but Rob stopped her, his hand on her arm. She could have pulled away had she wanted to, but she grew still, her questioning eyes meeting his.

"Jen, I really am sorry."

"I know—"

"No, I mean about everything. I never would have hurt you for all the basketball scholarships in the world."

"I know."

Her eyes held a different type of sadness but, like a murky pond in the summer, he couldn't read their depths. "I know I was selfish and blind, but I never would have hurt you."

She just laughed. "Rob, honestly, I do believe you. It's not like you refused responsibility. I never told you."

"But I was the one pressuring you to make love," he said. "It wasn't your idea."

She took his hand and it seemed like an anchor to cling to. "I wanted it just as much as you. Neither of us thought about the consequences, so we're both equally to blame for that, but it wasn't rape. It wasn't even undue pressure. It was like a celebration of our love, not 'sleep with me or I'll find someone else to love.' "

"So why do I feel so guilty? And why do I feel that you're still mad at me?"

She brushed the snow aside with her foot for a moment, before looking up at him again. "You feel guilty because you just found out. You won't hurt so much after a while and reason will set in. You'll know we were both to blame for our youth and foolishness." She looked away then, taking her hands from his to jam them into her coat pockets. "As for being mad at you, I'm not. Just sometimes I'm terrified of falling into the same old patterns out of habit."

There was such a stillness about her, a sense of underlying wariness. "Want me to leave town?"

Her laughter blessed the evening air. "Goodness, no. The boys would never forgive me."

Maybe not the best of reasons, but he felt a sense of relief, nevertheless. He reached into her pocket to find her hand and squeezed it in his own. "So, can we be friends again?" he asked. "No pressure, no trips down memory lane. Just somebody I can talk to who understands me."

"I'd like a good friend, too." Her hand tightened on his. "There are times the memories get hard. It would be nice to have someone to lean on."

He nodded, his throat tightening. He owed her that much. Without thinking, he pulled Jenna into his arms and just held her. She felt like she belonged there, like having her there would keep all the demons of the past away.

"We can lean on each other," he whispered. For a time... for a brief time.

Jenna moved slightly and he opened his arms ever so slightly allowing her to look up at him. "Happy Thanksgiving," she said and gently touched her lips to his.

Her kiss held the welcome warmth of a fire in winter. She would provide the comfort and feeling of home; a guide that would keep him safe. He, too, would keep her safe. It was time to go in for dinner.

Chapter Ten

"I'll be home late," Jenna told Gram as she shrugged into her coat. "I'm going to the frosh game to give them a hand, then I'm watching the film from my last game. Don't wait up for me."

Gram frowned. "I thought Peggy has her husband helping out. Man's been putting on weight. Do him good to get out of the house."

Jenna took her turn to frown. Darn woman knew everything about everybody in this town. "I just want to see how things are going. If they need help, I'll be there. Then I'll watch my film. Something wasn't clicking at that game and I want to see if I can catch it on the video."

Gram made a face and mumbled something that Jenna couldn't quite hear, something Jenna probably didn't want to discuss anyway, so she silently wrapped her scarf around her neck.

Susie came up, whining quietly and nudging Jenna with her graying nose. "Sorry, girl," Jenna said. "You can't come. You have to stay home and watch Gram."

"Susie doesn't want to go out with you in that snow and cold," Gram snapped. "She's disappointed in you like I am."

Jenna pulled her gloves on. "Good night, Gram."

"Town gets itself a world-class bachelor," Gram grumbled. "What young folks call a hunk, and you can't find anything better to do with your time than watch a game you've already seen."

"I'll leave a light on for myself," Jenna said.

"Folks think opportunity comes knocking on the door," Gram said. "It doesn't."

"Turn the heat down when you go to bed."

"It sneaks around, like some thief in the night. You want to get anything out of Old Man Opportunity, you got to grab him around the neck and drag him into your bedroom."

"See you in the morning, Gram."

"Got to wrestle him down and sit on him," Gram shouted after her.

The wind whipped Jenna in the face as she rounded the corner of the house on her way to the garage, stinging her cheeks with little bits of snow mixed with ice. It felt good. Jenna needed to concentrate on not falling down, not walking into the rose bushes, and not dropping her car keys in the snow.

She didn't need to think about Gram's comments, or the images they awoke. Since that talk she and Rob had had last week, on Thanksgiving, they were becoming friends again, getting to know each other all over. It felt right, no matter what the matchmakers in town thought.

The roads were on the slick side, but it only took Jenna a few minutes to get to school. She found she wasn't really needed at the game—Peggy's husband and a teacher were already at the timekeeping equipment, and two JV players had clipboards in hand to gather statistics. There was nothing for Jenna to do but sit on the far end of the bench and enjoy the game.

She tried to keep her mind on the girls and their play, she really did, but the memory of a crooked smile and sparkling blue eyes kept intruding in her line of sight. And no matter how Jenna dodged and weaved, they stayed there.

She was glad that she and Rob had resolved their problems. And it was kind of funny that he had thought she was mad at him, while she was wondering if he was angry with her. But there was no reason for him to still be lingering in her thoughts.

"What do you think of Jamie and Megan?"

Jenna looked up to see the team heading toward the locker room and Peggy standing in front of her. It was halftime already.

"I had to pull them in the second quarter," Peggy was going on. "Otherwise the score would really be out of line."

"They looked good, real good," Jenna said and got to her feet. Her mind had wandered through most of the first half; there seemed to be no reason to stay for the remainder of the game if she couldn't concentrate. "Looks like you have this game in hand. I'm going to be in the teachers' lounge looking at some film."

Jenna hurried through the dimly lighted corridor, glad that no one was around. Gram had unsettled her this evening and she needed some time alone, concentrating on basketball, to get back to her old self.

She unlocked the door and looked toward the corner, only to see a boys' basketball game on the large screen TV. "Hello?"

Rob turned around. "Jenna?"

"Oh hi. It's you." Who else would be watching a varsity boys' basketball game here? "I was going to look at the film of my last game, but I can do it later."

She should go. They might be building a new friendship, but alone in a dark room was probably not on the list of recommended ways to do it.

"I figured you'd want to watch it." Rob stood up, somehow filling up the room with his presence. His voice made her uneasy. "I thought you'd be at the frosh game now, so I slipped in to watch my film."

"I'll come back later." Good idea. She managed to slide one foot toward the hallway.

"That's okay," Rob said. "I'm almost done."

"No problem." She slid her other foot back.

"Actually I wouldn't mind having you take a look at this." He frowned at the screen where a boy was frozen in the act of missing a free throw, then turned back to her. "That is, if you have time."

She was being as skittish as a thirteen-year-old. "Our team is ahead by eighteen points at the half."

"Good." He waved her over to the sofa. "Have a seat."

She joined him on the sofa. Not too close, but not all that far away either. Thirteen years back, that distance wouldn't have stopped them for a minute.

"Jen, if you'd rather not, it's okay," Rob said, catching her unawares.

Was her uneasiness all that apparent? Why was she acting so foolishly anyway? "Why wouldn't I?" she asked, denying whatever he read into her body language. "I'm always on the edge of the seat when I watch a basketball game."

"Well, you can't watch this film unless you're relaxed and leaning back," Rob said.

Jenna gave him a look, but he just shrugged innocently. "I don't make the rules. I just live by them."

She knew what he was doing. He was trying to bring back the laughter they used to share. The realization disarmed her. He wasn't trying to seduce her, or make her feel guilty for the past, but make her smile again. Just like he used to.

"You're supposed to have your shoes off, too," he said, wiggling his stocking feet.

She was tempted, but fought it. "Start the film, Mr. Fagan."

"Okay, but don't blame me if something goes wrong."

She crossed her arms over her chest and forced herself to look at the screen. After the missed free throw, the boys started darting about in a semblance of a zone defense.

Blame him if something goes wrong. Hah. Something was certain to go wrong if she followed his advice and relaxed. She watched as Mike Sherwin went to the free throw line. He missed.

"See?" Rob said. "He made that shot in the actual game and missed it now because you aren't relaxed. We're going to lose this game, if you don't get with the program."

"Right," she said, but laughter was in her voice and she found herself leaning against the back of the sofa. "The real question is how it would affect the standings. Would you have to report it to the league or could it just be our secret?"

"Hey, I'm an ethical guy. I'd report it and report you." His arm was along the back of the sofa, moving closer to her as he leaned over. "You might be subject to disciplinary action."

"And that might hurt my girls."

He came even closer. "So?"

"So I'll relax."

Their laughter flooded the room, washing away whatever silly tensions she felt. Rob was as comfortable as ever to be with, and he still had the knack for making her laugh. He reached over and took her hand.

"It feels good to be friends again," he said.

It did. "Yep." Her hand felt good in his too, as if their bond was still strong.

He turned back to the game. "Now, coming up is where we had our troubles," he said. "See? That's the first of four turnovers that almost cost us the game."

She frowned at the TV, though her hand stayed in Rob's. It was how it had been and how it would be. Was this cause for worry or celebration?

"They were lucky," Mike shouted into Rob's ear as they stood cheering. The girls' varsity team had just won by one point, a desperation shot that went in at the buzzer.

"Shouldn't have been that hard," Rob agreed. "I thought our girls were the better team, but they didn't seem to be concentrating. Maybe they were dreaming about Santa Claus."

"I wouldn't know what they're dreaming about," Mike said as they started flowing with the crowd toward the exits. "Sara's always busy these days."

"I'm just joking," Rob said. "It simply looks like the girls are tight. Sara mention any problems?"

Once they reached the gym floor, they moved out of the crowd. "Not any problems really," Mike said. "Just that folks are too tense."

Rob thought back to that evening a few nights back when he and Jenna had watched the game films together. She'd been tense then, too. He'd teased her out of it, but only for the moment. She'd always done everything full speed and full strength, gave her all to whatever she was involved in. That hadn't left much time for fun back in school and might not now. Trouble was, her tension could be infecting her team and she might not even be aware of it. Looked like the situation required a little athletic-director-to-coach chat.

"You and Sara stopping for a bite?" Rob asked Mike.

The boy shrugged. "I don't know. I'll see if she wants to do anything." He frowned as he looked out over the jubilant crowd. "We haven't gotten together much lately. Been sort of busy. You know, basketball, homework. And with Christmas coming, we've both been working longer hours."

Rob stared off at the door to the locker room. He and Jenna had been busy, but look at the extracurriculars they'd managed to fit in. Maybe it was best Mike and Sara were drifting apart.

"They're coming out now," Mike said.

Jenna was walking between the two taller girls on her team, but left them to come join Rob.

"Congratulations," he said.

"Thanks, but we were lucky."

"Girls looked a little tight tonight."

"Yeah," she agreed. Lines of tension were still around her eyes.

"Want to stop at the Red Lion for a little something to warm the soul?"

Jenna hesitated a bit, but then shook her head. "No, thanks. I have a lot of things to do." She waved a pile of statistics sheets in the air. "We have another game the day after tomorrow and I have to analyze these before tomorrow's practice. Otherwise we'll go through the same thing we did tonight."

"Maybe all the more reason to go out with me tonight."

She frowned at him, confusion all over her face. "You lost me."

He did once and he wasn't sure he would ever get her back. But he just took her arm and led her toward the exit. "I'm going to share my wisdom with you, the benefit of all my years of experience. You don't need statistics because you have me."

"Aren't I lucky?"

"'Bout time you realized it."

She made a face as they went out into the night. Pulling her collar up around her head, she nodded in the other direction and said, "My car's over there."

"Yep. I see it. We're taking my car and then I'll bring you back for yours." He felt her rebellion. "Athletic director's orders."

She groaned but got into his car willingly enough. "So what's all this wisdom? We could save a lot of time if you would just tell me now."

He just shook his head. "You youngsters. So impatient."

"You're only six months older than me."

"And those six months make a lot of difference."

The Red Lion wasn't far from school and they got there quickly. Too quickly to suit Rob, for he liked the feeling of having Jenna here with him again. Different car, just as they were different people now, but it was still a good feeling.

They went inside the lounge, finding it almost empty, and took a table near the fireplace. A Christmas tree in the corner glowed with friendly cheer, while carols played softly in the background. The place seemed warmer and friendlier than most bars he'd been in.

"Perfect night for a fire," Jenna said and moved her chair a bit closer to the welcoming blaze. "December's been colder this year than usual."

"Nothing like an Indiana winter to remind you what cold is."

"No. Cold is a North Dakota winter. We just get kind of cool here."

He laughed, from the joy filling his heart from just watching her. The fire seemed to dance in her hair, turning it to gold. Her cheeks glowed with the heat and her smile seemed to come from her heart.

"Hi, folks." A solid, middle-aged woman came over to take their order. "How'd the game go?"

"Won with a last-second shot at the buzzer," Jenna said and Rob could feel her tension returning.

"Better than losing with their last-second shot," the woman said. "What'll you have?"

They both ordered Irish coffee, then were alone again with just the glow of the fire to keep them company.

"She's Maggie McDermott's aunt," Jenna said. "You know, my backup center. Maggie could be a great player if she'd just concentrate."

He reached over and took her hands in his. "Be careful, Jenna."

Her face registered confusion. "Be careful? What are you talking about."

"You. This team. Sometimes you can want something so bad that you kill the thing that makes your goal possible in the first place."

"That's a rather convoluted answer."

Rob paused and stared down at their hands intertwined. "You really want to make the Final Four."

She stared at him. "Every team in the state wants that."

"And you have a chance," he replied. "But don't make it the most important thing in your life."

She pulled her hands away, leaving him feeling bereft, but then the waitress came with their drinks. Was she rejecting him or merely trying to keep the gossip-mongers from gathering more fuel?

"I have a good team this year," she said as she sipped her drink. "The best I've ever had."

"But it's not just the goal that's important. The trip's got to be fun, too." He'd learned that the hard way, always looking ahead instead of enjoying where he was.

"That's a little hard to take from you," Jenna said.

"Why?" Could she see that well into his soul?

"I'm not the one running ten to midnight practices on Fridays," she said.

Oh, that. "The kids voted for it," he said. "And it was fun. We had pizza and watched cartoons afterward."

She cupped her mug with her hands as if to soak up the warmth that was inside. "I just think this is the year we can do it."

"Not if it's only your dream and not the girls' as well."

He finished the last of his coffee. So had Jenna, he noticed as he put down his empty mug.

"Thanks for the drink and the advice," she said. "I will try to ease up a bit, though I'm not giving up wind sprints."

"I meant attitude, not drills. If your girls have too much energy, my boys are uncontrollable."

"Ah, so that's the real reason behind this talk." Her face brightened with laughter, taking his breath away. "My girls are taking it out on your boys and they sent you to me."

"Hey, if it works, I get the last piece of pizza next time."

"Must be anchovies and mushrooms. Your fatal weakness."

No, his real weakness had been her, but he hadn't known it at the time. He put his hand out toward her again, but she seemed not to notice, and reached around behind her for her coat. The drink's warmth faded quickly.

"Thanks for the drink and the advice," she said as she slipped into her coat. "But I need to get home. Gram'll be worrying."

"Right-o."

He paid the bill and they walked out to his car. The wind had picked up, carrying a bit of snow along to emphasize its chill. Jenna moved closer to him and he slipped an arm around her shoulder as he spotted a familiar-looking figure trudging along the edge of the parking lot.

"Mike?" Rob called out. "You need a ride?"

The boy hurried over to them. "Uh, hi, Coach. Miss Lauren. A ride would be great. It's really starting to blow out."

"Sure," Rob replied. "No problem. Hop in."

Jenna turned to face Mike once they were in the car. "Nobody went out after the game?"

Mike shrugged. "Sara said she had homework, that she needs to concentrate better."

Jenna turned back around as Rob pulled out of the parking spot. He could have sworn that the chilly air from outside had invaded the warmth around him.

"It'd be easier to take me back to school first," Jenna said. "Then take Mike home."

"I don't mind a little extra driving."

"But I really need to get home."

Sounded like she'd decided to concentrate, too. Or was it just a desire not to give anyone anything to gossip about? Rob was getting tired of living his life under a magnifying glass.

He drove to school and exchanged polite goodbyes with Jenna, then waited until she got her car started. Mike came around into the front seat.

"We didn't have a date or anything," the boy grumbled. "I just thought we could get together for a few minutes. Have a hot chocolate or something." He glared at the swirling bits of snow in the air. "Women. Damn if I can ever figure them out."

"Homework has to come first," Rob pointed out.

They followed Jenna's car out to the street, then turned behind her. Mike lived the other way, but Rob wasn't going to go off and leave Jenna driving alone on slick roads. He glanced over at Mike, but the boy hadn't noticed. He was lost in his own gloom.

"I guess Miss Lauren is really on their case," Mike said. "At least, she's on Sara's case. Always yakking at her. And I think she's starting to get through."

"How so?"

Jenna stopped at a stoplight and glanced into her rear-view mirror. Rob could tell by the set of her shoulders that she knew they were behind her and wasn't happy about it.

Mike sighed. "I think Miss Lauren has a bug about being stuck in Warsaw all her life."

"Oh?" He couldn't imagine Jenna anywhere else. This town and Jenna were one and the same. Though she might have felt trapped after her father died, she'd certainly had chances to leave since then. She probably didn't because she hadn't wanted to.

"She keeps telling Sara about not giving up on her own dreams," Mike went on. "That there's a big world out there waiting for her. That kind of stuff." Mike slumped down in the seat.

Rob wondered uneasily if he had been that self-centered at eighteen.

"You're following your dreams," Rob pointed out. "Girls have a right to big dreams, too."

"Yeah."

They got to Jenna's house and she pulled into her driveway, flashing her lights in farewell. He waved and let a bit of Mike's gloom settle onto his shoulders. The real problem was that Jenna had been too close to someone with wandering feet and wanted to keep Sara from getting hurt the same way.

He shook his head in the darkness. Her great-grandfather was right. She had everything that mattered right here. Unless someone took your heart away with them.

A light snow was falling, putting the perfect dusting on the rows of evergreen trees. Jenna had always loved snow, especially in these weeks before Christmas, when everything seemed so magical. Of course, Rob being here with her didn't detract from anything.

"Turn up here," she said, pointing out the Santa Claus sign ahead.

Rob pulled into an old-fashioned farmyard, parking in an area marked off by ropes and stakes. A farm dog announced their presence and soon a woman hurried out to greet them.

"Anyplace over there in the south quarter," she said after taking their money.

After getting a saw from her, they drove down the lane. The snow crunched under the tires.

"These things are big," Rob said, frowning up at the trees they were passing.

Jenna found a smile lurking on her lips. "Why do you think I asked you to come along?"

"I was hoping my charm had something to do with it."

"Nope. Just your muscles."

"You women are all alike," he said, forcing a scowl. "All you want is our bodies."

A warm flush stole over her cheeks and Jenna looked away. She could remember all too well the wild passion they'd shared during that recent night of love, and the sense of peace she'd felt lying in his arms afterward. But a repeat wasn't on her agenda.

"How about parking over here?" She pointed to a clearing up ahead. "Those trees look great."

Rob pulled the car in and they got out, walking down the nearest row. She kept her stride brisk as if she would outpace her thoughts, but the trees seemed ever taller, more dwarfing. Rob took her hand and she looked at him. His eyes seemed to be peering into her soul, their depths dark and hungry. Or were they just a reflection of her own? It was time to find something else to think about.

"You were right, you know," she said.

"Oh?"

"I took a good long look at myself and decided I was getting too tense. That's why I'm having this party for my team tonight. We need to laugh together as well as work together."

She pulled her hand away and stopped to peer up at a tree, but moved on after deciding it wasn't full enough at the base.

"I think I ought to be invited as a reward," Rob said.

"You were." She was relieved that he was back to his playful self. "Invited to part of it anyway and this is the most important part. You can't have a tree-trimming, sleep-over party without a tree."

He eyed her with a strange gleam in his eye. "We could have our own sleep-over," he suggested.

Playful wasn't necessarily safe, come to think of it. She stopped to check out another tree, walking slowly around it. A sleep-over with the team would be lots of giggling about boys, scary stories told once the lights were out, and doing each other's hair. A sleep-over with Rob would be coming alive in his arms, feeling whole and happy. And vulnerable.

"How about this tree?" she said. "It looks pretty good."

"Looks huge. You sure this is a reward and not some sort of revenge?"

"We have twelve-foot ceilings," she said. "Anything smaller would look puny."

"That's exactly how I feel, about now," he grunted.

"I thought you were in better shape than this," Jenna said laughing.

"I can think of better ways to show you what kind of shape I'm in," he said.

His eyes captured hers again, fire blazing suddenly in her soul. Her hands tightened with tension, with the wanting to caress and touch, with the need to feel his strength. She'd always felt like kindling just waiting for his igniting spark to bring her to life.

Without a word, she moved into his arms. They closed around her, imprisoning her in the sunshine and springtime. His lips came down on hers as if there was no tomorrow, or no yesterday either. There was only now and the deep, nagging hungers of her soul. She needed his hands on her body, his mouth resuscitating her to full response.

They came nearer, if that was possible. Their arms in silent union pulled the other closer and closer as his lips moved over hers. His heat was burning into her. They weren't teenagers anymore, and her needs lay deeper. It wasn't just her body that needed satisfying, but her heart needed tenderness, her soul needed to be stirred. Everything was here in Rob's arms, but only for now. Only for this moment. She pulled slowly from his embrace, feeling as if she were pulling away from the sun.

"We really ought to get this cut down," she said.

For once, Rob had no smart-alecky quip, but just got to work. He cut through the base of the tree as she held the branches back. Then they half-carried, half-dragged it to the car, wedging it into the trunk before driving back to the farmyard. The woman came out to help them tie the tree on the roof.

"That's sure a big one," the woman said, once the tree was securely in place.

"We have twelve-foot ceilings," Jenna explained.

"Well, you certainly couldn't use anything smaller," the woman said.

Jenna heard Rob's silent groan, then, in panic, wondered how. Was she starting to read his mind, knowing his thoughts, not just seeing his actions? The idea was scary, delicious, nerve-racking.

They left the Christmas-tree farm and rode along in silence. Jenna was conscious only that Rob was so close, hearing his breath and seeing his hands on the steering wheel, yet feeling the memory of those hands on her skin. What was happening to all her brave thoughts?

After they'd gone a few miles, Rob cleared his throat. "You ever wonder what your life would have been like if you'd taken a different path?" he asked.

The question took her by surprise. "No," she said. "Not really."

He smiled, but it was a distant one. As if he were in a world that she had no entry to. "You always were a practical sort."

Somehow his manner made her feel left out, alone. Which was exactly how she wanted to feel, so why was her heart so sad? "Life deals you your cards," she said. "All you get to decide is how to play them."

He glanced at her briefly, his frown saying he wanted more than philosophy. "With your mother being so sick and all, you didn't have the chances other kids had. You had to help care for her and the house."

Jenna shrugged. "I'm not a heroine. My parents had given me a lot and it wasn't a big deal to help out a little."

"It didn't restrict you in any way?"

"I never looked at it that way."

They fell silent as Rob stopped for a caution sign and checked the traffic. They drove on, but the silence lingered with them. It grew, filling the car until Jenna wanted to cry out.

"I know I had a fence around me," she said. "In reality, everyone does. It comes from the community. Some people look upon that fence as restrictive, but to me it was protection."

She stared out the window at the snowflakes dancing wildly in the rush of wind the car made. They seemed to have no sense of purpose, no destination, just weak, little crystals that had to fly with the air currents. As she had felt back then. She had wanted to bury the past, but maybe it was never really over.

"I was pretty fragile right after the miscarriage," she said quietly. "I never talked about it to anyone but I knew that my family and friends were always there for me. Knowing that helped me heal quicker."

"I thought your mother wanted you to travel, see a bit of the world before you settled down."

"Yeah." Jenna saw the past, saw her mother with all her feverish dreams that she had known would never come true. "You have to understand Mom. Her kidney disease had her in its clutches ever since she was a teenager. It restricted her and grew worse over the years until she was totally imprisoned by dialysis. To her, traveling was a freedom she didn't have. Even going to Fort Wayne was a burden in her later years."

She looked at him a moment, but saw instead all the people who had helped to make her whole. Or as whole as she would ever be. "All in all, I'm satisfied."

"Maybe those who love you see needs that you don't. Needs you might not want to see."

"Mom's been dead several years now."

"Yes, but now your grandmother lives with you."

Jenna bit at her lip. Gram certainly saw lackings in Jenna's life, but did that mean they were there? "My life is fine," she said. "If I wanted to travel I could. I can go anywhere I please in the summers. I could even move if I wanted to."

"Could you leave Gram?"

"Gram is well able to take care of herself and if she weren't, the county's chock-full of relatives. She wouldn't have any problems finding care."

He didn't reply or comment. Did that mean whatever ghosts he was pursuing had been satisfied?

"I can do what I want," she said, as if the ghosts were pursuing her. "And coaching in my old high school is exactly what I want to do."

Some of the sparkle seemed to have faded from the day, the glittering snowflakes seemed dull and ordinary. What had he been trying to tell her? Why had he jumped on this traveling thing? Maybe he was trying to convince her that it was great, because it was so much a part of him. They stayed silent, each in their own cocoon, until Rob turned into her driveway.

"I'll just get your tree inside, then I'll be on my way."

"Do you feel up to it? We could leave it out here and the girls could carry it in."

"Are you implying they're stronger than I am?" he asked, the familiar teasing fire back in his eyes.

But it awoke the familiar hungry fire in her. "No, but you were complaining about it being heavy."

He pulled her into his arms, his strength like iron holding her fast to his chest as he kissed her. His lips took hers as if they were starving, like the desert takes up the rain. There was no chance to breathe, no chance to think or worry. All she could do was feel, and feel she did, as her heart went up in flames. Then just as suddenly, he released her.

"Well," he said, his voice as husky as her hands were shaky. "Am I up to it?"

She was so tired of fighting her feelings, of trying to keep her heart in line. She wanted to enjoy Rob's company and his love, not skitter about like a scared bird. The trouble was, she was going to have a houseful of teenage girls arriving in a few minutes. "Let's try those muscles on the tree."

Sighing, he exited the car. "You're a hard woman, Jenna Lauren."

Chapter Eleven

"Jenna, I think someone's at the door," Gram called over the laughter of the dozens of great-grandchildren around her feet.

Jenna nodded, and picked her way across the living room floor, stepping around aunts, uncles and cousins, and over gifts and wads of wrapping paper. Christmas was always a madhouse here, with every relative in the tri-state area dropping by to see Gram at one time or another. And every one of them brought eggnog. Homemade eggnog, complete with rum. Jenna was sure she would never be cold again.

Jenna and Susie reached the door at the same time, but not to greet Aunt Beckie from Kokomo. It was Rob with two small gifts, neither of which looked like eggnog.

"Hi. Merry Christmas," he said and looked past her into the crowded interior. "This is a bad time?"

"When isn't it?" The eggnog had made her brave, able to act on her feelings. She took his hand and pulled him inside. "It's good to see someone who won't tell me how I've grown, ask me when I'm going to settle down, or offer me some more eggnog."

"Boy, I can't remember when I've felt so welcome." But his eyes were laughing as he took off his coat.

Jenna knew there was no room in the guest closet and led him upstairs with it. "You can leave your coat in your choice of my room, any of the guest rooms or Gram's."

"Do you come with yours?"

His voice came from close behind her and the words tickled the back of her neck. How could he make his words so soft and sweet, wanting to melt away her worries into nothingness? She stopped at the top of the stairs and let him catch up. It was good to see him, she realized. Just what her holiday had been missing.

"I'm glad you stopped by," she said. "I wondered what you were going to do with your day."

He left his coat on her bed. "Forget how to use the telephone?"

She leaned against her dresser, picking up the piggy bank she'd gotten in fourth grade. Its plug on the bottom assured that it would never get too full, but it had such a happy grin on its face that she couldn't get rid of it.

"I thought of calling," she admitted to Mr. Pig. "But I don't know. I thought you might feel obligated or something."

"I'm pretty good at fending off unwanted social obligations," he said.

She shrugged and put Mr. Pig down. "All right. I was chicken." She dared a look up at him. "I don't know where we're going, all I know is where we've been. It seems safer to stay away from you."

"Is that what you want?" he asked, coming closer even as he asked.

"No."

She wondered if she'd spoken aloud or merely thought the answer, but somehow it didn't matter. She was here alone with Rob, the pleasant warmth of the eggnog had melted her wall of worries, and it was Christmas, the time for love and joy.

"We've got some mistletoe around here someplace," she told him.

"Ah. The old pagan customs," he said. "I myself prefer an old Fagan ritual."

"Which is?"

"When you're alone with a beautiful woman with eyes as blue as the sky and a smile as sweet as honey, you kiss her."

And that's what he did, pulling her into his arms as if it was where she belonged. His lips were gentle and kind, speaking words of tenderness to her heart even as they soothed the fears that lurked in the corners of her soul.

But then something stirred between them. A spark, a current, shot through the air and brought to life the passion that lay sleeping. Jenna moved deeper into his embrace, letting the scent of his aftershave surround her and was lost in his caress. The creaking of the stairs told them someone was coming up and they pulled slowly apart.

"Oops. Am I interrupting something?" A pregnant woman stopped in the doorway.

"Not at all," Jenna assured her; it had been time to let her heart breathe anyway. She turned to Rob. "This is Debbie Roegiers. She's a cousin on Mom's side. She used to be Debbie Barton."

"He doesn't remember me," Debbie said. "I was a freshman when you two were seniors."

"Nice to see you again, Debbie."

"I was madly in love with you back then," Debbie said, her voice matter-of-fact, as if she were discussing a former taste for chocolate chip cookies. "You didn't even know I existed."

"Sorry."

"Hey, I was just a freshman. Pond scum." She turned to Jenna. "I hated you. After school I would go home, pull the shades in my room, and sit in the dark dreaming about all the things I was going to do to you."

"Like what?" Jenna asked, laughing.

"You know, standard little girl things," Debbie said, smiling pleasantly. "Cut all your hair off. Tie all your nylons into knots."

"Sounds vicious," Rob said.

"But I got over it and married Richie Roegiers," Debbie said.

"He was a sophomore when we were seniors," Jenna said, knowing Rob wouldn't remember. "Played on the JV team."

"Oh, yeah," Rob said. "He was a pretty fair ballplayer."

"He played hard." Debbie laughed. "Actually gymnastics is his sport."

Rob looked at Jenna. "Did we have a boys' gymnastic team?"

"He only does private performances," Debbie said. "Very private."

Jenna joined Debbie in her laughter. "He's real cute when he blushes," Debbie pointed out. "So, what are you guys doing for New Year's Eve?"

Jenna hadn't been prepared for the question and felt Rob's eyes on her. Spending Thanksgiving and Christmas with him was one thing; New Year's Eve was different. New Year's Eve was like a promise for the future, as well as a celebration of the past.

"Secret, huh?" Debbie grinned at them as she picked through the coats on the bed. "Gonna stay at the Marriott in South Bend? Or Chicago? I bet it's Chicago. I hear Chi-town really jumps on New Year's." She pulled three coats out from the pile, then stopped in the doorway to smile at Rob. "I'm really glad you're back. Jenna hasn't had a decent date since you left."

"Thanks, Deb." But her cousin was already out the door.

Jenna turned, ready to defend her dating habits, but found that Rob's gaze wasn't teasing as she expected. The gleam in his eyes was gone, a sad murkiness clouding the depths.

"Something else to lay at my door?" he asked.

Jenna just frowned at him. "Don't be silly. Debbie doesn't know what she's talking about. Come on, let's go downstairs."

"Not yet." Rob put his hand on her arm to stop her. "Open your present first."

He handed her the smaller of the two packages he brought, a squarish box wrapped in silver and red. "The other one's for Gram. A soup mug."

Jenna slowly opened the gift. Hers for Rob—a Warsaw High School basketball jersey with his old number on it—was lying downstairs under the Christmas tree, but there was no privacy down there. She wished she'd thought to bring it up with them. The ribbons and paper off, she opened the box to find a wooden ball the size of an orange. It was painted like the sky with the sun and clouds over it.

"It opens," Rob said.

She twisted it apart to find another ball inside, this one painted like the night sky with the moon and stars. Inside that was one of snow falling, then a small raindrop.

"Oh, Rob, it's great," she said, and threw her arms around him. "Thank you."

Her exuberance quickly changed into something richer though as his arms closed around her. Happiness boiled over and their lips found each other. This was what Christmas was all about, sharing with those closest to you. His mouth moved against hers, sending shivers of delight down her spine, but she pulled away slowly. It was too tempting up here with him.

"Come on downstairs," she said. "I think Santa left something for you under the tree."

They went down. Jenna introduced Rob to some of the relatives there, and jogged his memory on the others who he already knew. The talk started with his winning shot against Northwood, moved on to his career at UCLA and in Europe, then came back to his winning shot. Jenna could see the amusement lurking in his eyes and left him alone with his fans to answer the door.

All afternoon and evening, relatives came and went. Most brought food along with gifts, and Jenna spent a good part of the time refilling the buffet that was set out in the dining room. Susie was parked under the table, ready to catch any scraps.

"That real eggnog?" Rob asked, coming up behind her as she was setting out a casserole some cousins from Bourbon had brought.

"Real yummy and really rummy," she said.

"Ah, the best kind." He filled a cup for himself, then leaned against the buffet. "Anything I can do to help?"

"What's the matter? Tired of reliving that shot?"

He grinned. "Tired of feeling that I haven't done anything worthwhile in the thirteen years since."

"Poor baby."

He followed her into the kitchen, and without a word, they began to wash some of the mountain of dishes that were stacked in the sink. How'd he know this was what she intended to do? Too often lately they seemed to act as one. It was scary, but also deliciously sweet.

About midway through the pile, Gram came into the kitchen. "Rob Fagan, what are you doing washing dishes?"

"I didn't make him," Jenna said.

"Actually, it was the best way to stay close to her," Rob told Gram. "She's too polite to go off and leave me here with all the dishes, so she's got to stay."

Gram just snorted with laughter, slapping Rob on the back. "I'm glad you're back," she said and went back out with her guests.

Rob was silent for a moment, then stopped washing dishes to grab a few cookies off a nearby tray. "The question is, are you?"

Jenna looked up from the platter she was drying. "Am I what?"

"Glad I'm back."

She was tempted to make some teasing remark, brushing aside his question like a joke, but there was a seriousness in his eyes that asked for the truth. What was the truth? How did she feel about him being here?

She thought of her days before he came back and they seemed to be shadowed. Since he'd come back, her life seemed to be in bright sunshine. So much so that even her worries and anger couldn't dim it.

"Yes," she said simply. "I am, and not just because you wash a mean dish."

His smile caressed her. "I'm glad I came back, too."

The kitchen door swung open. "Well, another Christmas."

Jenna looked over her shoulder at a cousin from her father's side and his wife.

"I never thought this house would be too small," Ben said. "But it seems a little tight this year."

"A shade over a hundred came this year," Jenna replied. "A bunch from out of town."

"Gram's looking good," Ben's wife said. "How is she doing?"

"Little stiff in the morning," Jenna said. "But mostly just fine."

Ben stood at the door while his wife sorted through the dishes for the serving bowl she'd brought. She picked it out, then stopped. "I know you two probably have more exciting things in mind, but if there's a bad snow or you don't want to leave town, you're welcome to come to our house on New Year's Eve. We might be a little quiet for you single folks but we have fun."

Jenna just nodded. "Thanks for the offer. We'll keep it in mind."

Once they left and the door swung closed, Rob started to chuckle. "Looks like we'd better come up with some New Year's Eve plans or your whole family's going to be disappointed."

"I haven't given New Year's much thought," Jenna admitted. "We've got two tournaments to get through first."

"Doesn't mean we can't work on some ideas."

"No." She finished drying a salad bowl, coming to the realization that she wanted to do something with him on New Year's Eve. That her heart couldn't conceive of spending the evening without him.

Jenna held her breath as the scoreboard clock counted down. Twenty seconds had never been so long. Nineteen, eighteen, seventeen. Sara passed the ball to Amy, who passed it over to Maggie.

Then a Washington player knocked the ball from Maggie's hands, shot a pass to an outside player who sprinted down the court for the lay-up that would win them the game. Jenna's hands were clenching into tight fists when

Sara flew down the court in time to block the shot and grab the rebound with seven seconds left. A pass to Amy, then to Cindy, then back to Sara and the buzzer went off. They'd won the holiday tournament.

The celebration started on the floor, continued on in the locker room and promised to last most of the night. Somehow Jenna settled the girls down enough to shower and change, herding them out finally with the reminder that they had to cheer the boys' team into victory for the tournament to be complete.

Rob already had his team on the court when the girls came out of the locker room, but they stopped their warm-ups to give the girls a round of applause.

"Good job, Coach," Rob said, giving Jenna a hug that made her victory all the more special. His eyes told her that he'd like to congratulate her in other ways, but not with their audience.

She hugged him back, her eyes promising him she'd wait. "Good luck, Coach."

She and the girls took their places in the stands, and settled down to watch the boys play. Their game was a lot rougher with Mike going down in the first half, grabbing at his knee. Jenna could feel Sara's tension, her prayerful stillness, until he reentered the game a few minutes later. The boys were ahead by four at halftime and kept the lead for the rest of the game. As the clock showed zero time left, the girls ran onto the court to celebrate.

Rob was mobbed by the boys and their parents, but Jenna saw his eyes looking for her over the crowd and made her way to his side.

"Great job, Coach," Jenna said.

"This calls for a double celebration."

His eyes were alight with excitement, the joy around them spilling into their smiles. He understood what the victory meant to her, how it was part of who she was.

Maybe that was why they would always be friends, no matter what life put in their way. They shared the same dreams, the same determinations.

The principal was suddenly there with them, shaking their hands. "I don't know if having both the boys' and the girls' teams win the South Bend Holiday Tournament is a first for Warsaw High, but it sure as heck is a first in my time."

"The kids put it together," Rob said.

"They did all the hard work," Jenna added.

"And who whipped them into shape?" Arthur patted their backs. "Listen, I was going to take the bus back with the kids and I thought maybe I could talk you two into driving my car for me."

"You're sure you don't need us?" Rob asked.

"Hell, yes, I'm sure," Arthur replied. "I've got teachers and parents up the wazoo. Most of them are taking their kids in their own cars, but we've got some riding on the bus."

"Okay," Rob replied. "Let me get my hoard into the locker room and cleaned up."

While Jenna waited for Rob to get the boys into and out of the showers, she spoke to parents congratulating her on her victory and Rob's, too.

"It must be nice for you both to have won," one parent said.

"What a great team you two make," said another.

It was silly to point out to each that the basketball victories had nothing to do with her and Rob's friendship, or that either of them could take even partial credit for the other team's performance. No one gave her time to speak, or seemed interested in listening to her explanations.

Besides, in some small way, she was feeling as if she and Rob were a team. They seemed always to be there for the other, ready to support or scold. They had been closer in some ways in their youth, but she never felt that they were more in tune than they were now. Life was perfect.

The boys' team straggled from the locker room, joining parents and girlfriends. Rob and his assistant were the last ones out, carrying bags of equipment that helpful parents quickly took from them.

"Great job."

"You really know how to win them."

They all headed out of the arena into the parking lot, where some people drifted off toward cars while others piled into the buses. Arthur gave Rob the keys to his car, but he and Jenna had to run a gauntlet of congratulatory handshakes and backslaps before getting away.

"Driving by ourselves is a good idea," Jenna said with a laugh.

"Yeah," Rob agreed. "Before our friends and neighbors beat us to death."

They left the stadium parking lot and headed back toward Warsaw. The traffic was light and it seemed like they were alone in the world. Jenna leaned her head against the seat-rest, closing her eyes. It had been a perfect few days. Maybe even a perfect few months since Rob had came back.

"Want to stop some place for something to eat?"

"Sure."

She opened her eyes as she felt the car turn into a lot. It was a small tavern, plush, dim, and subdued. Absolutely perfect for her mood. Customers hid in their individual booths scattered about the large room while a piano player played soft music in the background.

They ordered hamburgers and blush wine, then sank back into the warm comfort of the place.

Jenna yawned. "I'm sorry," she said. "I'm afraid I'm losing it."

He reached over and took her hands in his. She felt delightfully lost. "It'd been thirteen years since I'd seen you last. But take it from me, you haven't lost a thing."

Their wine came and she sipped at it, feeling the weariness slip away under his steady gaze. He could work magic on her with just a look.

"In fact, you've improved, like a good wine aging."

Jenna arched her right eyebrow. "That's almost old enough to be a cliché."

"Maybe sayings become clichés because they've proved their truth down through the years."

"Maybe."

They let the silence fall around them, sipping their wine and unwinding from the pressures of the last few days.

"So what are we doing on New Year's Eve?" Rob asked. "Chi-town or your cousin Sue's?"

"I don't know," Jenna said with a shrug. "I was thinking we could go see the Bulls play."

"Got tickets?"

She shook her head.

"I doubt we'd be able to get any at this late date."

"We could go down to Indianapolis. There's a New Year's high school tournament," she suggested. "We're going to be meeting some of those teams in the state tournament sectionals. Might be a good idea to scout them while we can."

He twirled his glass a moment, watching the bubbles forming in the wine. "Sounds like work."

Jenna frowned. "I thought we'd enjoy it."

Rob shook his head slowly. "I'm going to plan something special," he said. "A surprise. Dinner and whatever."

Her gaze wavered. He looked so intense in the dim light over the heat waves generated by the candle in the middle of the table. His eyes told her to trust him, to put herself in his hands and let him take care of her. And for the moment, that was all she wanted to do. She wasn't frightened or weak, her decision was just right.

"I'm game."

Their hamburgers came and they both dug into them as if they were starving.

"Your glass is empty," Rob said. "Want another?"

"Just one more," she said. "I don't have a high tolerance for wine and even if I sleep all the way home I still need to walk up the steps to my room."

"No problem. I can carry you."

"Be careful about making promises like that," she said. "I'm not a little girl, you know."

His eyes captured hers. "I'm well aware of that, Jenna. I'm very aware of that."

A delightful shiver raced through her and she couldn't do anything but enjoy it.

They stood on the crest of a slight slope, looking down at the cross-country ski trail illuminated by kerosene torches. In the distance, other torches winked like a line of stars leading far beyond the woods.

Rob stared at Jenna and felt his heart grow full of joy, almost to the bursting point. Her eyes glowed, her mouth was formed into the most beautiful smile, and the wonderment of a child hung all over her face. She was truly an amazing woman to have gone through the trials she'd had and yet still be so fresh, so vital, so alive.

"Well," she said turning toward him. "This is very impressive."

Rob had quickly turned away and was now looking down the trail. "Yes," he agreed. "It did turn out rather well."

"But to get all these things to come together." She shook her head and laughed, the sound as rich and joyful as sleigh bells on a horse's winter harness. "I mean you had to arrange for a solid base of snow, then last night you got all this fluffy new stuff dropped down."

"Yep. And I had to get the park district to schedule this torchlight cross-country ski thing even before we knew it was going to snow."

"Amazing."

"I told the gods I had to impress this lady," he said. "A lady who was not easily impressed."

"Sounds like a tough woman."

"Oh, she is."

They took a while longer to savor the Currier and Ives scene before them. "Well," Rob said. "Do you want to ski or watch?"

"Ski."

"Then let us proceed down yonder path."

They skied in unison, gliding along on the glittering snow. The torches threw wild shadows into the forest and a special glow into Jenna's eyes.

"I think this is the best New Year's Eve ever," he said,

"Oh? Better than the one we spent together in our senior year?"

He frowned and thought back, but all he saw was a long line of dull parties with too much liquor and too few friends.

"You had a bad cold," Jenna prompted. "But were determined we were going to Jerry Wray Bilecki's party anyway."

It all came back to him. "And I fell asleep in your living room because you took so long getting dressed."

"You were there less than five minutes before I was down," she insisted, then bit back her aggravation with a laugh. "You do remember."

Her eyes were so beautiful drenched in laughter. He had to look away. "I guess I owe you a good New Year's then," he said.

"Hey, my dad didn't mind that one. Said he liked knowing where we both were all evening."

Rob laughed, but his heart suddenly felt heavy. Jenna and her father had been close. How it must have hurt when she lost him, and Rob hadn't even known to comfort her.

At times, Rob suspected that his mother had purposely not told him right away about Jenna's father for fear that he would come home to be with her. Would he have if he'd known about Mr. Lauren's death? What would he have done if he'd known about the baby? He owed Jenna a lot more than just the special New Year's he'd so carefully planned for her.

For a time, they skied in single file, concentrating on the trail before them. Rob pushed himself hard, trying to rid himself of the ghosts of the past as he watched Jenna's trim figure. He had jumped at the chance to come back here, telling himself it was to repay old debts. But had it been? Had he been hoping Jenna would still be around? Or was he just cheating her again by pretending the urge to move wouldn't come over him again?

"Want to stop at the lookout?" Jenna called back to him.

"Sure."

They took off their skis and climbed onto the platform from which they could view the river. Its midnight blackness rushed beneath them, hellbent on getting away.

He'd been like that, only no place had ever felt right. No place but here and now. He turned to find Jenna watching him, waiting to move into his arms as if together they could fight off the wintery darkness.

Her lips were cool, but sent a rush of heat through his blood, firing up his hungers. It was heaven to have her in his arms, to be holding her close like this, and feel that the night could go on forever.

At times like this, he would have given almost anything to be able to go home with Jenna to a place of their own, filled with their own family, but for her sake, he'd never risk it. If he'd ever harbored hopes that he wasn't a nomad, the past few years had drowned them. The longest he'd been in one place was eight months. He'd thought he'd reach that mark here, but his feet had been getting restless lately. He'd had moments when the weight of his friends seemed too much to bear, when Jenna's smile seemed so precious that it scared him.

Don Parsons had been out of the hospital for weeks now, and had even started coming to some of the basketball games, so Rob knew it wouldn't be long now. Don would be back to his job soon and Rob would be gone, probably after basketball season. There weren't too many positions open in Warsaw for a former basketball player turned coach, but even if there were, he'd known he'd move on. He pulled away from her.

"Better keep on the move or the abominable snowman might get us."

"Is that why you keep moving?" she teased.

"Right."

It was almost an hour later by the time they had circled back to the beginning of the trail. If Rob hadn't totally exorcised his ghosts, he'd at least convinced them to go back to sleep. They turned in their skis and drove to his apartment.

"So now for your special dinner," Jenna said. "Did you plan it this way or was it accidental that I'm not very hungry after that workout?"

"Why do you always suspect the worst of me?" he asked. He was hungry, but not for the meal he had in the refrigerator.

After parking the car, they hurried inside where he started heating water for some hot chocolate. "I'm going to get out of these clothes," he said. "You want to get out of yours?"

Jenna just looked at him. A what-kind-of-a-dope-do-you-take-me-for? expression on her face.

"I meant I was going to take a quick shower and change into clean clothes," he explained with a teasing smile. "I've got a sweatsuit all picked out for you, if you want to do the same."

"And here I thought you'd lost your smooth touch," she said with a laugh. "All right. Who's first?"

"Ladies, of course."

He showed her to the bathroom and gave her his UCLA sweatsuit, then went back to finish making the hot chocolate. He could hear the shower running, his mind painting vivid pictures of the water streaming over Jenna. Dinner, he reminded himself. She came for dinner, not seduction.

He was reasonably calm when it was his turn to shower, but lost it again when he came back into the kitchen. His baggy old sweatsuit had never looked so good.

"Boy, you do things for this kitchen that no interior decorator ever thought of," he said.

She laughed and his heart caught on fire. He had never felt so alive as with her. He took another step into the kitchen and then she was in his arms, pressed against him and consuming the fresh clean smell of him.

"Ah, Jen," he said as his lips came down to take hers.

She was liquid flame, scorching hot, yet he was the one ready to explode. His hands slid under the sweatsuit, finding her skin so cool and soothing to the touch, but all too far away from him. He pulled her closer, ever closer, though he knew she could never be close enough for him to tire of her.

His hands moved upward, cupping her full breasts, even as her hands brought life to his body. Her caress was blessed torture, soft and oh, so slow. He wanted to cry out in joyful agony.

"You do know how to warm a person up after a chilly evening of skiing," Jenna murmured. "It's boiling in here."

"There are cooler rooms," he told her.

"Like the porch?"

"Like the bedroom."

His fingers had teased the tips of her breasts into hardness, and with each gentle brushing, he felt a shiver of delight course through her. The power he had to please her gave him joy, and a good dose of humility. How had he come to deserve someone like Jenna? Out of all the men around, why was it that he pleased her like no other?

"I vote for the cooler room," Jenna said, her voice a whisper that floated on the air.

Rob stopped, his eyes gazing into hers. "Are you sure?"

"What's there to be sure of?" she asked.

Her smile was soft, gentle and forgiving. The past rolled away from them, so that there only was now. Only the passion of the moment mattered.

He swept her up into his arms and carried her into the bedroom. The last time they'd made love it had been in a rush, as if their hungers had been growing for the past thirteen years and could only be satisfied in a rush. This time, they had all night.

Rob undressed her, kissing her breasts once they were free of the sweatshirt, then kissing a slow, steamy trail along her shoulders and down between the valley to her waist. His hands slid into the sweatpants, finding other warm valleys where he could stroke her fires into wild flames. She gasped beneath his touch, her breath coming faster and faster.

She looked so beautiful lying beneath him, a light haze of moisture on her face. Her eyes were deep pools, clear blue lakes that reflected her soul and all the goodness and generosity that rested there. He pushed the sweatpants off her so that his lips could take the place of his hands, bringing her pleasure.

"Rob, oh, Rob," she sighed.

He got out of his clothes to lie with her, to join with her and be one. She took him into her arms, into her warmth, and into her heart. Moving beneath him, in ancient rhythms, she climbed higher and higher into the night. Past the stars and the heavens until they exploded into oneness. She pulled life from him and gave him peace.

Much later she stirred in his arms and he opened one eye to peer at the clock. Midnight.

"Happy New Year, Jenna," he whispered into her hair.

"Happy New Year," she murmured and burrowed deeper into his arms.

He just held her and her presence kept the panic buried deep in his heart.

Chapter Twelve

"Well, you're here bright and early," Rob said as Jenna rushed into the school lobby, trying to escape the frigid winds outside.

"Who can sleep on a beautiful day like this?" Jenna said with a laugh.

Actually the morning was dark, gloomy and cold, with a promise of freezing rain later on, but in her heart the sun was shining. She'd finally stopped fighting her feelings for Rob and let things go as they would. No more worrying, no more imitating yo-yos.

"I'm hoping there's coffee in the teacher's lounge," he said. "I hate to make a pot at home just for myself."

"Anything that's there'll be left from yesterday," Jenna warned.

"I can handle it."

"Brave words."

They walked down the hall together, greeting the few other teachers already in the building. It was too early in the morning for real conversation, and forced talk just wasn't necessary between them. She'd known what she was doing New Year's Eve; she hadn't been swept away by the past.

"This is my stop," Jenna said as they got to the school office. "I've got to make copies of a test I'm giving today."

"See you later then."

His eyes kissed her even if his lips couldn't and she felt a glow surround her. The icy rain outside couldn't chill her.

It was hard to conduct business as usual anymore though. Her feet still kept her on paths that passed by Rob's classroom or his office, but it no longer bothered her. Or at least not in the same way. She enjoyed seeing him during the day, loved his teasing smile when words weren't possible.

"You seem mighty chipper today," Rita commented at lunch.

"We won the holiday tournament."

Rita just made a face. "That was last year. Since then, my washing machine has gone on the fritz, I've caught a cold and my freshman history class has forgotten how to read."

"You just don't live right," Jenna teased as she gathered up her lunch garbage.

The week seemed to fly by. Even though they got five inches of snow on Tuesday and temperatures fell below zero Thursday night, Jenna could have sworn spring was on its way.

"'Bout time you came by for dinner," Gram told Rob Friday evening. "You could have starved to death by this time."

"I'm pretty hardy," he said and hung up his coat.

"No thanks to Jenna."

"Gram," Jenna protested. "What did I do now?"

"You should have made him come over earlier."

"I can't make him do anything."

Gram clucked a reply and went back out into the kitchen. "Take him into the living room and make him comfortable," she called back over her shoulder.

Rob merely raised his eyebrows in comment and slipped his arm around her waist. "And how do you propose to do that?" he asked. "Need any suggestions?"

But they didn't even make it as far as the living room. Standing there in the foyer, arms wrapped around each other, his lips found hers. His touch thrilled and delighted her, made her heart sing, and even when they pulled apart to go into the living room she felt as if she was walking on air.

She still felt that way the next evening when she went to see Rob's boys play. Sitting up in the bleachers, she watched Rob as he coached. Somehow he knew what each boy needed to be motivated. One needed a pat on the back, on another a scowl worked wonders. Just as he read her moods, knowing when to make her laugh and when to just hold her.

"Team looks pretty good, doesn't it?"

Jenna looked up to find Don Parsons sitting down next to her.

"How are you feeling?" she asked.

"Not bad. A little older than I'd like to think I am."

"Isn't that true for all of us?"

They watched the game in silence for a few moments, while Jenna tried to force the chill from her heart. She was truly glad Don was up and about, but that could also mean the end of Rob's term here. All too soon he could be off chasing new rainbows.

"So when are you coming back?" she made herself ask.

Don winced as one of the Warsaw boys missed an easy lay-up. "Oh, I haven't decided yet. Rob's got such a good rapport with the kids, I wouldn't want to disturb that."

"Right."

She'd always known he was a roamer, here on temporary leave, and once Don claimed his own chair, Rob would be off searching for another rainbow. It was all right.

She told herself that all evening, but once the game was over and Rob joined her in the gym, he could read something was wrong.

"What's the matter?"

"Just tired," she said with a shrug. "Been a long few weeks."

"Just seven days in each of them," he pointed out.

"Maybe I'm getting a cold." She tried to sniff a bit. "Want to go over to the ice rink and rent some skates?"

"Not if you're getting a cold." He put his arm around her shoulder and led her out toward his car. "You're going straight home, and straight to bed."

"Gram will be shocked," Jenna teased.

"And you will be alone."

"That's no fun."

"If you're good, I'll come over tomorrow and read you the newspaper while you drink chicken soup."

Her bad-luck angel must have been listening because by tomorrow morning, she did indeed have a cold. After crawling into a sweatsuit, she lay on the sofa and felt miserable.

"Maybe you should stay home from school tomorrow," Gram said.

"I've got to run practice. We play Wabash this week."

"Can't run nothing if you're sick."

"I'm not that sick."

"And you want to be better for your birthday," Gram went on as if Jenna hadn't spoken. "Maybe Rob'll have a special present for you and you don't want to sneeze all over it."

"Gram, Rob doesn't even remember it's my birthday."

"A man remembers what's important to him."

Rob came over later, bringing sympathy and the Sunday paper. While watching football playoff games on TV, they read together. It was a nice afternoon, peaceful, relaxing.

"I can't believe that the pro football season's almost over," Jenna said with a sigh. "Soon basketball will be, too."

Rob was in the middle of an article about yesterday's boys' game. "Guess you've got to enjoy them while they're here."

She leaned back to watch San Francisco complete yet another pass. Maybe that was advice she should apply to everything.

"Happy birthday, boss lady," Peggy said as the three of them took their usual table in the teacher's lounge.

"I didn't know it was her birthday," Rita said.

"Yep, she's thirty-one."

"Wow."

"Thanks a lot," Jenna said.

"I don't mean that's old," Rita hastened to explain. "I just can't believe how everyone knows everything about everybody else in this place."

"Jenna." Arthur's secretary stood in the doorway. "Rob would like to see you. He says it's really important."

Jenna frowned down at her clipboard of notes and sighed. They had so much to cover. What could be so important that he hadn't thought to tell her when he saw her earlier today?

"We can take care of this," Peggy said, pulling the clipboard over to herself. "Go ahead."

"After all," Rita said. "He's our supreme leader."

Jenna got up. "I'll get this taken care of and be right back."

She walked slowly down the hall. Her cold was all gone, but she still didn't feel too perky. She could manage her classes and her practices, but when it came to the rest of her life, she just had no energy to spare. Her remedy for the situation had been to avoid all thought. Go, do, enjoy. Just don't think beyond today and now.

She knocked briefly at Rob's door before sticking her head in. "What can I do for you?" she asked.

Rob looked up from the papers he was correcting, and nodded toward a deep box on the corner of his desk. "Help me eat the pizza before it gets cold."

She stepped into the office, feeling just too weary to deal with his jokes. "Come on. I was in the middle of a meeting with Rita and Peggy and I—"

"Happy birthday." He had taken the lid off the box and there indeed was a pizza. With a basketball candle in the middle of it. As she stood there dumbfounded, he lit the candle.

"Want to come blow it out?" he asked. "Or do I have to sing 'Happy Birthday'?"

She walked over to his desk. "I could have eaten already, for all you knew."

"From what I've seen, you haven't been eating all that regularly these days."

"Have you been spying on me?"

"I'm your manager." His soft smile put a little bit of life back into her heart. "That makes me responsible for your welfare as well as your productivity."

"You take your job seriously."

"I take anything having to do with you seriously."

The smile remained in place but his eyes took on a more somber appearance. Jenna didn't want to guess what they were saying so she leaned over and blew the candle out.

"Did you make a wish?"

Always. The same stupid, impossible wish. "Sure. To win the next ten games."

"You weren't supposed to tell," he scolded her. "Now it won't come true."

"Sure, it will because I lied."

He just laughed and handed her a can of soda. "Come on, dig in."

Jenna sank onto the nearest chair and reached for a piece. It was still warm and the rich gooeyness revived her. This was just great. Just what she'd needed.

"Rita and Peggy are still in the teachers' lounge, planning our practices for this week." She licked her lips and took another piece. "I really should get back."

"Jenna. Today's your birthday."

"I know," she said around a mouthful of cheese. "But I have responsibilities."

"And good capable assistants. Do you honestly think they need you around every minute of their day?"

No, she was sure nobody needed her around every minute of their day and that was what saddened her. Even Susie, as arthritic and old as she was, did just fine while Jenna was gone for long hours.

She took another piece and Gram's words came back to her. Somehow when Gram had talked about a "special gift," Jen didn't think she'd meant a pizza with a birthday candle. More like a ring with a diamond.

"I never got a pizza for my birthday before."

"I was going to get you a scarf or some perfume or flowers." He made a face as he listed all the usual gifts. "But I tried to think of what you really needed and that was a pizza."

"And your fondness of it had nothing to do with it?"

"Hey, if I'd gotten it for me, it would have had anchovies and mushrooms on it."

"Well, it's great." And it was. Once again, he'd read her mood and her heart and come up with the proper medicine. But did he have the medicine to cure her love for him?

Jenna stopped cold, swallowing back the shiver of fear that raced through her. She was in love with Rob Fagan, just as she had been thirteen years ago.

No, that was wrong. It wasn't the same as it had been thirteen years ago. Then she'd been a child with a child's puppy love, an adoration of someone she admired. A sexual attraction to someone her hormones reacted to. Now, she was an adult woman with an adult's love.

She wasn't looking for sexual thrills or a date to the prom, but a lifetime of companionship and support. That was what adult love was. Being together through thick and thin, and Rob was a rainbow-chaser just like his father.

"Have you heard anything from Don lately?" she asked.

Rob took another piece for himself. "As a matter of fact, he was in this morning, going over some of the baseball paperwork."

"He must be feeling better."

"So he says."

Jenna forced herself to eat the rest of the piece of pizza she had in her hand, then stood up.

"I really have to go," she said. "Thanks for the break."

"Hey, no problem." He frowned at her. "You okay?"

"Just trying to adjust to the shock of being thirty-one," she joked.

He didn't press any further and Jenna left.

What an idiot she was, she scolded herself. Hadn't she learned from the past? Of course, she hadn't. Why else would she be seeing him everyday, making love with him, and not realizing that she was bound to fall in love? She was such a jerk.

Looking for someplace quiet to escape to, Jenna headed into the counseling office. It was quiet all right, with only one student there. Sara.

"Hi, Miss Lauren." The girl looked up only briefly from a college catalog she was studying. "Do you know where River Forest is?"

"It's a suburb on the west side of Chicago. Why?"

Sara held up the catalog. Rosary College. "I was just checking out some other options. You know, ones in the Chicago area so I wouldn't be so far from home."

"Dayton's not that far."

Sara just made a face. No, Dayton was too far, Jenna knew. Too far from Mike. History was repeating itself.

Jenna sank down onto the sofa next to Sara. "You can't hold onto him," she told the girl. "Love him while he's here, but don't ever fool yourself into believing you can hold on to him."

"How about a cola, Coach?"

"Sure," Rob replied as he reached into the cooler for a can of soda and handed it to the heavyset man at the counter.

"Keep the change," the man said. "The kids could use some new wrestling mats."

"Thanks," Rob said.

The man opened his can and drank from it. "Boy, you sure are the spitting image of your dad," he said. "He used to come out to our farm a lot and nurse our tractor along."

Rob felt the need to say something. "I guess he was a pretty good mechanic."

"Once he was gone, nobody could keep the old tractor running," the man went on. "We were living on a shoestring anyway, and it finally broke and we moved into town. But, boy, I can still remember how he could make the old motor purr like new."

Someone else his father let down. Funny, Rob'd never thought how others had depended on his father, too.

"Your boys are doing well."

"So far," Rob agreed.

"Heard you're a good coach, got a lot to teach the boys."

"I try."

The man nodded, apparently satisfied he'd fulfilled his obligation of sociability, and walked back to the stands. Rob turned his eyes, if not his full attention, to the two young men rolling around on the mat, faces red from straining to come out on top. Wrestling didn't draw much of a crowd but the coaches more than made up for it, bellowing their instructions to the combatants.

His father had been a good mechanic, that man was right. But maybe it would have been better if he'd been only average, fewer people would have been hurt by his leaving. Was he starting the same situation with the boys' team? Making them depend on him, only to pull the rug out from under their feet when he'd leave. But Don was a good coach. It wasn't like Rob would be leaving them stranded.

The LaVille lad pinned the Warsaw boy and the gym went near to dead quiet. Each boy went to the center of the circle, the winner had his hand raised for a moment, there was a quick handshake between the athletes and they vacated the mat for the next match.

It had seemed too simple when Arthur had contacted him about taking Don's spot for a few months. Come back, see everybody, have a few laughs, then go. What had gone wrong? Maybe he was just as blind to reality as his father had been. The next match started and Rob focused his gaze on the wrestlers.

"Hi there. A penny for your thoughts."

Rob quickly forgot the wrestlers, feeling joy drive everything else out of his system. "Hi, Jen."

He wanted to lean forward and kiss her but pulled up short at the last second. He didn't know what stopped him, but he knew it was the right thing to do. Two teachers smooching in the school gym was less than professional.

"What are you doing around here?" he asked.

"I had a team meeting," she replied. "Thought I'd drop in and see how the boys were doing."

"We're holding our own. I think we've won at least as many matches as we've lost."

Jenna nodded and stared at the match in progress. Rob watched her. She'd been different, quieter, for the past few weeks, since before her birthday, before her cold even. He wished he could help her find her smile again.

"No girls asked to be on the wrestling team this year?" Rob said.

"That happens about once in a blue moon."

She was taking his remark seriously so he did, too. "What would you think if one did?"

Jenna shrugged. "I don't know. I think the girls should be able to play any sport they want, but I also know that a girl who participated in wrestling would be considered a freak. And female athletes already have a hard enough time with acceptance."

Rob gazed at Jenna in her jeans and long-sleeved T-shirt. There was no hiding her sleek, womanly musculature. He couldn't imagine any man not accepting her.

"As a basketball coach, I wouldn't be awfully excited about another winter sport for girls," Jenna said. "The pool of female athletes is so small that I'd probably lose some of my good players if they had another choice."

"Which would you have chosen?"

Jenna frowned at him.

"If you had had the choice, would you have picked wrestling or basketball?"

Her face relaxed and she patted his hand. "Same old Rob," she murmured.

He didn't like the way that sounded. "Is that good or bad?"

Jenna went back to watching the wrestlers.

"It's not polite to ignore people," Rob said. "Especially when they ask you a direct question."

"Goodness," she said with a chuckle. "You've become quite the Mr. Manners in your maturity."

"I'm not old yet," he protested.

"Mature doesn't have to mean old."

No, it didn't. Jenna had reached maturity long before he even began to approach it. Maybe that was why he had needed her so. She'd served as an even keel for him, giving him stability and balance as he bounced from depression to exhilaration, and raged about the various inequities of life.

"To me, wrestling isn't a viable option for women," Jenna said. "There's no reason to speculate on something that's impossible."

His question might have been indicative of the same old Rob, but her answer was the same old Jenna. Practical, logical, filled with common sense.

She was watching the wrestlers again, so he got the chance to watch her. High cheekbones, generous mouth. Classically beautiful.

But there were also a number of things that were uniquely Jenna. There was sternness—yes—a toughness, determination. But there was also a gentleness, a softness, and most of all, caring.

He swallowed a small lump, at once facing a blatantly true fact straight on. He certainly was the same old Rob. Just like thirteen years ago, he was happiest when he was with her. She smoothed his ups and downs. She was someone to cling to, emotionally and physically.

Unfortunately, other things hadn't changed. Like him, like his fear of letting her down. The time for him to move on was getting close.

"A penny for your thoughts, pretty lady."

She smiled and turned to him, giving him a view that was so exquisite it almost hurt. "They're not worth all that much."

"Let me be the judge," he murmured.

"Well, okay." She paused a moment as if to gather her thoughts. "Susie's arthritis seems to be acting up again. So I have to get some medication from the vet."

"Uh, huh."

"Gram's caught my cold and I'm hoping she has sense enough to rest and stay in the house."

"She's a tough-minded lady," he said. "But she has a lot of common sense."

"And Sara's talking about going to school near Mike."

"She has a right to make those decisions for herself."

"I know she has, but she really doesn't have all that many options. Her family doesn't have the money. She needs a scholarship in order to attend college. Her grades are good but not outstanding so it has to be a basketball scholarship."

"There are a number of schools in Chicago," Rob pointed out.

"Yeah, but they seem to be either high-profile division I programs like De Paul or Northwestern, or division III. Sara's not good enough for a high-profile program and division III schools don't give scholarships. That scholarship from Dayton was her best option."

"Maybe she doesn't think so."

"I think she does. She's just lost sight of reality because of her feelings for Mike. She thinks she loves him."

"Love is really knowing the other person, their fears as well as their dreams," Rob said. "I think Mike's afraid of her clinging too tightly. Maybe I should talk to Sara."

"No, that's okay," she replied. "Sara's my responsibility."

"Mine, too," Rob said. "I'm responsible for all athletic programs. Remember?"

"Yes, but you're just temporary. I'm going to be here the rest of my life."

"So?" Irritation sprouted within him.

"So, I'll take care of it."

He wanted to argue, but just kept silent. Why should he want to argue? Did he want to say he wasn't temporary? But the thought of a white picket fence and people waiting for him each day, was like shooting ice into his veins. He'd vowed years ago never to let anyone down and the way to insure that was never to let anyone that close. He was going to stick to his promise.

"I should be going." Jenna stood up. "I don't want to leave Gram alone very long. Give me a call if you want to do something tonight."

She reached for his hand and held it a brief moment. He wanted to give her everything and see nothing but smiles residing in her eyes. He wanted her life to be filled with sunshine and springtime. He wanted to love her like she deserved to be loved, yet the best thing he could do was to free her to find someone else.

"I think I'll probably just vegetate at home tonight," he said.

She let go of his hand as her eyes caressed him with the saddest of smiles.

"You can vegetate with us if you want," she said, then left without waiting for an answer.

He watched her walk away, a bitter taste rising to his mouth. He suspected he was already too late to keep his vow not to let anyone close. He glared out at the wrestlers and their big mouthed coaches. He had to get out of here soon. One of the boys was quickly pinned and a sense of weariness pinned Rob's soul just as fast. The fact that leaving felt so wrong was proof that it was time to go, time to put some distance between him and Jenna before she really got hurt again.

Chapter Thirteen

The bell rang ending classes and Jenna's students dashed out like buffalo trying to escape from a prairie grass fire. She sat down, letting the vacuum of silence wash over her tired shoulders.

It had been a cruddy weekend and she'd carried the depression over into her workweek. Every place she'd looked there was gloom, doom and aggravation.

The more she tried to help Gram, the more irritable her grandmother had become. Then the weather had turned bitterly cold which didn't do Susie's arthritis any good. To top everything off, Sara was still talking about turning down the University of Dayton's offer and finding a school in Chicago.

Actually, Jenna knew it wasn't the weather, Gram or Sara that was the real problem. The real root of her depression was the fact that she'd hardly seen Rob in the last week. He didn't come by at all over the weekend, and he turned invisible here at school. How could she have let herself fall in love with him again? Hadn't she been hurt enough in the past?

She tried keeping busy, hoping that if she exhausted herself during the day, she'd sleep all through the night. Fat chance. She had yet to find a task that kept her so busy that her mind wouldn't wander back to Rob. And the nights, well, they'd never been so long.

She'd lie awake, watching the nighttime shadows dance on her ceiling and listening to Susie's quiet breathing from the foot of her bed. Thirteen years ago, Rob had been part of her social life, a friend and a confidante whom she had leaned on. No matter how she needed his support in those first few months after he'd left, she'd been too young to know anything about love.

Back then, love was a date to the prom and someone to commiserate with about a teacher's unfairness. It was not having to worry about filling your Saturday nights and someone to talk to on the phone while you did your homework.

Well, she didn't have any more proms in her life, she'd learned the world didn't revolve around her, and a quiet Saturday night at home was a joy, not a tragedy. That didn't mean she didn't need love, but that her definition had changed.

Love was feeling whole with someone, being alive when he was around. Love was someone to lean on when she was tired or grumpy or worried, someone to laugh with when the sun was shining. Love was Rob, except that he wasn't going to be around much longer. Not unless he was going to change his spots and decide to put down roots. And that seemed a pipe dream of the wispiest quality, especially the way he'd been acting lately.

"I got your message that you wanted to see me."

Startled, Jenna spun to see Rob standing in the doorway.

"Sorry," Rob said.

Jenna waved her hand as she sat down. "It's not your fault. I was just mulling over some new plays to try against Noblesville next week."

"Want me to come back later?"

And when would that be, next year? "No, come on in. Sit down. It seems like ages since I've seen you."

He came in and sat down in one of the student desks, but looked more like he was there to serve a detention than because they were lovers.

"What's wrong, Rob?" she asked. "You've really been distant lately."

He looked away the way the kids did when they were trying to pull a fast one. "Nothing," he said. "Just caught up in the season. Remembering how I hate winter, too."

Oh? He'd never hated it when they were in school. Snowball fights, ice skating, skiing and sledding were all part of his passions.

"I've missed you," she told him.

He looked at her then, his eyes meeting hers for the briefest of moments before he stared down at the top of the desk. What was the shadow she'd seen there? Regret?

"Should be glad of the free time you have now," he said.

She ignored the stupidity of that statement. "I was trying to see you today for a reason," she said. "The senior class is having their sleigh ride tonight. One set of chaperons ducked out at the last minute and we've been invited as a replacement."

They'd had a sleigh ride when they were seniors. A starry night, new fallen snow, and holding hands with Rob while sitting beneath a blanket. Another trip down memory lane, but then everything they'd done thus far was a repeat of what they'd done in the past. Necking in the cafeteria during dances, going to Ricco's after football games and now a sleigh ride.

"Sorry," he said. "I can't."

She'd expected him to refuse, but still it hurt. She got up and began to erase the equations she'd worked for her trigonometry class. "I see." Though she didn't. Jenna didn't see anything anymore.

He got up from the desk, but didn't move toward the door as she expected. "What was that for—trig?"

Jenna nodded.

"Want to explain it to me?"

"No, if you haven't gotten the concepts by now, you're a lost cause."

"That's a rotten attitude for a teacher."

"Realistic," Jenna assured him and erased the rest of the board. Why didn't he just go? Go back to his office, go back to his life somewhere else.

Rob waited until she was back to her desk before speaking again. "I'm really sorry about tonight. My team needs a lot of work."

"You were counseling me not too long ago to lighten up and my play-offs start three weeks before yours do."

"There's a lot I have to do."

"So much that you can't even take a few hours off to relax? Come along. Half your team's going to be there. Todd, Ricky, Don, Mike. They can help you plan strategy."

"Mike?"

"He's one of the senior class officers."

"Damn." Rob slammed his hand down on the desk. "After all his promises about taking things seriously, he's going to spend an evening sleigh-riding and staying up late. He'll be totally useless for our game tomorrow and he's got a recruiter from De Paul coming."

"Come off it, Rob," she said sharply. "Don't make a big deal out of nothing. Kids that age have a lot of energy. He'll just sleep late and be fine for the game."

His lips tightened and he looked away. She could see his shoulders heave as he took a deep breath. "I'm sorry, Jen. I'm just tired."

"I know you are. That's why I think the sleigh ride would do you good.

Rob shook his head.

"Hey, it's a small group of kids and the better-behaved ones at that. Chaperoning them will be a no-sweat gig."

"No. I'm tired. I may have caught your cold and really need to rest."

Jenna looked at him a long moment, almost long enough to make her blurt out the truth, that she loved him and that this silent treatment was killing her. But then he just turned and left.

"Take care of yourself," she murmured, but he was already gone.

It had to end, that was the conclusion that Rob came to after a night of restless tossing and a Saturday morning spent staring out a window. He couldn't keep telling himself that he was going soon; he wasn't going until the basketball season was over and Don Parsons was back to work. But he couldn't string Jenna along for all that time. It wasn't fair to her.

So early afternoon, he went over to her house. A couple of "woofs" greeted him when he rang the doorbell. He could see the old dog through the sidelights by the front door. At least, she was still happy to see him. But maybe that was because he hadn't done anything to her yet.

He squatted down by the sidelight. "Hi, Susie," he called.

The old dog wagged her tail, looking back occasionally. Rob stood up as Gram opened the door. In a way, he was relieved it wasn't Jenna. After a whole night of planning speeches, he still wasn't sure about what to say to her.

"Hi, Gram," Rob said. "It's a real pleasure seeing you."

"Quit flapping your gums and get on in," Gram ordered him briskly. "And wipe your shoes off. I vacuumed today. Don't want you tracking dirty old snow through the house."

"Yes, ma'am," Rob replied. He wiped his shoes thoroughly, even the sides.

"Jenna cracked a filling," Gram said. "She's over to the Eastside Dental Clinic right now."

"Hope she'll be all right."

"Ain't no reason she won't," Gram snapped. "Got the muscles of a plow horse and the disposition of a mule."

Rob wasn't sure how to respond. That didn't quite sound like a compliment in his book.

"Come on back to the kitchen, boy."

Rob hung his coat up and followed the old woman down the hall. He'd been down this hall many a time, but back in his youth, he'd never noticed the beauty of the fine oak woodwork or the brightly polished old oak floors. It seemed timeless. As if it would stand here forever.

Jenna belonged here, just as Gram did. They were the steady types. The ones you could count on in the long run. He was like a prefab house, up fast and not made to last.

"Sit yourself down, boy," Gram ordered. "I got some corned beef hash on the back burner."

"Thanks, but I already ate lunch."

"Ate?" The old woman fixed her eyes on him, peppering Rob with sharp arrows of accusation. "What and where?"

"I had a hamburger." He tried to avoid those dark eyes but they held him in a grip of steel. "Over by the mall."

"One of them fast food places? Good Lord, boy." Gram shook her head. "Even a cockroach won't eat at one of them places."

She put a heaping plate of hash before Rob and sat down across from him. The hash smelled delicious, the warm scents curling around him in the air and enticing him to relax. But he couldn't.

"You probably noticed I haven't been around much lately," he said, uneasy under the old woman's stare. "I've been fighting off a cold."

"Sure," Gram said. "That must be why Jenna's either biting my head off or hardly saying a word for days on end. She gets that way when her friends have the sniffles."

Rob stared at his food, playing with it more than eating. He should have known better than to try to pull one on the old lady. "Jenna tell you what's been going on?"

Gram shook her head and poured herself a cup of coffee. "Jenna ain't never been much of a talker, not since her daddy died. She changed then, turning inside herself where none of us could ever reach her."

"His death must have been hard on her, since she was driving and all."

"She's a strong woman and came to grips with most things, but there was a darkness about her then that none of us could pierce. And Lord knows we all tried. Girl came home on the bus just about every weekend to see her Momma."

Rob felt his stomach turn. He should have been there to help Jenna through that darkness. But true to his genes, he'd been gone.

"We finally went and bought the girl a car," Gram said. "Got a passel of relatives to pitch in. Saved her a lot of time."

Rob took his plate to the counter, hoping Gram wouldn't notice he'd only eaten about half. "I guess she felt her mother needed the care."

Gram shook her head. "I was here. And we got ourselves a couple acres of kin nearby. Mary had all the love and care she could tolerate." Gram shook her head again. "I think Jenna was just using her Momma to fill the empty spaces in her life."

Empty spaces that he'd inconsiderately caused.

"All she did was study and play basketball. Girl that age, single and away at school, ought to put a little foolishment in her life. A body don't get too many chances for that."

They sat in silence, Gram sipping at her coffee and Rob lost in his thoughts. He thought he'd cared about Jenna years back, thought he was the world's greatest boyfriend, but what had he given her? Nothing but pain and emptiness. The same type of gifts his father had passed on. The same things he'd leave her when he pulled up stakes.

"It ain't like the girl ain't had no offers," Gram said. "I mean she's pleasing to the eye and a nice firm bundle to wrap your arms around." Gram looked sharply at him. "You been looking her up and squeezing her proper. Ain't that right?"

Rob gulped at his coffee. Was he supposed to agree or disagree?

But Gram just sat there, shaking her head. "And she's a strong girl, too. The kind a man can love all night and then help him plow the back forty afore breakfast."

Rob'd never had a conversation like this before and fought back the urge to find a place to hide. Maybe Jenna would come home and rescue him.

"Jenna seems rather worried about Sara," he said quickly. "She's the captain of the varsity basketball team."

Gram grunted. "Girl would do well to get some children of her own. Then she'd get all the aggravation she needs. Wouldn't have to go looking for more."

He sensed the conversation was drifting toward animal husbandry again so Rob picked up his cup and silverware. If Jenna wasn't home in a few minutes, he'd keel over on the floor. Then he'd stagger to the door, after telling Gram that he was coming down with the Mongolian spotted fever and needed to get to bed, alone.

"You know, now that you've filled out, you look a lot like your daddy."

Rob looked up to find Gram smiling and staring at him with her sharp, dark eyes. He wasn't up to returning her smile.

"I mean you always had his twinkle in your eyes and that silver tongue, but now you're the spitting image of the man. If your momma were alive now, she wouldn't have to explain where you came from."

Rob just put the silverware in the sink, his heart silent. Nothing like reality smacking you in the face.

"Hi, Gram." Jenna came in through the back door, slipping her coat off her shoulders before she noticed Rob. "Oh, hi. What are you doing here?"

"Having some lunch," Gram snapped. "What does it look like?"

"I dropped by to see you," Rob said. "And your grandmother started feeding me. Just like when I was back in high school."

"You ought to have the man over more often," Gram said.

"Hey, now," Rob protested. "I've been here a whole bunch."

"Not recently, boy."

He looked at Jenna. She seemed to have picked up his weariness. It was time for Gram to take her badgering elsewhere. But the old woman was already standing up when Rob turned toward her.

"I made some gelatin in case you want something soft and cool," Gram told Jenna. "I'm going to watch the television for awhile. I'll be in to clean up afterwards." They heard the floorboards creak and then the soft sighing sound as she sank into her favorite chair in the living room.

"She sure is some mixture," Rob said.

Jenna nodded. "She can wear on a body but she's full of love."

The silence stretched and filled the big old country kitchen. There were so many things he wanted to talk to Jenna about. He should apologize for yesterday, make her understand that he never meant to hurt her. But now that he was here the only thing Rob wanted to do was take her in his arms. She looked so vulnerable. What she needed was a massage, a little sleep, and a whole lot of love. His desire to give them to her stunned him with its intensity.

"You had a hard week," he said. "Losing a filling was the last thing you needed."

Jenna shrugged. "Wasn't a big deal. It happened halfway through practice this morning. Slipped right out into the gum I was chewing."

"Halfway through practice?"

"Bothered my assistants and the girls more than it did me," Jenna said. "They just about picked me up and carried me to the dentist."

He somehow had known she hadn't bothered to leave, enduring the pain rather than give in to it.

"I don't know why everyone's got this compulsion to take care of me lately," she said with a laugh. "This close to the play-offs, everyone's got to pull their weight and then some. As head coach, I sure don't want to be a Freida Freeloader."

Ah, Jenna. Why do people want to take care of you? Because they care about you. His eyes misted slightly and he suddenly felt tired himself, although he didn't know why. He should be happy so many people cared about her. That meant she'd always have someone looking out for her long after he was gone.

"I'd better be heading on home," he said, abandoning all his speeches. "I just came over to tell you I was sorry about yesterday."

She just shrugged. "No big deal."

He got his coat and paused, wishing courage would force the words out of his mouth. But for a sweet moment, they just stared into each other's eyes and anything was possible. He forgot all his plans. All he wanted was to take her in his arms, to soothe and comfort her. She certainly didn't look like the plow horse her grandmother had talked about. She looked like a soft, fragile little girl who needed care. His care.

"Want to take some pie home?" Jenna asked.

He shook his head. "No thanks."

"Doesn't matter, take some anyway." Jenna went over to the counter and wrapped a large chunk of pie in some foil. "Gram will just fuss at me if you don't."

He took the plate and murmured a barely audible thank you. This house was filled with strong women. They sure didn't need him. The world had plenty of helpless critters for them to care for and he could go on his way without worrying.

"Two fast laps around the gym," Rob shouted at his team. "And if I see one person dogging it, everybody does an extra set of five."

Jenna came up behind him. "Boy, I'm glad you're not my coach," she teased.

She expected his eyes to be laughing when he turned around, or maybe she just hoped they would be. He didn't do much laughing or even smiling lately. Not that she saw much of him to know what he was doing.

But Rob was his same old serious self when he turned. The ever-present twinkle in his eye was no longer ever-present and she didn't think a smile could crack those lips with a crowbar. If only he would talk to her, tell her what was wrong. She didn't really think it was something she'd done, but rather the demons of the past that he carried around with him. Whatever it was, she needed to know to be able to help him.

"Aren't you being a bit hard on them?" she asked.

"We can't afford to slack off," he said. "Not in the least little bit."

"Don't want them to burn out either."

"They won't."

They silently watched the boys finish their final lap, none slacking off as if they'd heard Rob's comment and were intent on proving him right. Actually, she was less concerned about the boys burning out than she was about Rob. Something was eating at him, and pulling him away from her.

The silence continued as they watched the boys pick up their sweats and head for the locker room, followed quickly by the managers with the team equipment. The silence became oppressive now that she was alone with Rob in the gymnasium,

"I'm going to turn off the lights, then I'm gone," he said, turning to escape into the boys' locker room.

"I can get them," she said.

He shrugged and continued toward the locker room door at the far end of the gym.

"Rob."

Her voice, soft as it had been, seemed to echo in the huge empty space. Rob seemed to pause, hesitate as if weighing whether or not he wanted to stop, but then did. She hurried over to him.

"There's a good snow base this year," she said.

Rob's face was expressionless, distantly polite. "Yes, the cold's holding on."

She just looked at him, trying to read what lay deep in his eyes. They were still, motionless lakes that gave her no clue as to his thoughts, but still she refused to look away.

"There's going to be another torchlight ski this Friday night," she said. "Let's go."

She tried to make her voice light, paint it with pictures of their times together during New Year's Eve. A clear winter sky with the moon and the stars shining bright. Candles blinking like a thousand eyes on into the woods. Exercise that washed the tension out of their bodies and love that brought them ecstasy.

For a moment Rob seemed to weaken, but then he stiffened his back. "I really can't do it," he said quietly.

She forced her smile to stay in place. "I thought the last time we skied, it was great."

He shrugged. "I guess it was fun."

Her vision blurred as a film of moisture covered her eyes. Fun? How could he call it fun? The laughter, the joking words, the delicious tiredness to her muscles when every shred of tension had been put to rout, and finally laying by Rob's side, feeling totally fulfilled. It wasn't fun, it was heaven.

"I just can't take the time," he said.

"It's only a few hours," she said, holding his eyes tight with hers. "We'll have dinner—you have to eat anyway—then some skiing and before you know it, I'll have you in bed."

Rob's face closed in some undefinable way.

"Whosever bed you want, alone or together," she said. "You pick."

He didn't say anything for the longest time, just staring off into the distance at some invisible vision. Then he sighed, seeming to sag from within for a moment, before his eyes turned rigid and cold.

"It's not just the time for the skiing itself," he said. "I don't want the distraction right now."

Distraction? He didn't want a distraction? What did he think this whole mess was for her, but a distraction? His voice followed her down the empty corridors of school after her practices. His eyes danced for her among the papers as she corrected tests late into the night. Then, when the world was dark and she lay in her bed staring at the ceiling, her body reached out and screamed for the warmth of his flesh.

"Our state tournament play-downs begin in a few weeks," he said. "And I want myself totally dedicated to doing our best."

"Damn it, Rob. This isn't healthy. Everyone needs a break, both you and the kids."

"We're fine."

Jenna didn't know what to say. She wasn't fine, hadn't been fine for weeks now. He'd come back into her life, laughing and teasing until he swept away all her arguments and she was in love with him again. Then suddenly, he turned and acted as if they were barely acquaintances. She hadn't wanted to come right out and ask if he no longer cared about her, but all of her little hints and hopes sure weren't working.

"Rob." Her voice came out hoarse, just above a whisper. "I thought we were starting to build something, you and I. Something that we'd started thirteen years ago."

His shoulders stiffened and he looked back to that distant vision. "Thirteen years ago you helped me pass algebra," he said coldly. "And we played one-on-one against each other."

Jenna stared at him, her heart slowly cracking into a million pieces. "We did a bit more than that," she pointed out.

"And you paid a high price for it." He swallowed hard, then went on. "What we had was in the past. Neither of us play ball anymore, and I'm sure I know enough algebra to get by."

"It doesn't sound like it was much of a relationship," she said.

"Not enough to keep these feet from wandering," he said before turning on his heels and striding out of the gym. It was so empty that even his soft-soled heels boomed in her ears.

Chapter Fourteen

"Damn."

Rob stretched his long frame but still could just barely reach the top of the basketball rim. Changing the nets wasn't going to be as easy a job as he had thought. But then what had been easy lately? Everything he touched seemed to turn sour.

It had been days since he'd seen Jenna, really seen her, that is. Yet the stricken look in her eyes when he'd finally gotten the courage to push her away still haunted him. He saw it in his dreams and heard her pained voice in every whisper of the wind. Damn. He'd done it all wrong. But if he'd been gentle, explaining about his need to wander, wouldn't that have just given her false hope? It would hurt her so much more if he let their relationship continue to grow. He reached up again to try to loosen the old net.

"That's a forward's job," a young cocky voice said. "You guard types are too short."

Rob drew himself up to his full six feet two inches on top of the small stepladder, and glared down at Mike Sherwin and his six feet four inches on the floor. "All I need is a bigger stepladder."

"The ladder's fine," Mike replied. "All you need is me up on it."

"There has to be a bigger ladder around here."

"Nope." Mike shook his head. "That's the one we always use."

"Don Parsons is shorter than I am," Rob pointed out.

"Like I said, Mr. Fagan. That's a forward's job. Mr. Parsons always had one of us frontline guys change the nets."

Still frowning, Rob came down off the ladder. He bowed slightly to Mike as he took Rob's place.

Mike quickly scrambled up the ladder and began unhooking the old net. "See," he said, grinning down at Rob. "Any job's easy if you have the right tools."

Rob gave Mike a scowl in return but there was nothing fierce in its delivery. "How come you're here so early?" he asked. "I thought you and Sara usually got here around quarter to eight."

Mike shrugged as he handed down the worn net and took the new one from Rob. "I came with Mr. Fidler. He saw me walking and gave me a ride."

He knew that Mike usually came to school with Sara, whose father dropped them off on his way to work. Apparently the two were having problems. Rob could well appreciate what they were going through. His life wasn't going too smoothly right now either.

"I had to do some homework," Mike explained, studiously concentrating on stringing the new net properly. "It's easier to study here in the morning. You know, it's really quiet."

"Then why aren't you working on it?" Rob asked.

"I finished it." Mike stepped down off the ladder. "Went faster than I thought it would."

Mike picked up the ladder and they walked in silence down to the basket at the other end of the court. Rob could see that there was a definite touch of fatigue in the boy's expression.

"How are things between you and Sara?" Rob asked, when Mike was up on the ladder again, unhooking the old net.

Mike waited until he had taken down the net and accepted the new one from Rob. "I don't know," he said. There was a noticeable sigh in his voice.

"Senior year is a tough year," Rob said. "Your world is so neatly put together. Friends, school, girls, sports. And then in a few months, it's going to get all wrecked to hell."

The job of replacing the net complete, Mike nodded and sat down on the ladder.

"On one hand, you're looking forward to a new, exciting world. Yet, on the other hand, you hate leaving something you know that appears safe and secure."

"Sara's been talking about going to school in Chicago," Mike said. "But she is still interested in taking that basketball scholarship at the University of Dayton." He shook his head. "She doesn't know what she wants."

"What would you like her to do?"

A pained look came to Mike's face. "I don't know."

"You know what you want to do?"

The pain vanished, replaced by a look of hard determination. His body stiffened. "Yeah, but now Sara's talking about me going to school near her. You know, since she hasn't got as many offers as I have."

The pain had returned to the boy's face but it was nothing near the pain Rob felt in his own heart. The world was like a merry-go-round, with Mike and Sara playing out a later version of his and Jenna's senior year. But was there ever a time when the merry-go-round stopped? It hadn't yet. He and Jenna were still on it, still hurting.

"You haven't committed yet," Rob pointed out.

"I know." The words came out in sort of a moan as Mike sat there shaking his head. "I don't want to hurt anybody, most of all Sara. But I don't want to hurt myself either and I think playing in Chicago would be just great for me."

"No more small towns for you," Rob said with a chuckle.

Mike just ducked his head and Rob moved closer to put his arm around the boy's shoulder. "Hey, I don't mean to pick on you. I just wanted to lighten things up."

"I know, Mr. Fagan," Mike murmured. "You've been real cool for me all year."

"I'm just a cool dude."

Mike twisted his face into a half-smile but then retreated into silence. Rob followed but brought along his own pain. The kids' problems weren't that different from his and Jenna's. But he couldn't solve his own dilemmas, so why did he think he could solve theirs?

They obviously cared for each other but so many things were pulling at them right now. Different talents and different dreams were pulling them apart while pleasant memories and fiery hormones were pushing them together. Was he thinking of Mike and Sara or him and Jenna?

"The main thing you have to have," Rob said. "Is a respect for each other."

Mike shook his head. "Sara wants to come back to Warsaw," he said. "She wants to teach and coach."

"Everybody has their own dreams."

"I want out of here," Mike muttered.

Rob looked at the boy's grim face and didn't know whether to laugh or cry. "This town is going to be a part of you the rest of your life. It's a major part of what made you who you are."

"Ain't my fault."

UCLA, Europe, Paris, London, Tokyo. To many those names conjured pictures of glamour, excitement. There was some of that but in looking back Rob could also see the endless string of look-alike hotel rooms and nameless restaurants. He'd cut himself off from his past and drifted around the world like a tumbleweed.

"Don't burn all your bridges behind you, old buddy."

"What difference does it make?" Mike asked. "I ain't coming back."

"None of us knows what the future holds," Rob said firmly. "So don't get so positive about things. Your relations with Sara don't have to be an all-or-nothing situation. At your age, each of you should follow your own dreams."

The boy nodded.

"But that doesn't mean you have to cut each other off. Stay in touch. Call, write. You'll be home for some of the holidays. Hop on a bus and visit each other. Chicago and Dayton aren't that far apart."

Mike was silent a long time before finally standing up. "I'll put the ladder away, Mr. Fagan."

"Thanks."

He was almost at the door when Rob called out. "Mike." The boy turned around. "I've been down your road. A lot of things will be happening, a lot of pressure." He looked at the kid a long moment. "Just be sure to leave Sara with memories, nothing else. Neither of you are up to carrying any extra baggage at this point."

Something went through Mike's face and Rob was sure that he understood, although he just nodded before he walked out. Rob just sighed and rubbed his face with both hands. Oh, how fast the years went by. It seemed like one minute he was the smart-mouth punk and the next he was the wise old man. But if he was so wise, why had he bungled this whole thing with Jenna?

"Rob?"

He turned. "Oh, hi, Arthur."

Arthur walked farther into the gym, his face bathed with a big grin. "Talked to Don Parsons just a few minutes ago. Says he's feeling fine."

"That's good." Rob felt himself steeling, as if to ward off a blow. He knew what was coming and was glad, he told himself, even as his heart sank.

"But he figures the best way to keep on feeling fine is to take things easy. He's retiring."

Rob paused, knocked from his train of thought by the news. "Things aren't going to be the same without him," he said after a moment.

"You've been doing a super job," Arthur said, his grin growing. "And the board would like to offer you the job permanently."

Rob took a deep breath, exhaling slowly as if he could rid himself of all his woes and start afresh with the new breath of air. Take the job permanently. Stay here with Jenna and Gram, watching kids like Sara and Mike grow and mature.

But he'd been on the road so long and liked it, liked being able to pack up and go whenever people got too close. The offer dangled before him like a carrot on a stick. He wanted to grab at it, to reach for a life he'd never had, but then he heard his mother's voice laughing about his father's need to chase rainbows. He saw Jenna's wounded eyes when he tried to save her from greater hurt. He felt his own anger and pain when his father left them, because the call of the rainbows was stronger than his love for his family.

"Can I think on it a few days, Arthur?" he asked.

Arthur smiled and nodded. "Sure."

* * *

"I'm going to the boys' basketball game, Gram," Jenna said. "I should be home by ten."

Her grandmother smiled and looked up from her needlepoint. "That's good, dear. Have a nice time."

Was that possible? Since Rob had ended their relationship, she didn't think nice times existed, not for her. She hurried out to her car, shivering from the cold.

The girls' state tournament started next week and Jenna could hardly wait. The girls were primed and ready, but more than that, Jenna was ready. The tournament would consume her, giving her no time to think about Rob, and once it was over, the boys' tournament would start. Then she could start counting down on her fingers the days until Rob was gone.

It wasn't that she wanted him to go, but he obviously did. And it would be easier not to see him everyday. It was funny how he had railed so against his father as a teen yet became just like him. Well, maybe not just like him. He wasn't leaving a wife and family behind, but a broken heart nonetheless.

And whose fault was that? a little voice inside her asked. Her own, she knew very well. She heard all his stories, knew what his track record was, yet kept right on seeing him, right on falling for his charm. Maybe this time when he left, she'd be cured. She parked her car and hurried through the crowded gym lobby.

"Hey, Jen, how're your girls doing?" someone called.

"Fine."

"How's the great romance going?" someone else asked.

"Fine, just fine."

"Hey, Jen—"

She gave a quick wave in the direction of the voice, then darted into the gym. After a deep steadying breath that also gave her a moment to check the layout of the land, she took the long route to the bleachers so as to avoid Rob where he was working with his team.

"Miss Lauren."

Jenna looked up to see Sara, sitting at a table just behind the team bench, waving at her. She'd rather sit somewhere else, anywhere else, but Sara probably needed help with the stats and it was something all the coaches helped each other with. Jen put a stiff, plastic smile on her face and walked past Rob and his team, then climbed up next to Sara.

"Want to help me with stats?" Sara asked.

"Sure. Where's everybody else?"

"Ruthie and Nan have colds, so they didn't come. Debbie doesn't want to, she says she gets too excited during the game and forgets to keep track of things."

"Fine with me," Jenna said. It would be easier to keep Rob out of her gaze and her heart if she had to carefully watch the play. "What do you want me to do?"

"How about assists and steals?"

Jenna took the clipboard from Sara and marked in the date, location, and game opponent. The buzzer sounded the fifteen-minute-to-game warning and the boys ran over to pick up water and/or sweat jackets before running off to the locker room. Mike smiled and waved to Sara.

Rob followed more slowly behind them. He had his game face on, and showed little emotion beyond an intensity, but she thought she could see shadows in his eyes. He looked tired. Not just his face, but in the way he held his body. If he was unhappy, why not change things? It was in his power to make them both happy.

"Mike says this is going to be a tough game," Sara said. "He said that Penn is big this year and fast."

Jenna swallowed and forced a small smile to her face before she turned to face the girl. Sara's eyes were bright and her cheeks flushed with excitement. Snapping her gum, teeth flashing in a broad smile, she looked very pretty, a Norman Rockwell image of a small town teenager, watching her boyfriend play basketball.

"How are things going with you and Mike?" Jenna asked.

"Fine."

Fine? Such a good, all-purpose answer. Who cared if it was a lie?

Her skepticism must have overflowed onto her face because Sara hastened to assure her. "No, things really are in shape. We've been talking and things are mellow."

Jenna smiled at the intensity in the girl's voice as much as the words. "That's good," she said.

She tried to turn her attention to the stat sheets before her but the names and boxes sort of flowed together.

Fine. Mellow. Words of comfort if one didn't understand teenagers and the things that could be going on with them. After working with them for eight years, Jenna felt that she understood teenagers very well, maybe too well.

"Better be careful that things don't get too mellow," Jenna said.

Sara's face wore a mask of bewilderment for only a split second. Then the girl smiled, reaching for worldlywise and almost making it. "No need to worry, Miss L. Everything's cool."

They exchanged stares, over a generation gap, over that gap that separates teacher and student. Jenna could read her own history within the gleam of Sara's green eyes. Rebellion, love, dreams, fear, all the pain of growing up.

"Mother Nature has a way of playing tricks on us ladies," Jenna said quietly. "She can wreck dreams with the best of them."

Sara just smiled. "I'm not gonna let her." She let her look fade to serious. "I mean, I'm just learning now to take care of myself. You know, like separate the colored clothes from the whites so that my blouses don't come out all pink. And a whole bunch of other stuff."

Jenna just stared at the girl and started to laugh. "Well, I won't worry about you anymore." And she wouldn't. Sara was going to make it, just as she would. She did thirteen years ago and she would now. Being alone wasn't so bad.

The cheers of the crowd told them that the boys were coming back on the floor and the two of them stood up and joined in. Jenna looked down at Rob going from player to player, slapping them on the back and encouraging them.

She was glad to see the anger fading from Sara and Mike's relationship, not that they were out of the woods yet. Doubt and second thoughts would always sneak in but it looked as if they were going about it more maturely than she and Rob were.

The whistle for the tip-off blew and it was with a great sense of relief that Jenna turned her attention to the game. She interspersed her critical watchfulness and record-keeping with encouraging cheers for their boys, but tried to avoid watching Rob.

The trouble was that the gym would always be haunted by him now. Whether he left tomorrow, every time she came in here, she would see him. Every time she passed his office, she'd hear his voice. It was a pain she'd learn to live with, she guessed, but it wasn't going to be easy.

The Warsaw boys won by five points, and at the final buzzer the crowds descended down onto the gym floor. Sara ran up and hugged Mike while Jenna stood back and waited for a reporter to finish interviewing Rob.

Once the reporter was gone, Rob noticed Jenna.

"Congratulations," Jenna said.

Rob nodded curtly. "Thanks."

She didn't wait to be dismissed, but stepped aside to let others speak to him. This time, she would do the walking away.

People were still milling around in the parking lot, waiting for the players and reliving moments of the game, when Jenna stepped out of the school building. She paused on the steps. There wasn't any reason to push through the crowd just to get home and have Gram grill her on why she was home so early.

"Hey, Jenna."

She turned to see the principal pushing toward her. "Hi, Arthur."

"Boys did well tonight."

"They certainly did,' Jenna agreed.

"We got ourselves two good teams this year," Arthur said. "Boys and girls."

"Thank you."

"How are you ladies going to do in the state play-offs?" Arthur asked.

Jenna shrugged. "Fine." There was that word again. "Good, I hope. We're young though, Sara's our only senior starter."

Arthur laughed heartily and hugged her shoulder. "You coaches are all alike," he said. "Getting your excuses set up beforehand."

"I've had a master teacher these past eight years."

He laughed again and let go of her shoulder. "I try, Jenna. I surely do."

They watched the crowd for a moment before Jenna spoke. "Rob's doing a real fine job with the boys."

"Yes, he is," Arthur agreed. "We're hoping to keep him."

"Isn't Don Parsons coming back?"

Arthur shook his head. "He's says his body's been telling him to slow down for years. Figures it's time to listen."

"So he's retiring."

"Yep. Board authorized me to offer Rob the job permanently."

Rob? Oh lord, could that be the incentive he needed to stay? With a permanent job under his belt, would he see that there was no reason for them to pretend that they didn't care about each other? Jenna felt her fingers start quivering and she thrust them, gloves and all, into her jacket pockets. Although 'permanent' and Rob might be a contradiction in terms. She swallowed hard.

"Is he taking it?" The words came out strained and Jenna coughed into a gloved hand, pretending she had something in her throat.

"I don't know yet. He told me he wanted to think on it."

Her balloon of happiness came crashing down to earth, brought down by the cold winds of realism. Rob wanted to think about it. What was there to think about? If he wanted to stay, he'd know that immediately. If he wanted to go, he might need time to come up with a soft rejection.

"Why don't you talk to him?"

Jenna turned to stare at Arthur. "What?"

"Talk to Rob," Arthur explained. "You know, convince him."

"Oh." Jenna looked away.

"I can't think of anyone better to persuade him. You and Rob have had a special thing going for most of your lives."

She flexed her hands, as if the movement could remove the chill from her heart. She stood there staring at the thinning crowd for a long moment.

"I'm not sure that I would know what to say," she finally said.

"Maybe talking isn't the best way to convince him," Arthur said, then patted her on the back. "See you on Monday."

Jenna considered running away herself but her feet stayed put, obeying her heart that very much wanted to know whether Rob was staying or not. She walked up and down on the steps, trying to ward off the cold. The crowd was down to a few diehards before Rob finally came out. Cheers greeted him and he stopped to wave.

"Hey," somebody shouted from just beyond the steps. "You two coming to the Red Lion for a little celebrating?"

He quickly glanced her way, proving that he'd known where she was even though he hadn't seemed to look her way. But the expression on his face wasn't a soft and easy one. That same shuttered look was in his eyes and his mouth was a grim line.

"I have a lot of work tonight," Jenna called down to the parent.

"Me, too," Rob joined in.

"That's convenient," someone shouted and the crowd joined in laughter.

The night was cold so the laughter was short-lived as the group hurried toward their cars, leaving Jenna and Rob standing on the gym steps.

"Arthur told me about the board's offer," Jenna said, once they were all alone.

Rob just nodded.

"Are you taking it?"

He shrugged. "I doubt it. Warsaw's not the place for me. By the time the season's over, it'll be time to move on."

"It doesn't have to be," she said.

"Sooner or later, the time'll come."

She watched him in the dim lights from the parking lot, but all she saw were shadows. He'd always been good at hiding his emotions. Maybe it was time for real honesty though. Maybe, he needed a real reason to stay here, to fight the urge to wander.

"I wish you would stay," she told him, putting her gloved hand on his arm. Even through the leather of her glove and the thickness of his coat, she could feel him tense. "I care about you, Rob. I care a lot. We could build something very real if we tried."

He shifted the bag in his hand as if it were heavy, but she knew it was to escape her touch.

"That's all the more reason for me to go," he said.

"That's crazy. I love you, so that's reason to leave? And you care about me, too, I know you do."

"Jenna, leave it be," he said, and for a moment the real anguish in his heart came through in his voice. "I like the excitement of a new place, of meeting new people and facing new challenges. I hate it when things fall into a rut, when people know me too well and start pushing in too close."

"So take me with you." She blinked back the tears that were threatening.

He shook his head; she could see that well enough in the dim light. "I travel on a ticket for one. Besides, you belong here. You said it yourself; if you'd wanted to leave, you would have, anytime in the past eight years. You'd be miserable on the move, and I'd be miserable here. I'm my old man to a T, right down to the wear on the soles of my shoes."

"You don't have to be him. You hated what he was."

"And so I won't cause the hurts he did. I'm going to tell Arthur that I'm leaving after basketball season."

There seemed to be nothing left to say. She'd humbled herself and had been turned down. She supposed worse things could happen, but she wasn't sure what.

Rob didn't love her, that was the bottom line. He used the excuse of wandering feet, but it was only an excuse. No one could really believe that just because their father had been a roamer, he was destined to be one as well. All it came down to was that he didn't love her. Very simple.

"Well," she said. "I'd better get on home. Gram's expecting me."

"Yeah, I've got a pile of papers to correct."

They walked toward their cars together but not really. The night was turning frigid. They'd said it was going to be one of the colder winters on record and she believed it.

Chapter Fifteen

The girls sat on the benches in front of the lockers. Exhaustion was etched in their faces, sweat-soaked hair hung down in strings, and their eyes were covered with a dull glaze. Sara sat at one end, a boot filled with ice wrapped around her left ankle.

Jenna could feel the sting in her eyes. They came so close, losing the sectional game by one point. And playing without Sara, their senior point guard and floor leader, for well over half the game. She was so proud of them that she could cry.

"You guys played a heck of a game," Sara said.

"Wait until next year," someone else shouted.

The gloom and depression didn't vanish, but it seemed to lift a fraction. The tears slowed and a few girls began to loosen their shoelaces.

"We have lots to be proud of," Jenna told them all. "You all played a great game and tried your hardest. That pride will make you feel good longer than your disappointment will make you sad."

"I think winning the game would have felt even better," someone quipped and they all grinned somewhat.

"A hell of a lot better," Jenna agreed and the slight grins turned into quiet laughter.

"Are you going to be back with us next year, Miss Lauren?" one of the sophomores asked.

Jenna looked at the bright, shining faces surrounding her, childlike enthusiasm framed in the determination of approaching womanhood. "I couldn't think of any other place that I would rather be."

Everyone cheered.

"We were afraid you'd be leaving."

"Yeah, going off with Mr. Fagan."

No chance, but not for lack of trying. But somehow she kept her smile in place and didn't flinch from the pain. "Nope. This is where I belong." That much was true.

"Now we just have to get Sara to come back."

"Yeah, Sara. Start flunking your courses."

"Give her an F in math, Miss Lauren. We need her."

Jenna laughed and looked at her captain, the glue that had held their young team together all year. There was a touch of concern lurking in the girl's eyes, a worry of the future. But mostly there was maturity. An eagerness for the excitement and adventure the future would bring.

"You still thinking of the University of Dayton?" a girl asked.

"Not thinking anymore," Sara replied. "I've made my decision." She and Jenna locked eyes for a long moment. "I sent my commitment letter in last night. That's where I'll be playing this fall."

The girls rushed over to offer congratulations and hug Sara. A lump rose in Jenna's throat and she found herself blinking rapidly for a moment. There wasn't enough money on earth to pay for a moment like this, being able to cross that threshold into maturity, hand-in-hand with a great kid.

"Is Mike coming with you?" a teammate asked.

"He hasn't decided for sure yet," Sara replied. "But he's really leaning toward De Paul." She paused. "In Chicago."

Silence jumped into the locker room as every young girl's dream of perfect love seemed to be precariously perched on the line.

"We're still going to be friends," Sara said.

Her words burst through the dam of silence.

"Oh, that's great."

"You two are so perfect together."

"Long-distance love is so romantic."

Not hardly, but Jenna was not going to push reality into their dreamworld. "Okay, everybody," Jenna shouted. "Let's hit the showers. Your parents are waiting for you."

The girls slowly dispersed to undress and wash. Jenna was going to miss them all, and the frantic pace of the season. They'd helped fill a void in her life that Rob had left, but all too soon the void would return. She'd have to find other ways to keep busy. She gathered up the uniforms that girls had dropped and noticed Sara was still sitting on the bench.

"Need any help?" Jenna asked Sara.

"Nah." Sara looked down at her booted ankle. "It doesn't feel too bad. I can get along just fine."

"Tough, huh?"

Sara smiled broadly. "I'm just a country girl, Miss L. My daddy always says that's what makes country girls so great. They're strong, work hard, and are really tough."

"Yeah," Jenna said. "I guess we are."

They shared a moment of silence, letting the singing and shouting from the showers wash over them. Jenna sat down on the bench across from Sara.

"I'm glad you and Mike worked things out," she said.

Sara nodded. "Yeah, Mike's been talking with Mr. Fagan a lot. He says that Mr. Fagan's helped him the most."

Rob helping a troubled teen? That shouldn't be surprising. Rob had been through so much trouble himself that he could relate to just about any problem a kid could bring in.

"Is he going to stay, Miss Lauren?"

Jenna blinked, trying to comprehend Sara's words.

"Mr. Fagan," Sara went on. "Is he going to stay as coach?"

Jenna looked away. "I don't know Sara. I don't think so."

"Oh, he's got to, Miss Lauren. Mike says he's the best coach in the whole world and he's just so cool."

Jenna forced a smile to her lips. "Yes, he is a good coach."

"Why don't you talk to him?" Sara said. "I bet he'll listen to you."

She was through laying her heart on the line, but she wasn't going to say that to Sara. She looked up just in time to see some of the girls drifting back from the showers.

"The showers are emptying," she said. "You better get cleaned up."

"Right." Sara rose and began walking slowly and stiffly. A couple of the girls moved in to help her.

Jenna left the locker room, knowing that a crowd would be waiting in the gym to commiserate and maybe it was best to face them all now.

"Tough loss," someone said, shaking her hand.

"How're the girls taking it?"

"Okay," she said. "We're tough."

"Wait 'til next year."

"Right," Jenna said with a laugh.

Rob was off to one side and came over once girls started exiting the locker room to claim their parents. "How's Sara?"

"She'll be fine," Jenna said. "It's not a bad sprain, just bad enough to keep her out of the rest of the game."

"She might have made the difference."

Jenna shrugged. "Maybe. Cindy played real well and scored more than she normally does."

"So it's wait until next year, then?"

She nodded and looked away, her eyes suddenly moist. Would he know how she did next year? Probably not. Warsaw results were published in South Bend and Fort Wayne, but that was about the extent of their range.

"I'd better check out the locker room," she said. She flashed a bright smile and hurried away.

The locker room was peaceful and quiet, a haven. Jenna leaned against a locker and took a deep breath. She'd make it, she had to. No man, not even one she loved as much as Rob, would ever defeat her.

After a moment the teariness faded and she went around checking the lockers. Two mismatched socks, a brush and three cans of hair spray were all that was left of the season. And one broken heart.

She put her clipboard and other game paraphernalia into her bag, then slipped into her coat. Why had Sara and Mike been able to resolve things so amicably when she and Rob couldn't? Maybe if they'd had someone to advise them, they could have been able to manage their emotions. Maybe they would still be friends. A friend who could talk to Rob, tell him that the community wanted him to stay, tell him that they would help him tie down his wandering feet. Maybe, maybe, maybe. And maybe the moon was made of green cheese. And maybe there was a pot of gold at the end of every rainbow. She turned off the lights in the locker room and left.

* * *

"I thought you were going to sleep late," Gram said, looking up from her Wall Street Journal.

"I have a headache," Jenna replied, rubbing her temples. "I must be coming down with something."

"What do you want for breakfast?"

"Nothing," Jenna murmured. "Maybe just a cup of coffee."

"Want me to make you some pancakes?"

The nausea washed over Jenna, causing her to move quickly to the kitchen sink. She gripped the edge of the sink and stared out at the snow-covered yard, swallowing hard. Sweat beaded on her forehead and she prayed she wouldn't be sick.

"Please, Gram," she whispered hoarsely. "Don't mention food of any kind."

She was sure that her grandmother was looking at her, but Jenna just stared hard out the window. A male cardinal hopped around on the bushes in back and she concentrated on him, fighting back the queasiness.

"You might be coming down with the flu," Gram said. "Lot of that going around lately."

Jenna nodded, still not daring to speak.

There were rustling sounds behind her as Gram turned a page. Some of the tension eased in Jenna and strength began flowing back into her limbs.

"I think I'll take a shower."

"Want me to draw you a bath?" Gram asked.

"I'd like a shower better."

"That's fine, dear. Call if you need any help."

Jenna slowly worked her way upstairs, pausing a couple of times to rest. Gram was probably right. She was coming down with the flu. Too bad it had to come on a free day.

Arthur had given the school a day off to celebrate the girls winning the regional and coming in second in the sectionals. Jenna had planned on catching up on her cleaning and other chores, but now it looked like bed-rest would be the order of the day. Good thing basketball season was over. She couldn't have afforded to be sick then.

The shower was revitalizing. By the time she stepped out and briskly wiped herself, she began to think she could do some of those chores after all. Her eyes strayed to her bathroom closet. Dusting was becoming a necessity. She could write her name on the tops of some of the boxes.

Suddenly the towel fell from her hands and a new sense of impending gloom came to settle on her shoulders. Oh, God. Jenna kept a personal calendar but there was no need to check that. One of those dust-covered boxes in her bathroom closet contained her sanitary napkins. The thick layer of dust on the box told her what she didn't want to know. Jenna dressed herself under remote control and slowly walked downstairs.

"I thought you were going to rest today," Gram said.

Jenna turned away to pour herself some coffee. "I thought I'd do some shopping instead," she said, staring out the window.

Some chickadees had joined the lone cardinal at the bird feeder providing black and white contrast to his blood red cloak.

Her grandmother was looking at her. Jenna could feel those sharp eyes boring in, peeling back the layers, plunging into the very furthest depths of her soul.

"Are you sure that's wise, dear?"

Jenna spilled the more than half cup of coffee down the drain. "I feel fine, Gram. I think maybe the taste of the toothpaste hit me wrong this morning." She turned around and tried to meet those eyes. She didn't quite make it.

"I'd best head out," she mumbled. "Get an early start."

"Jenna. Are you sure you're up to it?"

"I'm fine, Gram. Just fine." Jenna grabbed her coat and hurried out the door, shutting it on poor Susie who'd wanted to follow her out. Today was not the time for leisurely strolls up and down the shoveled driveway with the old dog.

Once she was out on the road, a giant cloud of gloom settled itself on Jenna's shoulders. She exchanged the nausea in her stomach for the pain of tension.

She was vaguely aware that she'd missed a period but that happened sometimes during basketball season. The tension, plus driving herself as hard or harder than she drove her girls, often did that to Jenna.

Thirteen years ago she would've had to go to a physician to confirm her suspicions, but not anymore. The years might not have brought her wisdom, but they had brought home pregnancy testing kits.

Of course, she couldn't purchase such a kit in Warsaw. Half the people in town would know by the time they broke for lunch. Following lunch, the discreet little phone calls would start. And she sure as hell couldn't say she was buying the kit for Gram.

She turned east onto US 30 and headed toward Fort Wayne. She hesitated in Columbia City, halfway between Warsaw and Fort Wayne, considering buying the kit there, but fear caused her to push on. She'd coached in the area for eight years and was well known in all the small towns in northeast Indiana. Made it nice when she wanted a friendly face, but it didn't help her privacy any.

Even in the faceless anonymity of a suburban shopping center on the north edge of Fort Wayne, Jenna was still nervous. The middle-aged female clerk took her money with no more expression than if Jenna were buying a box of aspirin, but it didn't help. Jenna hurried for her car as if she was being chased.

"Home or here?" she asked herself, but knew that she couldn't wait.

She drove to a large department store and went up to their rest room. After only a few minutes of waiting, she knew. She was pregnant.

Somehow she made it home, though she felt like she was in a fog. Susie greeted her at the door and Jenna mechanically petted her, then hung up her coat.

"Hello, dear," Gram said. "How are you feeling?"

"Fine. Just fine." She almost laughed aloud as she said the words, but knew that would just provoke too many questions.

Gram frowned. "You didn't buy much."

"Not much." Enough though. "I think I'll spend the day cleaning."

"Maybe you should go over and see Rob."

For a moment, Jenna's heart stopped, as if Gram could read her mind or somehow see into her. But that was impossible. "Why would I do that?"

"See if you two could smooth out your differences. It isn't natural you being apart when you both care for each other so much."

Jenna picked up the paper and pretended to read an article. "A high school romance, can go only so far, Gram. We've both changed and things just sort of petered out."

Gram's snort was her only reply.

Jenna put down the paper. "I'm going upstairs to clean out some drawers."

She escaped before Gram could say anything else, but she just stretched out on her bed rather than get to work. What in the world was she going to do? Thirteen years ago, she'd vowed that she wouldn't tie Rob down here, but maybe this was the tie he needed. Was forcing him to stay the answer? Not if he didn't care for her as deeply as she loved him.

If she knew he loved her, she'd fight like the devil to make him stay, but the very fact that he was planning to leave said he didn't. How could you love someone and leave them? But then, how could she love him and let him go?

"Hello." The authoritative voice came booming over the telephone lines.

"Hello, Gram. This is Rob Fagan."

"I know who it is, boy. No reason to announce yourself like that."

"I just thought after being away for thirteen years it wouldn't hurt none."

"Get to be my age," Gram said. "Thirteen years ain't no more than yesterday. Besides, I have a good memory. Always did. Was the first one in my class to learn the ABC's. Anyway, you sound just like your daddy. Always have."

Rob opened his mouth but quickly closed it. There was nothing he could say to that. Unfortunately, he resembled his father in all kinds of ways.

"Why are you calling so late anyway?" Gram asked.

"Beg your pardon, ma'am?" It was only eleven o'clock in the morning.

"Jenna's up and gone already. She's always up early on Sunday," Gram said. "Women these days got their own cars and money. They don't wait around."

"I guess not." He cleared his throat, hoping to derail her philosophizing. "Could you tell Jenna that I called?"

"Why don't you come over for lunch?" Gram asked. "She should be home around then."

"I...I really can't," Rob replied. "Just tell her I have some questions about her team banquet."

"Making sloppy joes. They're your favorite lunch."

"Thank you, ma'am, but I can't today."

"You've been to Paris and now you don't like my cooking?"

"Oh, no," Rob insisted. "It's not that at all."

"You're gonna waste away to skin and bone."

"I'm eating just fine, ma'am," Rob said. "It's just that I have a touch of the flu, stomach flu."

"Folks that eat just fine don't get sick."

"I have to go," Rob said hurriedly. "Please tell Jenna I'll see her on Monday."

"You've been looking peaked, boy," Gram said. "I want you over here for dinner."

"I'm sorry, Gram. Gotta go."

Rob hung up the phone then, sighing deeply, walked slowly to the front of his apartment where he leaned against the wall and watched the traffic move along the street in front.

It was stupid of him to call. He was trying to stay away from Jenna, and then what does he do? Calls her up on the flimsiest of excuses. He'd have to be a lot stronger than this to get through these last few weeks. But then he was beginning to wonder just how strong he was.

He remembered when his father had his bouts of depression. Then the old man would hit the bottle, hard and heavy. When Rob was older and stronger, he'd help his mother undress his father and put him to bed.

When the gremlins of the dark had first come to perch on Rob's own shoulders, those memories of his childhood kept him away from the liquor cabinet. He learned that from his father's experience, but that was about all.

Clouds were coming in from the west. Probably were going to drop something on the fine citizens of Warsaw. Being that it was February, that could be rain or snow, or anything in between.

His depression called for his attention and Rob turned away from the weather outside. Don't drink when you're down, that was the single thing he'd learned from his father. Was that how improvements came to a species, one fix per generation? If he had a son, what would he improve on?

Rob turned angrily from the window and went into his kitchen to sit down. He didn't have a son or daughter and never would have. There was more to fatherhood than putting the biscuit in the oven. You had to stay for the long haul and he was genetically incapable of that. He doubted that his father's wandering feet would ever be eradicated from his bloodline.

Though feeling old and tired, Rob pushed himself up and took his coat from its hook. Time to take a little walk, a long little walk. Maybe if he was lucky, he would get caught in one of the midwest's February specials. Snow mixed with sleet and rain. Perhaps he'd catch himself a death of cold and let his soul be released from this sorry old earth. Let it go someplace where no-nonsense blue eyes wouldn't challenge him to take roots, challenge him to become something he was not and could never be.

The February slush came but not soon enough to do any good. It came early the next morning, just in time to make a mess of his six a.m. practice. Kids came straggling in until six-thirty. All brought harrowing tales of slip-sliding down the roads, passing other cars in ditches. It was a good way to start the week.

Arthur was waiting for him when Rob exited the gym. "Hey, Rob," he said in a voice disgustingly full of good cheer. "How're the boys doing?"

"Anymore days like today and we might as well hang up our jockstraps," Rob grumbled.

Arthur laughed. "Cheer up."

"Yeah, I know," Rob replied. "Things are bound to get worse."

The principal slapped him on the back and hurried away. Rob watched him move down the hall, dropping a word and a smile to students and teachers along the way. He felt the bitter taste of envy on his tongue. The man had been in Warsaw for thirty years now and he was still happy. Rob wished he could be like that.

He saw Arthur several times during the day and the principal always had a snappy greeting for him. Never once did he ask if Rob was going to take the job on a permanent basis. And he knew that Arthur wouldn't. That just wasn't the way things were done around these parts.

He'd already decided he wouldn't take the job, but wasn't going to say anything until after the season was over. Making that kind of announcement now would just hurt the team. And there was no way of keeping it a secret. Fact of the matter was, there were no secrets in a town like Warsaw.

Jenna presented a different challenge to him. He would have preferred not seeing her at all, yet he found himself taking circuitous routes just so their paths could cross, like some lovesick high school stud.

But seeing her didn't help his depression. She looked so wan and woebegone that he wanted to snatch her into his arms and protect her from life's hard jolts forever and ever. When he did come close though, like that lovesick high school stud of yesteryear, Rob became tongue-tied and found himself fleeing in confusion.

By the end of the week, he was a wreck himself. He didn't know whether Jenna was sick, down because of her girls being knocked out of the play-offs, or just afflicted with the mid-February blues, a very common midwest ailment. Finally he gathered his courage and walked in on Jenna as she sat in a classroom, doing her end-of-day routine.

"You got someone planning your team banquet?" he asked.

She looked up at him before speaking. "Yeah. Sara's mother volunteered," Jenna replied. "I think she's looking at the end of the month."

"Okay." Rob nodded. "Just hoped it wouldn't conflict with the boy's tournament."

"No, she said she'd make sure it didn't."

Silence came in and took hold of them. "You look tired," Rob finally said.

"A touch of the flu."

"Your grandmother told me that people who eat right don't get sick."

"She's been telling me the same thing," Jenna replied with a wry smile.

"She's lived a good many years. Maybe she's right."

"Most likely is." Jenna turned her attention back to the papers in front of her.

Rob stood only a moment in the silence. It was obvious that Jenna didn't need him, appeared that she didn't even want him. "Well, take care."

"Yeah," she said, looking up quickly. "You, too."

Rob quickly left the room, then slowed down to a crawl once he was out in the hall. Probably nobody in this damn town needed him. He should tell Arthur about his decision soon, so that he could leave right after basketball season. They could always get a substitute to handle his classes for the rest of the year.

Time to sent out a few letters. Probably best to get himself a traveling man's job. That sporting goods outfit always said they'd be glad to take him back if he was interested. Well, he was interested, Rob told himself firmly. Very interested.

Chapter Sixteen

Jenna sat slumped on the floor in front of the television. The cheering of the crowd told her the Bulls had done something good, but she had no idea what it was. Nor did she care.

"You ought to go to bed if you're tired, dear," Gram said.

"Who said I was tired?" Jenna had the set of nested balls that Rob had given her for Christmas and was tossing them from one hand to the other.

"Well, you haven't said a word for almost forty-eight hours now, so I thought it must be that."

Jenna grinned at her grandmother. "I distinctly remember saying that I didn't want anymore soup at dinner and that was only two hours ago."

"That doesn't count."

"Oh no? People shouldn't make up the rules as they go along," Jenna said and found herself slipping back into the mire of her gloom again. That's what Rob had done, made the rules after they'd begun playing. Or maybe, she was the one who did that. Maybe they had still been playing by the old rules, but she'd thought they must have changed.

The cheering from the TV grew annoying, and she slumped down farther on the floor. The outside ball of the set was a sunny sky with just a few clouds. Too cheerful. She took it off and stared at the nighttime sky. Better, but the stars made it feel full of hope and romance. The next one was snowflakes. Not enough to make even a halfway decent snowball, but too many to feed her depression. There'd been snow on the ground when they'd gotten the Christmas tree, and on New Year's Eve for the torchlight ski. The snowflake ball had to go.

That left her with the raindrop. Or teardrop, she thought. This was the one that was most fitting. This is what Rob had left her with last time, and this time, too.

She let the raindrop/teardrop roll around in her hand. Raindrops nourished the earth, helped things to grow. Teardrops didn't nourish anything. She should know; she'd shed her share over the last few days and had come no closer to any answers.

"Alice said that Rob hasn't given Arthur an answer yet," Gram said. "Think he's waiting for a push from you?"

"No, Gram. He's not. He's probably waiting until the end of basketball season. Now's not the time to disrupt anything with either good or bad news."

Did that mean she shouldn't tell him about the baby now? She had to tell him. He had a right to know.

Susie got up from her spot on the sofa and came over to join Jenna on the floor.

"How'd you know I needed company," Jenna asked.

The old dog leaned against her and let her body slide to the floor, then quivered to settle everything into the right position. It was her usual pattern, but this time, her foot hit Jenna's hand and the raindrop fell to the floor.

"Susie, Susie, Susie," Jenna muttered, but as she reached out for the drop, she stopped. A crack around its middle had appeared.

She picked it up carefully. The drop wasn't the heart of the set. She carefully loosened the bottom, and opened the drop up. A tiny rainbow lay inside.

"What's that, dear?" Gram said.

But sudden tears had blinded Jenna and she could just hold out her hand.

"Oh, isn't that precious? But true, I guess. Rainbows come after storms, after all."

Jenna nodded, and closed her hand around the rainbow, afraid almost to let it go. Rainbows came after storms. Always?

She'd been through a lot of storms in her life, none quite so bad as the present one, but she'd never seen a rainbow afterward. Or was it that she'd never looked for one?

Rob had always liked to tease her about being the practical one, never one to indulge in dreams, while he always seemed to be going after something impossible. Why did she always like things cut and dried, and obvious? Was it because it was easier to take things as they were, than to risk hurt by hoping for something that was out of reach?

She opened her hand to stare down at the tiny rainbow. There was no pot of gold at one end, but that was as it should be. The rainbow was reward enough, a kind of blessing on the world. She'd like to have the courage to chase rainbows, not by leaving town as Rob did, but by believing that the impossible could come true.

Rob knew her better than she thought. All too often, she hid from the raindrops and missed the rainbows in life. She didn't have faith in miracles.

Even as Jenna began to put the rainbow back into the raindrop, she heard Rob's words in her mind. If you love someone, you know all their fears and dreams. She stopped, afraid almost of letting the rainbow be hidden again.

Could it be that he knew her so well because he loved her? But why was he leaving then?

"Gram, do you remember Rob's younger brothers much?"

Gram put her knitting down and frowned off into space. "Oh, some. Nice boys, but they didn't have that cockiness Rob had."

"What were they like after their father left?"

"Pretty much the same. A little less confident, a little less trusting."

"Did Mrs. Fagan ever date after her husband was gone?"

Gram just laughed. "Gracious no. Lady had more than her share of woes from that one man. She wasn't about to set herself up for more from another."

Jenna stared at the rainbow, fingering its curved edges. "Rob and his father were close, weren't they?"

"Close as you can get to an irresponsible alcoholic." She sighed. "Man had such a way about him. He'd do you wrong, then cry and plead and promise never to do it again, then the next day he would. Adults just got to not believing him, but a child would be hurt a lot of times before he'd learn not to trust."

Rob had learned, Jenna thought. It might have taken his father a while to teach it to him, but Rob knew very well not to trust anyone's feelings for him. She thought back to all his speeches about his traveling life. He'd leave before people got too close; he liked the excitement of new places. He liked being on his own. Where no one could let him down again.

Jenna put the rainbow back into the drop, then all the other balls together and into her pocket. "I've got some errands to run before the stores close, Gram. I'll be back in a while."

Rob dragged himself into the building Monday morning. He was tired, irritable and ready to stomp anybody who gave him a kind word. Even a win over tough Tippecanoe Valley last Saturday couldn't perk him up.

"Howdy, Rob," Arthur called as they passed in the hall.

Rob gritted his teeth and nodded as he kept on going. Coffee was what he needed, though he'd been living on coffee and little else all weekend.

"Great game," Rita said as Rob came into the teachers' lounge.

"You guys should be unbeatable in the tournament," someone told him.

Rob just nodded, not even pretending to smile as he hurried over to the coffeepot. Jenna wasn't in the room yet and with luck, he could get his coffee and leave before she came.

"Hear Mike Sherwin's going to De Paul," someone said.

"Yeah." Rob filled his cup.

"That's quite a coup."

"Yeah." He added some powdered creamer, then picked his cup up. Jenna still wasn't here. It looked like he was going to make it.

"Baseball season's just around the corner," the baseball coach said. "I need to see you about some preseason tournaments."

"I'll be around." Not for long but there was no need broadcasting that news just yet.

He made it to the door without meeting Jenna, but rather than experiencing the feeling of relief, his heart was sad. Damn. He should never have come here.

The halls were relatively quiet as he stomped down to his office. Even if they went downstate and won the championship, the season would be over in a month. He could last here another month.

Balancing his folder under his arm and his cup in one hand, he reached into his pocket for his keys. A light was coming from under the door though; someone was inside. Rather than bother with his keys, he turned the knob and opened the door. Jenna was inside, along with about a hundred thousand rainbows.

"Hi," she said.

He just stared around him. Hung from the fluorescent lights were dozens of prisms, each one sending rainbows all over the walls.

"What's all this?" he finally managed to ask.

"Rainbows," she said, waving her hand to include them all.

He knew that much and just shook his head. "But why?"

She grinned and some of her lightness, her joy, seeped into his dark mood. "To show you that there are rainbows everywhere," she said. "You can chase them all you want without ever leaving town."

He didn't understand any of this.

"I wouldn't chase them too vigorously in here though," she added. "It could get dangerous since it's such a small space."

He came into the room then, slowly as if there were things to be wary of inside. "I don't get it," he said. He looked over at Jenna, a rainbow lay across her golden hair, making her look all the more beautiful with a touch of mysticism.

"It's simple." She sat on the corner of his desk. "You want to chase rainbows. I want you to stay. If you'd see that everyplace is filled with rainbows, then you wouldn't have to keep running off in search of new ones."

"Jen, it's not that simple." Despite the golden aura about the room, Rob felt some of his gloom returning. "I wish it were."

Her smile dimmed, but her radiance didn't. "Sit," she said, and pointed at the student desk. He obeyed.

"The main thing is that I love you," she said softly, her eyes aglow. "And you love me."

He opened his mouth to speak, but she just put her hand up. "No you may not have the floor until I have my say. I'm the teacher."

He closed his mouth, making do with a glare.

"I know you love me, so don't bother denying it. It's not the real problem, anyway. The real problem is that I love you and you just don't trust that emotion. I don't know why I didn't see it before."

She came over to the other side of his desk, so that she was close to him. So close that he could feel her warmth spill out over him, starting to banish some of the cold in his heart.

"You got your looks from your father and maybe the shape of your feet and their size, but not anything else. You've been wandering because it's safer. If you don't get close to people, they can't betray you."

"I never said you'd betray me."

She reached over and took his hands. "No, not consciously, but our subconscious can be awfully strong. You admitted that you like to leave a place when people start getting too close. You're more comfortable keeping people at a distance."

"Obviously it didn't work with you."

She grinned. "Nope. You let me get close and now you can't push me away. You have to trust me. It may take time before you really do, deep down inside, but that's okay.

You can teach me how to dream and reach for impossible wonderful things. I can teach you how to trust.''

''This job could take a long time,'' he said, feeling a small flame of joy trying to take hold in his heart.

''The longer the better,'' she said. ''Because you can't leave me until the lessons are all over.''

He was holding her hands now. ''Aren't you afraid though that I am like my father? Isn't there a little bit of fear in the back of your mind that I'll walk out some day?''

''No,'' she said and stooped down so that she could look straight into his eyes. ''You've never run from responsibility or from a challenge. You aren't going to start now.'' Then an impish little smile took her lips. ''And if you try, I'll just run you down. We jockettes are pretty fast you know.''

''Oh, Jen.'' His words were a sigh, a prayer, a bit of heaven as he stood up and pulled her into his arms. Their lips met and clung, drawing strength from each other, strength enough to fuel their love for a lifetime.

''I love you so much,'' he whispered into her hair as he held her close. ''But I was so afraid I'd hurt you. I don't want you to end up miserable and alone like my mother.''

''It won't happen because you aren't your father. No matter how much you look like him, you aren't him. You aren't doomed to make the same mistakes.'' Her arms tightened around him just a bit. ''Besides, if he'd been a high school basketball coach, maybe he would have stayed around. There's nothing more like chasing rainbows than aiming for the Final Four every year.''

Rob laughed out loud, feeling the rest of the shadows disappear. Rainbows filled his heart as he kissed her again, a light little kiss because he couldn't help himself when her lips were so near.

''We're going to get married after basketball season,'' he said, and kissed her again. ''And we'll live with Gram so she's not all alone, but we won't discuss plow horses with her."

Jenna just stared at him, shaking her head in obvious confusion. "Okay."

Rob laughed again, the joy and gladness in his heart welling up to explode. He hugged her tightly, whirling her around in the tiny confines of the office.

"I can't tell you how miserable I've been without you," he said.

"Me too," she said.

"I kept telling myself it was the flu, but I knew better."

"That's what I told Gram, but I knew better, too." Jenna grew still for a moment, then eased a bit from his arms so that she could look up into his face. "You know how so much of what we did seemed the same as it was when we were going together in high school?"

He nodded, missing her and wanting her back in his arms.

"Well, there's something else that happened just like it did back then."

For a long moment, Rob had no idea what she was talking about and just stared into her eyes for a clue, then suddenly her meaning came clear. "Jen," he whispered and eased her back down so that she was sitting on the corner of the desk. "You are?"

She nodded, worry warring with happiness on her face, until he broke into a smile. "Is that okay?" she asked.

"Okay? It's great." He put his arms around her gently, as if she were suddenly fragile and might break. "We really have been given another chance."

He closed his eyes against the emotion surging inside him. He hadn't known it was possible to feel so happy.

"Hey, Mr. Fagan—"

Rob and Jenna turned, still in each other's arms, as the door opened. Mike and Sara were framed in the doorway.

"Wow, radical," Mike said, whistling softly as he gazed around the room.

"Uh, we're sorry to interrupt," Sara said, tugging at Mike's arm. "We'll talk to you later."

Mike frowned at her. "Yeah, but—"

"Later," Sara hissed at him. She pulled him free of the doorway and started to close it. "Can't you see that Miss Lauren's trying to convince him to stay?"

Jenna and Rob just looked at each other and began to laugh.

"So they put you up to this?" Rob accused.

Jenna nodded. "They offered the last slice of pizza. And it wasn't even mushrooms and anchovies."

He just folded her back into his arms as if there wasn't any other place in the world she belonged.

"Not even mushrooms and anchovies," he marveled. "It must be true love then."

Epilogue

The rain had stopped when they came out of church, Jenna on Rob's arm and surrounded by all their friends and family.

"Land sakes, I thought this day would never come," Gram muttered.

"Neither did I," Sara agreed. "I mean, anybody could see those two were head over heels in love with each other."

Jenna just smiled. "Thanks, you two. Since you both were so sure things would end up this way, it would have been nice if you had let me know."

"That would have taken the joy out of your courtship," Gram said.

"That was fun?" Rob asked, pulling Jenna into the circle of his arms. "Next you're gong to be telling me coaching basketball's fun."

"Hey, we won the state title," Mike protested.

Jenna looked around at all her friends and wondered if it was all a dream. She'd never been so happy, and come fall, she'd be even happier.

"Come on, you all," Rita called out. "Let's line up for some pictures." She good-naturedly bossed them all around, lining them up on the church stairs.

"Happy?" Jenna whispered to Rob.

His eyes answered even before his lips. "Yeah."

He bent down to kiss her as she moved into his arms. It was a heaven she couldn't get enough of.

"Come on, guys, you can do that later," Rita protested over the laughter and applause.

"We have to get in shape for later," Rob said. "You know practice makes perfect."

But they stood still for her picture, smiling with all the joy bursting from their hearts. She took another, and still another.

"Come on," Jenna mocked, but then stopped.

The sun was coming out and blue sky was peeking through the clouds and over in the distance was a rainbow. A real rainbow.

"You know what that means?" Jenna whispered to Rob.

"That the storm's over now." He swept her back into his arms, a broad smile grew on his lips.

* * * * *

COMING NEXT MONTH

#709 LURING A LADY—Nora Roberts

Barging into his landlord's office, angry carpenter Mikhail Stanislaski got what he wanted. But, for the hot-blooded artist, luring cool, reserved landlady Sydney Hayward to his SoHo lair was another story....

#710 OVER EASY—Victoria Pade

Lee Horvat went undercover to trap Blythe Coopersmith by gaining her trust. She gave it too freely, though, and both were caught...struggling against love.

#711 PRODIGAL FATHER—Gina Ferris

It wasn't wealthy, stoic Cole Saxon's wish to reunite with his prodigal father; it was A-1 wish-granter Kelsey Campbell's idea. And from the start, Kelsey proved dangerously adept at directing Cole's desires....

#712 PRELUDE TO A WEDDING—Patricia McLinn

Paul Monroe was a top-notch appraiser. Sensing million-dollar laughter behind Bette Wharton's workaholic ways, he betrayed his spontaneous nature and planned...for a march down the aisle.

#713 JOSHUA AND THE COWGIRL—Sherryl Woods

Cowgirl Traci Garrett didn't want anything to do with big shots like businessman Joshua Ames. But that was before this persistent persuader decided to rope—and tie—this stubborn filly.

#714 EMBERS—Mary Kirk

Disaster summoned Anne Marquel home to face the ghosts of the past. With tender Connor McLeod's help, could she overcome tragedy and fan the embers of hope for tomorrow?

AVAILABLE THIS MONTH:

#703 SOMEONE TO TALK TO
Marie Ferrarella

#704 ABOVE THE CLOUDS
Bevlyn Marshall

#705 THE ICE PRINCESS
Lorraine Carroll

#706 HOME COURT ADVANTAGE
Andrea Edwards

#707 REBEL TO THE RESCUE
Kayla Daniels

#708 BABY, IT'S YOU
Celeste Hamilton

"INDULGE A LITTLE" SWEEPSTAKES

HERE'S HOW THE SWEEPSTAKES WORKS

NO PURCHASE NECESSARY

To enter each drawing, complete the appropriate Official Entry Form or a 3" by 5" index card by hand-printing your name, address and phone number and the trip destination that the entry is being submitted for (i.e., Walt Disney World Vacation Drawing, etc.) and mailing it to: Indulge '91 Subscribers-Only Sweepstakes, P.O. Box 1397, Buffalo, New York 14269-1397.

No responsibility is assumed for lost, late or misdirected mail. Entries must be sent separately with first class postage affixed, and be received by: 9/30/91 for the Walt Disney World Vacation Drawing, 10/31/91 for the Alaskan Cruise Drawing and 11/30/91 for the Hawaiian Vacation Drawing. Sweepstakes is open to residents of the U.S. and Canada, 21 years of age or older as of 11/7/91.

For complete rules, send a self-addressed, stamped (WA residents need not affix return postage) envelope to: Indulge '91 Subscribers-Only Sweepstakes Rules, P.O. Box 4005, Blair, NE 68009.

"INDULGE A LITTLE" SWEEPSTAKES

HERE'S HOW THE SWEEPSTAKES WORKS

NO PURCHASE NECESSARY

To enter each drawing, complete the appropriate Official Entry Form or a 3" by 5" index card by hand-printing your name, address and phone number and the trip destination that the entry is being submitted for (i.e., Walt Disney World Vacation Drawing, etc.) and mailing it to: Indulge '91 Subscribers-Only Sweepstakes, P.O. Box 1397, Buffalo, New York 14269-1397.

No responsibility is assumed for lost, late or misdirected mail. Entries must be sent separately with first class postage affixed, and be received by: 9/30/91 for the Walt Disney World Vacation Drawing, 10/31/91 for the Alaskan Cruise Drawing and 11/30/91 for the Hawaiian Vacation Drawing. Sweepstakes is open to residents of the U.S. and Canada, 21 years of age or older as of 11/7/91.

For complete rules, send a self-addressed, stamped (WA residents need not affix return postage) envelope to: Indulge '91 Subscribers-Only Sweepstakes Rules, P.O. Box 4005, Blair, NE 68009.

© 1991 HARLEQUIN ENTERPRISES LTD. DIR-RL

INDULGE A LITTLE—WIN A LOT!

Summer of '91 Subscribers-Only Sweepstakes

OFFICIAL ENTRY FORM

This entry must be received by: Nov. 30, 1991
This month's winner will be notified by: Dec. 7, 1991
Trip must be taken between: Jan. 7, 1992—Jan. 7, 1993

YES, I want to win the 3-Island Hawaiian vacation for two. I understand the prize includes round-trip airfare, first-class hotels and pocket money as revealed on the "wallet" scratch-off card.

Name ______________________________

Address ______________________ Apt. ______

City ______________________________

State/Prov. ____________ Zip/Postal Code ____________

Daytime phone number ____________________
(Area Code)

Return entries with invoice in envelope provided. Each book in this shipment has two entry coupons—and the more coupons you enter, the better your chances of winning!

 3R-CPS

INDULGE A LITTLE—WIN A LOT!

Summer of '91 Subscribers-Only Sweepstakes

OFFICIAL ENTRY FORM

This entry must be received by: Nov. 30, 1991
This month's winner will be notified by: Dec. 7, 1991
Trip must be taken between: Jan. 7, 1992—Jan. 7, 1993

YES, I want to win the 3-Island Hawaiian vacation for two. I understand the prize includes round-trip airfare, first-class hotels and pocket money as revealed on the "wallet" scratch-off card.

Name ______________________________

Address ______________________ Apt. ______

City ______________________________

State/Prov. ____________ Zip/Postal Code ____________

Daytime phone number ____________________
(Area Code)

Return entries with invoice in envelope provided. Each book in this shipment has two entry coupons—and the more coupons you enter, the better your chances of winning!

© 1991 HARLEQUIN ENTERPRISES LTD. 3R-CPS